Carol Clay
Yvonne White

Welcome Home

Book Five of the Lincks Series

Carol Clay

Published by Hear My Heart Publishing

ISBN: 978-1-945620-58-4
A product of the United States of America.
Written by Carol Clay, carolclaywrites.com

Chapter One

The plane landed ten minutes ahead of schedule, something almost unheard of anymore. Andrew Thomas stood and grabbed a carry-on bag from the overhead space setting it next to the woman seated beside him. She grinned as she stood gazing at his face the entire time.

"Andrew, you are going to make a wonderful husband and father." She smiled as she caught his face between her hands and pulled him toward her. The blush already started to creep up the man's face as she gently kissed his cheek. She patted his face lightly before moving to take her bag.

"I have this. You go ahead." He blocked the aisle for her to step in front of him. He noticed she seemed a bit stiff from sitting, but she straightened up and moved quickly keeping up with the passengers in front of her. He picked up the two bags and fell in line right behind her. They made their way to the end of the concourse before turning toward each other. He wasn't sure if she had checked any luggage or not.

"Do you have baggage to pick up?" He smiled slightly as he waited for her response.

"I do, but you have done enough. I can manage now." She reached to take her bag from his shoulder.

"Nonsense. I have to go down there as well. We might as well keep each other company while we wait for the luggage to be unloaded." He put both bags in one hand and offered his arm to the woman beside him. Both of them ignored the curious looks of the people they passed.

As they made their way slowly toward the luggage pickup area, he thought back to the beginning of the flight at Raleigh-Durham airport.

His companion was already seated when he boarded. She smiled softly at him as he stowed his bag. Then, Andy noticed the tears in her eyes.

"Are you okay, ma'am?" He had really hoped to find himself seated beside a self-absorbed business person not at all interested in talking, but somehow, he didn't think that was going to happen now.

"I'm sorry. Soldiers always remind me of Harold, my late husband. He was killed in the war." She dabbed at her eyes stopping the tears that threatened to fall. Andy hoped she wouldn't start crying. He never knew what to do when a woman cried. She looked at the other passengers as they loaded the plane before saying anything further.

"Are you going home on leave?" Her words were hardly more than a whisper. The lieutenant looked at her again before he realized she was addressing him. Her eyes were still sad, but no longer threatened to spill over with tears.

"Well I'm heading home, but not on leave. I just finished my tour of duty and will officially be a civilian in twenty-four hours." The comment made him wonder even now. He hoped he had done the right thing. As much as he enjoyed his career and his platoon, it was the best thing for him to do. Captain Gabriel Morgan had also decided not to re-up before Andy's last tour. The service just wouldn't be the same without his captain and good friend. Before he could delve further into the pros and cons of his decision, the passenger beside him spoke again.

"I'm Ruth, Ruth Simmons." She reached across to extend a hand he shook automatically.

"Lieutenant Andrew Thomas, ma'am. It's an honor to meet you." He returned the smile she gave him. They spent the next three hours discussing his decision and her husband, mostly her husband.

The luggage carousel in front of them brought his thoughts back to present. Ruth told him she had one matching bag to her carry-on piece. The floral print was easy enough to spot when it circled in front of them. Grabbing both of their suitcases, he attached the two of his together and extended the handle. Hers were older and had no wheels or straps to connect them. He slung one bag over his shoulder as he tucked the suitcase under his arm and grabbed the handle of his bags.

"Do you have someone meeting you?" Andy hadn't asked before now. He looked at the woman beside him. Not for the first time, he realized how she made him think of his grandmother, the same kind features, wrinkles earned from hard work and lots of hours in the sun year after year. Both of them were slightly humped from age.

"My son should be here any minute. Don't worry about me. I'm sure you have someone special waiting, glad you're coming home." She patted his arm as she held it. Just then Andy noticed a tall, dark-skinned man in a suit walking toward them. Ruth grinned and waved as she spotted him, too.

"There comes Jerome now." She tugged slightly on his shirt sleeve and he bent toward her. "You remember what you promised, Andrew. You have to come visit me when you are in St, Louis again. I gave you my address and phone number on that sheet of paper." She kissed his cheek just as her son approached them.

"Lieutenant Andrew Thomas, this is my son, Jerome Simmons. Jerome, Andrew kept me company from Raleigh. He finished his Army career at Fort Bragg yesterday." The men shook hands before Jerome took his mother's luggage.

"Take good care of yourself now, Andrew."
"You too, ma'am. It was nice to meet you, sir."
"Same here, soldier. Welcome home."
With that, Jerome turned back toward the doors, mom in tow. Andy heard Jerome ask if she were in the habit of kissing white boys in the airport. Ruth was cackling as they went through the outside doors. Andy grinned and went in search of his ride.

Chapter Two

Chuck Thomas scanned the groups of arriving passengers looking for his son. Andy would be in the throngs of people somewhere close. As proud as he had been when Andrew finished college and went into the service, he was thankful his boy was coming home for good. He spotted the soldier standing off to the side of the crowds. Andy had not yet seen the truck. It gave Chuck a chance to watch his child as he waited for a place to pull next to the curb. Dad noticed how nice his son looked in his fatigues as he followed Andy's eyes. The soldier tipped his cap, grinning at two young ladies flirting with him as they passed. Chuck was still laughing as he pulled to the curb and called his son's name.

Andy turned from watching the two women sashay by to the direction of the voice calling him. He saw his dad and waved as he reached for his baggage. Stowing the bags in the bed of the truck, he climbed in beside his father.

"Welcome home, soldier."

"Thanks, Dad." Andy grinned and leaned over to wrap his arms around the man sitting beside him, hugging him as if he were ten again. Maybe it was Ms. Ruth that made him feel so nostalgic. Whatever the reason, he was certainly happy to see the man next to him. Judging from the hug, his father felt the same way.

Coughing to clear the lump suddenly cutting off the air to his lungs, Chuck straightened himself in the seat and reattached his seatbelt. "Are you ready for that drive home?"

Home was almost three hours away in Lincks, Missouri, although it wasn't home to Andy, not yet anyway. His parents had moved there from Chicago about two years ago after passing through town on a trip. They had spent two days in Lincks, checking out the town and the surrounding area. The couple had been ready for a change in their lives and felt drawn to that area of Missouri almost immediately.

Chuck Thomas had owned a construction company in Chicago, providing custom-built homes in the more affluent suburbs. The year before they had moved, the contractor had fallen from the second floor of a house when a rafter slipped. His back had been injured, and he still had problems when the weather changed. Supervising all of the construction held no appeal for the builder.

Nora Thomas, his wife and Andy's step-mother, had always wanted to open a bed and breakfast. After spending time in Lincks, they sold the company and moved the family to the small town, building her dream business on the lake located outside of the township. Andy's two half-sisters had relocated with them.

"I'm looking forward to some of Mom's home-cooking." Andy thought about the woman married to his dad. He had been seven years old when Nora Gomez had come to work for his dad as the housekeeper and nanny to Andy. A year later they were married, and Hope was born on Andy's ninth birthday, July fourth. Faith was born exactly two years later. Andy enjoyed his birthday with the girls. It wasn't often family members shared the same event.

"Are those sisters of mine at home, or are they gone again?" Andy asked. The last two times he had been home on leave, both sisters were on mission trips in Mexico. He hadn't seen them in almost four years.

"They're home. The church here isn't as big and can't sponsor trips like the girls took in the past. I'm rather glad. I

6

like having them around during the summers. It will be nice to have all of my children at home for a while." Chuck grinned at his son as they merged onto the highway.

Discussing a little bit of everything, Andy was surprised when he noticed the exit sign just ahead. At the bottom of the ramp, Andy started noticing signs along the roadside. *Welcome home, Andy. Our hero returns. We missed you.* There had to be one almost every mile. The soldier looked at his dad.

"We missed you, son." Chuck wiped a tear he hoped Andy didn't see.

"I love it, but we had better stop and pick them up as we come across them."

Chuck laughed and turned the truck around at the first clear stretch in the highway. Andy had always been his environmentalist. He knew the signs would bother him until they were all picked up no matter how much he appreciated them.

When they approached town, storefronts all along the square had signs in their windows welcoming the GI to town.

"This is a special place, Andy. The people are friendly and really care about one another. Only downside is everyone knows everybody's business. Don't say I didn't warn you." Chuck grinned at the younger man beside him. "We'll need to come in soon, so I can introduce you around. There are a few people I know you'll be happy to see."

Before anything more was said, his dad turned the pickup down a long drive toward a huge Victorian-style home. It was large enough that the word home didn't really fit it. The structure was more than twenty-thousand square feet. The place had a long porch across the front with several pieces of white wicker furniture sitting on it. Flowers of every variety and color filled pots, planters and flower beds scattered across the lawn. The lodge looked like Nora. He saw her

7

hand in everything his eyes scanned. The two men grinned at each other as Andy grabbed his suitcases and headed toward the house with his dad.

"We're home." Chuck called out. They had made good time, but he had expected someone to have heard the truck and been there to greet them. Andy sat his bags on the floor and followed his father toward the kitchen. Just as the older man started to speak, Andy touched his shoulder, putting his finger to his lips. He walked quietly toward his step-mom, wrapping his arms around her waist. Nora heard the whisper before she could turn around.

"Hi, Mom." Andy stepped back, giving her space to turn in his arms. She grabbed him around the waist and hugged him tight as the tears started to flow. She had always been an emotional person.

"Aw, Mom, don't cry." He kissed her cheek before releasing her.

"Just look at you, Andrew. You are way too thin." Then she smiled and took his face in her hands. "Welcome home, sweetheart." The three of them stood talking for a few minutes before he heard laughter coming from the backyard.

"Are the girls down there?"

Seeing Nora's nod, Andy slipped out the back door. He noticed two women in recliners on the dock. Neither of them had heard him approach. He had waited almost four years to see them, and they were sunbathing. Lifting the one closest to him, Andy growled as he threw her into the air to catch her again.

"What kind of a welcome is this?" He swung her over the water just as he heard a scream and something about not swimming. Twisting the way she was, Andy lost his grip, and she fell into the water. He saw her arms flailing as the other female hollered.

"Andy, Casey doesn't swim!" Hope screamed as she sat

8

up ready to jump into the water.

"Who—" He swore as he dove into the water fully dressed. Surfacing, he reached the woman, thrashing in the water. It took all of his military training to keep her head above water while swimming toward shore. The woman fought him with everything in her.

Laying the young lady on the shore beside the dock, Andy rolled her onto her side as she began coughing. After a couple of minutes, she was breathing deeply but evenly. Hope and Faith knelt beside her.

"Casey, are you okay?" Hope moved the wet hair from her face. "Do you want to sit up?"

Seeing her nod, Andy placed his arm behind her shoulders and helped her. He still watched her face for signs of distress. "We need to get her to the hospital and make sure she's alright." He was already lifting her into his arms once more.

"I don't need a hospital. Really, I'm fine." The sensations going through her body from the man holding her were almost as strong as the fear she had moments ago. "Please put me down." She pushed against his chest feeling the muscles bulging as he held her.

Andy looked once more into her beautiful brown eyes before he allowed her to slip down his body. His hands kept her in place until she was steady on her feet.

"I'm Andy Thomas, former Army Lieutenant, current idiot." He took the towel Hope had given her and wrapped it around her back as he used each end to rub up and down her arms. "I can't even begin to tell you how very sorry I am. I knew my sisters were down here at the dock, but never thought about someone being with them. Are you sure you are okay? I'll be happy to drive you to a doctor. I would give you my blood, my life, my first born child." Andy grinned knowing he blushed as the last part of the sentence slipped out. He watched the fear in her face replaced with something else he wasn't sure he read correctly. *Was that attraction?* Hopefully, his comment would relieve some of the tension.

"My name is Casey Newton. Hope is my best friend. She told me you were due in town today. I really didn't expect such a dramatic introduction, but with Hope, nothing surprises me." Casey grinned back at Andy.

"Hey, none of this is my fault." Hope tried to act outraged. "Seriously, I'm thankful you're okay, Casey. Glad to have you home, Andy." She hugged her brother before stepping away.

Faith, his youngest sister, had stood watching the entire event. "Andy, I'm excited you're home, too." Andy received a hug from her as well.

"This is Tuesday, why aren't you at the clinic, Faith?" Andy knew his sister was normally at Doc Miller's, working as his nurse.

"We finally got that man to take a vacation. It was only two days, but that was something anyway," Faith told him as she headed toward the house.

Andy looked again at the woman still standing beside him. Her eyes were closed and her lips were moving slightly. He wasn't sure if she was shivering or praying. "Casey, are you certain you're alright?" He never felt so bad or so embarrassed about a situation before.

It was a few seconds before Casey opened her eyes. "I'm good, Andy. Please stop worrying. Let's get in the house and change out of these wet clothes. Oh, and welcome home, soldier." She stepped closer to him and kissed his cheek before walking away.

With the adrenaline wearing off, Andy thought about how fortunate he was things had turned out like they did. He took time to thank God himself before following the women into the inn.

Casey leaned against the wall in the bathroom connected

to Hope's room trying to get her nerves under control. She didn't want to think about the past. But as much as her heart tried to stop the thoughts of the incident, her mind grabbed on and brought them back to the present once more.

"Richard, I'm not really comfortable in the water. I never learned to swim."

"Casey, it will be fine. I won't let anything happen to you." *He moved further into the water pulling her with him.*

Just then a barrage of fireworks sounded all around them. Casey saw the kids shooting them only a second or two before she felt strong hands pushing her down into the water. Her mind registered it was Richard holding her down as she struggled against him. She fought for what seemed like eternity until she felt herself floating. Then people were screaming, someone was carrying her.

The next memory was in the hospital, bright lights shining in her eyes. "Welcome back, young lady. You gave us quite a scare there. We weren't sure if you were going to make it."

A knock on the bathroom door brought her back to the present. Hope was asking her if she was alright.

"I'm fine. Just about changed. I'll be out in a minute," Casey said. *It's time to pull yourself together. Andy got you out of the water. You're just fine. Richard's not here any longer.*

Chapter Three

Nora and Chuck hadn't mentioned the welcome party the family had planned for Andy until the day of the party. They knew he wouldn't want a big deal made of his return to civilian life, but they thought it would be the best way for him to meet as many people as possible in the shortest amount of time. Even though he appreciated the party, he wished they wouldn't have gone to all the trouble. But then, he knew how his mom loved any excuse to have company. The bed and breakfast inn was the perfect business for her. The event would also help take his mind away from the constant thoughts of what to do with his life after the service.

Andy had talked about possibly moving to St. Louis to find work, but his parents hoped he would find something in the area. He wasn't sure what he wanted to do yet. He had worked with Chuck every summer and was good at remodeling and new construction projects. He didn't have the capital needed to start his own company, and he didn't know if there would be that much business available in a small town. Right now, he wanted to spend time with his family for a few days before anything else. He had prayed about his future and knew God had a plan for him. He hoped he would know what that plan was soon.

By the time Andy came downstairs, a few guests had begun to arrive. As he walked out to the back deck, he looked at the couple talking to his dad. The man was tall, well over six feet. The woman beside the man looked up at Andy as he looked at her.

"Dani?" Andy couldn't believe his eyes. It had been more than four years since he had seen her, but he would know her anywhere. She flew into his arms, wrapping her arms around his neck as he held her close. "What are you doing here?" He was shocked to see her after so long and this far from Chicago. His parents had never mentioned her being in Lincks.

"I live here now. I want you to meet my husband, Garrett Austin. Garrett, Andy was Micah's best friend. They went to high school and college together. They even went into the service together. If Andy hadn't gone into a different field of training, he might have been killed with Micah." Micah was her half-brother who died at the beginning of his third tour of duty in Afghanistan.

Garrett smiled and extended his hand to her friend. Dani had told him about Andy and Micah's friendship. She had shared several stories about the two of them.

"Dad had called me when everything happened, Dani. By the time I was able to try reaching you, you were already gone. I'm so sorry I wasn't there for you." Andy hugged her close as she once again wrapped her arms around his neck.

"I know how much you loved him too, Andy. There is so much more I want to tell you, but let's save that for another time. Right now, we're here to welcome you back and hope you will make this your home. Lincks needs good men like you."

"What are your plans, Andy?" Garrett spoke up for the first time.

"I don't really have many ideas yet, Garrett. I only know construction and the Army. My degree in law enforcement didn't come in too handy for either of those. I thought I would end up with the military police, but the Army appreciated the fact that I could shoot more. My unit tracked down snipers most of our tours."

"Andy, I happen to be the sheriff here. We need to talk if you're interested in putting that degree to use."

"I just might. I'll stop by and see you in the next few days if that's okay with you."

"I'll look forward to it." Garrett slapped him on the back as they turned toward the couple coming through the door.

"I heard that good-looking Andy Thomas was in town." The woman said as she walked through the door.

"Amanda Black, are you here too, beautiful?" Andy lifted her into the air as his hands encircled her waist.

"She lives here with her husband and precious daughter," the man following her stated, smirking at the guy holding his wife.

"Well, you two are very lucky men. You have married wonderful ladies. Andy Thomas," he stated as he extended his hand to the man.

"I couldn't agree with you more, Andy. I'm Owen Jones. It's nice to meet you. Welcome to Lincks."

"Thanks, Owen."

"Andy, Casey Newton just walked in the front door. I think you might want to try erasing her first impression privately." Dani had walked close to him almost whispering.

"How did you…" Andy stammered, wondering how they knew what had happened.

"I warned you the town knows everything, son." Chuck commented as he moved past to get drinks for the group.

"I guess I'd better go see if she will even speak to me. Excuse me, please." He grinned sheepishly at them as he turned to re-enter the house.

Casey noticed Andy talking to the two couples as she walked toward the kitchen. She had stopped to check with Nora to see how she could be of help. Pine Trees Bed and Breakfast had been like a second home to her since its conception. She and Hope taught together at the early childhood center and had become as close as sisters. She turned to look at the man as he walked into the room.

Andy gazed at her long legs below the pair of hot pink shorts she wore today. The pink checkered top somewhat hid the shapely figure he had felt while carrying her from the water. Her dark hair laid across her shoulders as if caressing them. Her eyes showed none of the fear from the incident two days ago. Today, they sparkled with mischief.

"I don't think you have officially met Casey Newton, Andy. Casey is like a third daughter around here, darling." Nora grinned at her son. She knew something happened at the water when Andy came home, but she and Chuck had been busy with guests leaving, and didn't see what occurred. None of their children had talked about it.

"It's very nice to see you again, Casey." Andy offered his hand feeling the tingle go through his body as she touched him. "Could I talk to you just a moment, privately?" He didn't want to have an audience when he apologized another time.

Casey liked the feel of Andy's strong hand as he clasped hers. It caused the same electric shock she felt two days ago. She didn't want to feel this again. The attraction was stronger, different than those feelings a year ago. She pulled her hand out of his reach and walked to the great room, knowing he would follow. His voice whispered close to her as she turned to face him.

"I owe you a huge apology. The more I think about it, the worse I feel. I haven't seen either of my sisters in almost four years. When I heard them laughing and not at the house to welcome me home, I—"

"You just picked up the first one you saw to throw in the water, huh?" Casey interrupted him, as he stumbled through what he was saying.

"No. Yes, I guess I did." Andy grinned at the woman in

front of him. "I only made your fear of the water worse."

"Who said I'm afraid the water?" Casey hated the fact someone might know.

"I could feel it in the way you fought me. I don't think the girls saw it, if that bothers you. It will be our secret. Do you think you can ever forgive me?" he asked, reaching out to run a finger down her arm.

"I don't know. What if I had had a date that evening? My hair was a mess." She shivered slightly as his finger lit up her skin. She couldn't let him see how his touch affected her.

"Your hair looked beautiful clinging to your neck the way it did. Any man would consider himself lucky to be going out with you. Did you have a date that night?" Andy continued to run his finger up and down her arm.

"That isn't any of your business." She tried to put him in his place, but she could barely think with him touching her the way he was. She wanted to run her hand across the stubble of a beard he had let grow the last couple of days. His hair was so dark, she felt sure he normally shaved twice a day. *Why am I thinking about these feelings?*

"Would you let me take you to dinner Monday night to make up for ruining your day?" He moved a step closer.

"That isn't necessary—," she started talking until he laid a finger on her lips.

"That's the very least I can do. I'll pick you up at six. You choose the place since I don't know the town." He smiled at her once more before he removed his finger.

"Now, let's go enjoy this party." He slid his fingers down her arm taking her hand in his before leading her outside.

Nora watched the two walk through the kitchen and smiled. *Those two will be good for each other.* She turned to pick up a tray of food and took it outside for the party.

Casey wasn't sure what had just happened. Hope had made her promise to give him a hard time, and he ended up certain she would go out with him. She had to admit she looked forward to the date though. Despite her misgivings, she couldn't help but be attracted to the man. But was she ready for another relationship, especially with a soldier?

Several other couples arrived, and the party went well into the evening. Andy learned that Owen was also on the police force, as was Tom Wallace. Andy remembered meeting him and his wife, Maria, earlier. He thought about his desire to work in law enforcement. In college, he was sure that was what he wanted to do with his life. He wanted to be part of a SWAT team someplace. He didn't expect much went on in Lincks requiring that type of training, but he was interested in talking to Garrett just the same.

He heard a laugh across the deck and turned toward the sound. He knew it was Casey. He had heard her soft laughter several times throughout the evening. It always caught his attention.

"She's quite a woman, isn't she, Andy?" Dani had walked up to him while he was watching Casey.

"You caught me staring, huh?" He grinned sheepishly. "You seem to know everyone around here. Is she dating anyone?"

"She and Hope are best friends. Have you checked with her?"

"If I asked my sister, I would receive all kinds of grief about it. She still brings up the water incident every time I come into the room." Andy laughed. He noticed Casey turn to look in his direction and grinned.

"I don't think there is anyone important in her life right now. She's been in town two years. She's active in church, but Lincks doesn't offer a lot of social life. You need to ask her out." Dani told him.

"I already have. We have a date Monday night."

It was Dani's turn to laugh. "I'm so glad you haven't lost

17

your touch, my friend. You were always the first one to ask the pretty ladies on a date."

"Yeah, but I let the beautiful ones get away." He reached out and side-arm hugged Dani.

"You know we were too much like brother and sister to ever date. You had better be nice to Casey, she's special." Dani hugged him back.

Garrett walked up to them as they stood talking. "Dani, the girls are asleep on their feet. We had better get the kids home. Andy, come see me soon. I have a deputy retiring next month, and I need to replace him."

"I'll be by in a couple of days for sure. Thanks, Garrett." The men shook hands before Garrett led Dani over to tell Chuck and Nora goodbye.

"We're going to head home as well, Andy. Stop by the bakery when you come to town. Maria and I are always there." Mandy hugged him as Owen shook his hand. "We're glad you are home safely. You'll really like Lincks if you give it a chance," she said as Owen picked up their toddler.

Within thirty minutes, the entire group of guests had gone. Faith and Hope had both left earlier with dates. Nora and Chuck carried the leftover food into the kitchen while Andy and Casey started picking up the dishes.

"You don't have to help with this, Casey." Andy took the dishes from her hands and sat them on the table with his.

"Are you trying to get rid of me, Andrew Thomas?" She grinned as he took her hands in his.

The door opened and Nora walked out. "You two go take a walk. We'll get these dishes."

Andy didn't wait for Casey's reply. He took her hand and led her down the steps toward the lake. The sun was setting over the water creating a postcard-worthy view with enough breeze to cool the air making the evening comfortable. The two walked down the grassy slope toward the dock.

"Would you trust me enough to go in the canoe with me?" Andy stood behind her slightly, whispering close to her ear. He heard her giggle as she turned to face him not realizing he was quite as close. They stood inches apart. Andy looked from her mouth to her eyes and back to her mouth, moving closer to her. Just as he started to kiss the lips that looked so inviting, something big bumped in between the two of them almost knocking them off of their feet. The something was a large shaggy dog, fighting for Casey's full attention.

"Sherman, what are you doing out here this late?" Casey laughed as she removed the dog's front paws from her shoulders. "Andy, this is Sherman, your neighbor's dog. Greg must have just come home. He travels, and Sherman is boarded a lot. He loves to explore when he gets home. Sherman is just a sweetheart, aren't you, baby?" She cooed to the dog.

Andy knew he didn't appreciate the dog as much as Casey. He had wanted to kiss her since he first met her, and somehow he didn't think that was going to happen, now anyway. He heard a man calling the dog. Sherman thought about ignoring the command, but turned toward home after a good scratch behind the ears from Casey.

"Can I take a rain check on the canoe ride? I really do need to get home. Tomorrow is church, and I haven't finished my Sunday school lesson yet. I have procrastinated on it longer than I should have."

They headed toward the house hand in hand. Walking around the structure to the drive, Casey pulled her keys out of her pocket.

"Are you sure you'll be alright driving home this late? I could follow you if you want." Andy hated to think of her on the road by herself.

"I appreciate it, but I drive this road all the time. I'll be just fine. Will I see you at church in the morning?"

19

"We'll be there. Dad told me how much the family enjoys it. I'm anxious to meet the pastor."

"Good. I'll see you then." She reached back to open the door, but Andy reached it before she could. Before he opened the door, he ran his hand down the side of her cheek and around to the back of her neck.

"Sherman interrupted something I have to do, or I won't sleep at all tonight." He pulled her toward him as his lips captured hers. Casey moaned slightly as his other arm encircled her waist moving her closer still. She wrapped her arms around his neck. By the time Andy lifted his head, both of them were gasping for air.

"Be careful, Casey." His lips brushed hers again briefly before stepping back to open the car door for her. Casey wasn't sure her legs were going to hold her long enough to get into the vehicle.

"Goodnight, Andy." She looked away from him and started the car while he shut the door. She wasn't sure she would sleep now. As she drove home, she thought about the kiss and the man. She had never been more attracted to a man, and she thought of Andy's last statement as an omen. "*Yes, be careful, Casey, or you might lose your heart to this man.*

Chapter Four

Andy was accustomed to waking early and was ready for church before the others were out of bed. He let himself out the back door and headed for the dock with his Bible and a cup of coffee. The morning was as nice as the evening before. The sun was just beginning to peer over the horizon, offering the start to a beautiful day. He sat in one of the loungers and began to pray. He thanked God for his life and for the direction He planned for him. He was lucky to have a family to come home to and the promise of good friends, old and new. Andy knew how special his life was, and he certainly didn't want to take it for granted.

As the sun climbed high enough in the sky to make it light, he opened his Bible to read. He missed the opportunity to read like he used to, and he looked forward to making that a habit again.

He had always enjoyed reading the Psalms, and when his Bible opened to Psalm 116, he found new meaning to the verses 1-4.

"I love the Lord, for he heard my voice; he heard my cry for mercy. Because he turned his ear to me, I will call on him as long as I live. The cords of death entangled me, the anguish of the grave came upon me; I was overcome by trouble and sorrow. Then I called on the name of the Lord; O Lord, save me."

He was reminded of the month before his company returned from their last tour of duty. He had never told his family about the day the men were surrounded and expected to die. But the Lord had been with them. Two men were wounded, but everyone had escaped. The enemy had fled as if another company of soldiers came after them. God had surrounded them with His angels that day, Andy was sure. He had even talked to his captain about the feeling. Gabriel Morgan had felt the same way. God had spared their lives. He had saved them as the verses read. He didn't want to dwell on his time overseas, but he knew there would be times like today when he would be reminded of what God had done for him, and he thanked Him for it. He was so deep in thought, his dad was halfway across the yard before he heard the footsteps.

They sat and talked for a few minutes before Nora called them to breakfast. Thirty minutes later, the family headed for church together. While walking into the building, Andy was surprised at the number of people he already had met. The girls took him with them toward the young adult's class. Hope taught a Kindergarten class, but Faith was in the class their brother would be going to. Dani and Garrett walked in right behind them.

The hour passed quickly with a lively discussion about equality. The class was still buzzing as they headed toward the sanctuary. Hope and Casey were already seated with his parents. Faith moved to sit beside their dad leaving Andy to sit next to Casey.

"Do you want to sit with your family?" she offered.

"I'm perfectly happy right here." Andy grinned back as he noticed a man making his way toward the group, shaking hands as he walked along.

"Good morning. I'm Bill Jenkins, the pastor here. You must be Andy Thomas." He extended his hand, while placing the other one on the man's shoulder.

"I am. It's nice to meet you, Reverend Jenkins. I've heard

some wonderful things about you." Andy remarked.

"I can say the same about you, Andy. Maybe we should agree to believe half of what is said and get to know each other well enough to form our own opinions about the other half." The man grinned. Andy was surprised. He expected the pastor to be an older man, but Bill Jenkins looked to be just a couple of years older than he was.

"That might be the best idea, for sure, sir."

"My friends call me Bill. Hope I can count on you as one of those."

"Thanks, Bill."

Just then the music director took his place at the podium to begin the singing. The pastor patted Andy on the shoulder once more and scooted down to shake hands with a few others before he quickly moved out of the way.

Andy was happy to see that the church still used hymnals. The church they were going to when he left Chicago had an orchestra, and all of the music was on big screens. He had missed the books.

Casey picked up the one in front of them, turning to the page of the first song. She looked at him to see if he was willing to share a book with her.

He took one side moving closer to her and wrapped his arm around her waist. She looked at him once again, this time questioning his familiarity. He grinned sheepishly whispering to her that it made sharing a book much easier to stand close together. She grinned, accepting his explanation before turning to look at the book once more.

All too soon it was time to sit down. Andy placed his arm across the pew behind Casey, telling her it would make it handier in case they needed to share a book again. They sat close enough their shoulders and thighs were almost touching.

After church services, Nora turned toward her son.

"Andy, do you want to ride back to the house with Casey?" She had joined the Thomas' every Sunday for the last two years. Nora had insisted there was no reason for her to eat alone when they had plenty for her, too.

"Nora, thank you, but I'm sure you would rather it be just family today for Andy's first Sunday back." Casey felt like she was intruding.

"Darling, it will be just us. You know we consider you family as much as any of our children. Now you two ride together, and we'll see you at the house in a few minutes. I need to talk to Betty Lucas for just a moment." With that, she took Chuck's arm and headed them toward the couple talking to Dani and Garrett.

"Did Mom say her last name was Lucas? The man looks remarkably like Micah." Casey told him what she knew about the Lucas family, and how Dani had come to live in town with her young son. He knew they had the two boys and twin girls. He assumed the older boy was Garrett's by a previous marriage.

"It really is a small world, isn't it? Andy commented after hearing the story.

"It is," she answered, thinking about the voicemail she had last night when she got home.

"Have you decided where we're going for dinner tomorrow night?" Andy had his arm lying across her seat as he played with a lock of her hair while she drove. He was having a terrible time keeping his hands off the woman.

"I know a great place to eat, but it's in St. Louis. Would you be willing to take a drive with me for dinner? I have to make a stop before we can eat though. We would probably need to leave by noon or so to get everything done and get back before it gets too late."

"Hmm, a full day in your company. I guess I can handle that." He chuckled as she swung an arm out to hit him in the chest. They arrived at the house just a few minutes before the others. Both of them went upstairs to change. Casey was at the house so often that she kept some clothes in Hope's bedroom.

They had the table set and were dishing up the meal by the time the others arrived. Everyone sat down to enjoy the food and the company. As they each took the hand of the person beside them, Chuck led the family saying grace. Bowls were passed, and the conversation was lively. Andy was happy to be home for good.

"I'm going to wash my car. It needs to be clean for tomorrow." Andy stated as he finished drying the last dish. Casey had volunteered them for KP duty.

"We can take my car, Andy. I don't mind driving."

"I can still remember which side of the road to drive on and have a reasonable knowledge of the way to drive. Of course, it has been a year since I have driven in the states. I'll have to get used to not dodging things as I drive. Think you can trust me to keep you safe?" he teased.

"Hmm, a whole day of placing my life in your hands, I guess I can handle that." She replayed his words for him. Andy scooped her around the waist picking her up and swinging her around. Her breath caught just before she started to laugh at his response.

"Okay, if I have to ride with you, I had better help you clean the car. I'll be right back." Casey ran upstairs to put on her swimsuit and a pair of old cut off jeans. She had a feeling she would be wet before the afternoon was through. Andy was wearing a tee shirt and jean shorts already.

By the time Casey got outside, Andy had the car pulled out of the barn on the property and onto the yard. She had seen the car in the building before and knew it belonged to him. After meeting the man, she thought the black Mustang convertible fit him perfectly. She heard it running and knew he must have modified the motor, as well as the exhaust. The car was certainly his pride and joy.

Andy connected the hose and gave her the nozzle. "If you'll wet it down, I'll wash it with the soap, and then you can rinse it."

She grinned with mischief, thinking about how cold the water would be. She needed to decide if she was ready for any retaliation. They worked together removing all dust the car had collected in the last few months. She knew Chuck had washed it a time or two while Andy was gone, but mostly it sat in the barn.

Casey was rinsing the car when the water overshot hitting Andy on the other side of the car. "Oops." She giggled not really trying to hit him, but not minding that she did either.

He looked up from the side of the car he was washing and grinned before squatting down to wash more of the side panel. Again, the water splashed onto his back as he bent over working. Casey walked around to the other side of the car ready to rinse the soap from the car when Andy jumped up, scaring her. The hose was aimed right at him soaking the front of his clothes. Casey giggled again and headed back to the other side of the car with Andy close behind her.

"That was your fault. You shouldn't have scared me." She tried to take off, but Andy had the hose in his hands. She wasn't about to let go of the nozzle. She turned toward him. "I have a weapon, and I'm not afraid to use it." She started laughing and pointing the water hose toward Andy's bare feet.

He kept advancing, and she moved the water up higher on his legs. The closer he came, the higher she shot the water. He still didn't stop. Casey knew he was going to take the hose away and turn it on her. She dropped the hose and started running, shrieking as Andy sprayed her legs from behind. She didn't take into consideration his longer stride until he had caught her around the waist spraying her as he threw her over his shoulder in a fireman's hold.

She could hardly catch her breath between the screaming and the laughing. He swung her around just as Sherman headed toward her. He bumped into the pair sending Andy sliding on the slick grass. He rolled over, holding Casey as best he could. They ended in a heap with Sherman in the middle of them, licking Casey's face.

Andy's side hurt from laughing so hard. He and Casey were covered in grass and she had doggy slobbers all over her face. She still looked beautiful. Andy sobered, looking at the woman. She didn't worry about how she looked, she was having fun. He knew he was feeling more and more for her by the day. He hadn't known her a week, and he was halfway in love with her. Casey was the kind of woman he had waited to meet his whole life.

"Sherman, sit. Be a good boy." Casey was trying frantically to stop the dog from licking her face as she sat mostly in Andy's lap. *He must think I'm crazy.* She pushed the dog as his owner came walking up to the pair.

"I see Sherman found you, Casey. He has been pawing for the last fifteen minutes wanting outside. I think he heard your voice." He reached down to pull the dog off of the woman and gave her a hand standing up. "You must be Andy Thomas. I'm Greg Parsons, your next door neighbor." He took Andy's hand and helped pull him to his feet as well.

Andy looked at the man, shaking his hand. He was about the same six feet, three inches that Andy was. His hair was sandy blond and brushed his collar making his look more casual. He had a strong chin and good build. He wondered if Casey found him attractive. He guessed his age to be between thirty and thirty-five. He was trying to get Sherman to sit long enough to get Casey away from the dog, but Sherman wanted to play.

27

Casey finally took matters into her own hands. "Sherman, sit." She told him in her best teacher voice. The dog immediately stopped and sat. The men looked at each other and chuckled. Casey looked at both of them.

"You take Sherman home and get him dried off. And you need to get the soap washed off of your car." The men stopped chuckling, and once again looked at each other before they did as they were told. Casey took the hose and washed the grass from her legs and arms as best she could. Then she washed the dog slobbers from her face before she turned toward Andy. He was watching her. She grinned and asked if he wanted the hose to wash off the grass.

He took it and washed the grass from himself before turning the hose on the car. He had finished washing everything. It just needed to be rinsed. Casey started drying the areas as he removed the soap. They had it shining in no time. Andy pulled it back into the barn as Casey turned off the water and coiled the hose. After they had cleaned up the bucket, sponges and towels, they decided to walk down to the dock to dry off.

"Have you dated Greg Parsons? Is that why Sherman seems to love you so much?" Andy hoped he asked the question casually enough to not betray his true feelings.

"Last summer, Greg spent a lot of time here. He was between assignments and was home more than usual. He and Hope dated most of the summer. She hoped it would become more than it did, but Greg thought he was too old for Hope. He broke it off and started taking more assignments."

"How old is he?"

"He would be thirty-five now, I guess. That's only ten years difference. Hope felt like his age was not a problem, but she could never convince him."

"What does he do?"

"He is a freelance photographer for several magazines.

He goes on locations all over the world. You should see his work. He takes some beautiful photographs. He took some of Hope one time. You could see how much he cared about her in his work. She loves Sherman, as much as I do, and she would marry Greg in a heartbeat if he would ask her. It makes me so sad for her. She tries going out with other men, but they don't mean anything. Maybe one day he will realize what he's losing."

Andy thought about Casey and what she had said. He thought Greg was too old for Hope, as well, but if they truly loved each other, maybe the age shouldn't make a difference. He figured he was at least eight years older than Casey. He would try to find a way to get to know his neighbor better. He wanted Hope to be happy, but he wanted to be sure about this man, too.

He looked over at Casey to find her fast asleep. He loved watching her. Even sleeping, she was exciting. Her mouth curved into a slight grin, and he wanted to taste her lips again so badly he thought about kissing her awake.

He heard the boat before he saw it. An inboard ski-craft came into view. The occupants waved, and he realized it was Dani and Garrett. They were by themselves. Garrett pulled the boat along the dock as Casey stirred.

"We were going for a ride around the lake. Do you two want to go with us?" Dani issued the invitation.

Casey grinned at Andy. "Do you want to see the lake?"

"Sure. Thanks for inviting us." He helped Casey into the boat as he stepped in himself pushing away from the dock at the same time. Garrett started the engine as the couple put on their life jackets and got seated. The three of them pointed out different things to Andy as they took their time cruising from one end of the lake to the other and back again to the dock where they started.

"Do you have time to come in for a drink and some

29

dessert? Mom always has something for eat."

"Thanks, Andy, but we have to get back. Betty and Lucas are watching the kids, and we don't like to leave them too long when they have all four of them. The girls can be quite a handful." Garrett told them.

"They must take after their mother, then." Andy laughed as Dani placed her hands on her hips.

"Just you wait until you have children, Andrew Thomas. You will be paid back in spades for everything you did to your parents," Dani told him, giggling.

Having children was not something he had given much thought to before now. After meeting Casey, he wasn't as nervous about the idea. "I'm in no hurry, Dani. Garrett, thanks for the tour. I'll be in to see you in the morning, if that would be a good time."

"Tomorrow morning will be fine. Owen and I are just a quarter of a mile down the road. We run at least three to five miles most mornings, if you are interested in joining us. We usually take off about five-thirty."

"That would be great. I had planned on running in the morning. I'll see you then. Thanks again." They waved as the boaters headed back toward their house.

"Are you really getting up to run at five-thirty?" Casey couldn't believe people would want to do that. She had a yoga workout she tried to do each day, but never that early.

"I'm up by five every morning. That will give me some time to read my Bible and then get in a run. It sounds ideal." He grinned at her expression.

Chapter Five

Andy spent thirty minutes reading his Bible before he took off down the road toward Garrett's place. The sheriff was just coming out of his house when he reached the end of the drive. Owen waved as he cut across the yard from the house next door. The men greeted each other and took off at a leisurely pace before increasing their speed. They ran almost two miles before turning back to retrace their steps for the last part of the run.

"I'll be in a little later this morning, if that works for you, Garrett," Andy stated.

"Good. I look forward to talking with you." Garrett waved as Andy continued back to the lodge.

He cleaned up and headed into town by nine o'clock. His first stop was going to be the bakery before heading to the police station. He parked in front of the building with a sign 'Lucas' Deli' above the awning. He wondered if they were the same people his mom had talked to at church yesterday. The bakery was next to it, so Andy moved toward that door. As he walked in, he saw not only Mandy and Maria, but Owen and Tom, the deputy he had met at the party the other day.

Mandy gave him a hug as he approached the group. "You're right on time. We just took a fresh batch of apple fritters out of the oven. I can't run these two off until they each have one. I'll be right back." Maria went to help Mandy glaze and place the fritters on a tray for the display. Each man received their own fritter on a small plate.

"If these taste half as good as they smell, I may become your best customer. Apple fritters are my favorite, but I have never had them baked before." Andy bit into one rolling his eyes as the flavor melted in his mouth.

"Maria makes them. They're our best seller, hands down. So are you going to talk to Garrett about working with these crazy guys?" Mandy asked.

"I want to talk to him, anyway. I'm certainly interested in law enforcement since that's what my degree is in. But I'm feeling drawn to the construction as well. I enjoyed helping my dad with remodeling and building projects every summer. I doubt that there is a market for that type of work here anyway. That and I don't have the capital to buy everything myself yet."

Tom couldn't help but get excited. "Andy, we need to talk. I think you would be surprised by how much remodeling skills are needed in Lincks. My friend, Cody and I have been toying with the idea of starting a remodeling business ourselves. The work is there, but like you, parting with the money to buy all of the tools needed is expensive. Cody is also on the police force. Maybe it would be something we could look at as part-time work to supplement our incomes." He and Maria were making ends meet, but barely. Cody and Ava were struggling even with his job and hers at the deli. Plus, they were expecting a baby in a couple of months.

"That sounds promising, Tom. Let me talk to Garrett, and then we can sit down and discuss this some more. Would your friend be interested in a third partner?"

"Actually, it was Cody's idea. We've been trying to get Owen interested for months now. Of course, having someone actually bring skills to the table is even more exciting," Tom teased his friend.

"Hey, now. I have to resent that, can't deny it, but have to resent it." Owen pretended to be upset.

"We can teach you the trade if you are willing to work with us, Owen." Andy liked the way the men were so comfortable with each other. If the rest of the force were this easy to be around, he knew he would enjoy the job whatever it was. It reminded him of the platoon he left in the Army.

"Okay, then. Let's all go talk to Garrett. We need to get these things settled. Is Cody on duty yet?" Owen was finishing the last bite of his fritter as he kissed his wife goodbye. Tom handed his empty plate to Maria, kissed her and headed out the door right behind Owen.

"Looks like you have a job, want it or not, Andy. They have already decided you're one of them." Mandy took his empty plate and kissed his cheek before she pushed him out to follow them.

Andy trotted to catch up with the two deputies. Both men had on their uniforms, so he wasn't sure if they were already working or just going on duty. Tom could even be finishing his shift for the day. Nothing more was said until they entered the police station.

"Andy, this is Bethany Snider, our day dispatcher. Bethany, Andy is here to talk to Garrett about replacing Dan since he has decided to retire. Is Garrett in his office?" Owen was moving toward the back of the building as he talked. Andy was between him and Tom, walking with them. He figured this was going to be a group interview at this rate. Bethany never said anything, just waved as the men escorted him past the office containing the dispatch console.

Owen walked into Garrett's office and took a seat in one of the chairs across from the desk. He motioned for Andy to sit in the other one while Tom parked himself against the cabinet behind them. Garrett looked at Owen and Tom before grinning at Andy.

"Do you want to do this as a group, Andy, or should I run these two mother hens out while we talk?" Garrett asked.

"Either way is fine with me, Garrett." Andy wasn't sure what to say. He hoped he didn't have to make a decision in the next five minutes. He was still waiting to hear from God about the plans He had. He quickly prayed for the right words to say when he was told about the position.

"Garrett, you know this is just a formality anyway. We've already talked about hiring Andy if he wants the job. Our concern now is when he's going to start and what his schedule will be, so we can work out the details for our other job." Tom was the one to speak up first.

"What other job?" Garrett looked confused.

Tom and Owen quickly filled the sheriff in on the conversation they'd had earlier at the bakery. The men were excited, it seemed, about getting started with this venture. Andy had to admit he was as well, but he wanted to make sure the men really knew what they were doing. He didn't want his name associated with poor quality work.

"I know neither of you goes on duty for a couple of hours, but find something to do while we talk for a few minutes. Go back and harass your wives. Andy will meet you there if he wants to talk more about this." Garrett felt like he needed to take control of the situation.

The men told Andy they would meet him in a few minutes. They left the room talking about how to get the business off of the ground.

"Andy, I know with a degree in law enforcement, you were expecting to do bigger things than be a deputy in a county sheriff's office. The pay is not the greatest and the hours stink sometimes, but you couldn't ask to work with better people. Is this something you think you might be interested in?"

"Garrett, to be perfectly honest, I don't know. I have prayed about it since I met you at the party on Saturday. I was stunned when Tom and Owen talked about the remodeling business. Both of these positions are something I had thought about doing, really the only things I knew I wanted to do. I just hadn't thought about doing them in a town this size. I talked to Mom and Dad about going to St. Louis, maybe getting on the police force there. I'm discovering there are a lot of things I like about Lincks though."

"I don't want to try to persuade you either way. We don't have a SWAT unit where your shooting skills would be used more. We don't have detectives. It's just us. We do what has to be done. We give tickets, we take care of domestic disputes, do searches for lost children, we save lives. Whatever it takes, we are there to make it happen. Not everyday is exciting, but not every day on the St. Louis police force would be exhilarating either. Day to day, we're not much different except that you get to know the people you serve. They become friends. I'm glad you are looking to God for answers. I wouldn't want a man on my squad that didn't rely on God first. Andy, we would be pleased to have you work beside us, if you decide that is what you want. But don't let any of us pressure you into taking this job. I want it to be right for you. Do you have any questions?"

"Nothing I can think of right now. I know where to find you, if I do think of something. I appreciate you taking the time to talk to me and the offer. Hopefully, I will have an answer in the next couple of days." Andy stood to shake hands with the man sitting across from him.

"Have Tom take you to his house. You need to see their work before you talk about a second job with those three men. They're great to work with, but you need to know the type of work they're capable of doing." He shook Andy's hand as he walked around the desk to stand with him.

"Thanks, Garrett. I'll do that." Andy left the office and headed back to the bakery. It was ten o'clock. He was supposed to pick Casey up in two hours. That gave him enough time to visit with the men about their discussion. He was definitely interested in both positions. Garrett was right. When it came right down to it, he knew day in and day out, all positions would become routine. Casey was as much of a reason to stay in Lincks as his parents and the job opportunities. He was anxious to discuss them with her.

"Well, when do you start?" Owen and Tom walked out to meet him before he reached the sidewalk.

"I'm still talking to God about this, guys. I don't have an answer yet. Tom, Garrett suggested I see your house. I take it you have renovated it?" Andy decided to be straightforward with them.

"Do you want to drive or walk over there? It's about three blocks away." Tom didn't hesitate. He would feel the same way if he didn't already know what Chuck Thomas was capable of. He knew if Andy could do work to his dad's expectations, he was a good carpenter.

"Let's walk, if you two have the time. I have to be somewhere by noon, but if you men go on duty before that, it's fine. We can do this later."

"I have to relieve Dan in an hour. We have a suspected drug house we've been watching. Problem is the people know who we are. They haven't slipped up yet. Tom doesn't go on duty until noon, right?" Owen talked as they walked toward the house.

They reached a street lined with houses, some had been renovated, but several more were in need of repairs. Three of the houses needing to be remodeled had 'for sale' signs in the yard.

"Our house looked a lot like that one when I purchased it." Tom pointed to one as they passed by it. "I worked off and on over fifteen months to finish what I wanted to do. Then Maria became pregnant with our son. We are in the process of building two bedrooms and another bath on the back of the house. Maria's father is going to move in with us when I get the rooms finished." Tom opened the door and invited the two into the house.

Andy was immediately impressed with the place. He liked the stained moldings and the crown work. Tom led them through to the kitchen.

"I gutted the kitchen and started over. Like most older homes, the kitchen was a good size, just not functional." Tom was proud of the workmanship. "I'll show you one of the bathrooms, and then show you the new addition."

Owen followed the men through the house. He knew how to do minor repairs now, but he didn't have the skills to bring to the business. As much as the extra money would come in handy, he wasn't sure it would be fair for him to think about joining the team. The only thing he had done was help Tom and Cody when they built the extra bedrooms on the back of Cody's cottage and then help with the addition on Tom's house.

Andy was impressed with the work Tom did. The quality of the addition was first rate. Tom had mentioned Chuck gave him some pointers and had helped with the walls. That didn't surprise him. He saw some of the extra things his dad insisted on adding when he was in construction. He was interested in talking to the men more about the possibility of starting a business.

"What are they asking for the houses on the market, Tom?" Andy wondered if renovating a house might bring in fast capital. When Tom told him how much they were, he was surprised.

"There aren't a lot of homes available in Lincks. It seems high, but the value of my house doubled after remodeling it. That was before the addition. Thing is, so much has to be brought into town from St. Louis or other large towns. We don't have wholesalers or the big chain stores around here to buy from. Jack, down at the hardware store, is the best we have when it comes to ordering lumber. He sells it to us at next to no profit because it costs him so much to purchase it himself.

"Or we have to drive to St. Louis and get what we need ourselves." Tom knew these facts would be discouraging to Andy, but they needed to be honest with each other. He figured they could recover their expenses and make a good profit, but the cash layout at first would be expensive. He saw that Andy realized the same thing by the look on his face.

"So, do you think doing renovations for other people are a better alternative than purchasing a place ourselves and doing the remodel?" Andy asked. He knew the investment wouldn't be nearly as great, and the customer would pay for things in installments, where a house remodel could be a waiting game. They discussed the pros and cons until it was time for Tom to go on duty. Owen had already gone to relieve the other deputy.

"Let's talk to my dad, Tom. I respect his opinion. He might have some ideas we haven't talked about yet." Andy wanted to see what his dad thought about the venture. He would know if it was worthwhile or could cause them to lose everything.

"I agree. Chuck Thomas is a valuable source of knowledge. Just let me know what you want to do next." Tom was excited about the idea, but he knew he couldn't push, and they all had to take things slowly to make sure their bases were covered.

Chapter Six

It was five minutes until noon as Andy pulled up in front of the address Casey had given him. She was outside pulling weeds in front of the apartments when she heard the car coming. She looked up and waved as he parked and climbed out of his vehicle.

Andy's heart skipped a beat as he looked at the woman before him. Her long hair was pulled into a high ponytail and white shorts graced her long legs. She wore a red sheer shirt over a white tank top. Her sandals were red, matching the shirt. It was all he could do to keep from wrapping his arms around her standing there on the sidewalk.

"Hi. I was ready early, so I thought I would get some of these weeds pulled before they get carried away." She walked back toward the apartment two doors down. "Come in while I wash my hands." She opened the door to the apartment and walked in ahead of Andy.

"Those weren't your weeds you were pulling?" He was surprised when she didn't go into the apartment beside the flowerbed where she was working.

Casey shook her head. "Mrs. Johnson lives there. She's elderly and can't get around to care for them herself, so I try to help where I can. It's no big deal. I'll be right back."

Andy thought about what a nice person she was as he looked at the photographs Casey had sitting around the room. There were pictures of a couple with Casey and by themselves. He wondered if the man and woman were her parents. Within a minute or two, she returned.

"Who is the couple with you, Casey? Are they your parents?"

"Yes. They live in Florida, now. Dad retired after being a bank officer in St. Louis for thirty years. They love the life of leisure as they put it." Casey grinned. "Are you ready?" Andy nodded, and they walked out the door.

"Let's stop by and have a sandwich at Lucas' Deli. I would like to introduce you if he's there." Casey waited for Andy to unlock the car door and opened it for her.

Although the deli was busy, they were able to get a table right away. Andy saw Mandy and waved. She came over to the table just as the waitress finished taking their orders. She wanted to tell Casey hello and see how their meeting went.

"I wanted to introduce Andy to Lucas if he's around." Casey told Mandy.

"I'll go get him. He's in the back playing cook today. Ava is gone. The baby is really active and giving her fits. I'll go take his place so he can come out here. See you later." Mandy headed toward the kitchen.

"What meeting is she talking about?" Casey grinned at him.

"It's a long story. I'll tell you all about it on the way to St. Louis. Here comes Lucas now." Andy stood as the man approached the table with their sandwiches.

"You must be Andy. I've been wanting to meet you." Lucas ignored the hand Andy extended and wrapped his arms around the man hugging him close. "I'm sorry we didn't make it to your party. Betty, my wife, wasn't feeling very well. I understand you were my son's best friend."

"Micah and I were like brothers. I'm so sorry you never had the chance to meet him. He wanted so badly to get to know you one day. He talked about it often. It's comforting to realize he's waiting for us in heaven." Andy noticed the tears in the man's eyes.

"I'm grateful to meet another person who can tell me about him, his hobbies, the things he liked or didn't like, that kind of thing. Dani has told me so many stories about both of you. I hope we can sit down and have a long conversation one of these days." Lucas didn't bother to hide his tears.

"I would like that very much, sir. I'll make sure it happens soon." Andy hugged the man again before he sat down, and Lucas turned back to the kitchen. The couple ate their lunch and asked the waitress for the check.

"That's on the house per Lucas' instructions." She smiled. Andy gave the waitress a generous tip as they left, thanking Lucas when he reappeared from the kitchen.

As they drove to St. Louis, Andy told Casey about his morning including all of the different conversations. They discussed both renovating a house for resale and for clients. Casey saw the merits in both and knew Chuck would be able to give them better advice.

"You might want to talk to Adam Reynolds. He has a large construction company in town. I think all he builds are large commercial projects, but he might have a line on places to get the lumber and materials cheaper. Adam built the school where I teach and the apartment complex where I live. He's building a small strip mall right now. You probably saw it coming through town today," Casey told him.

They reached the exit Casey was watching for, and started giving Andy directions. All further talk about job opportunities would have to wait. She was excited and nervous about their destination. She knew Andy would be charming either way, but she hoped she was right about the surprise. She told him to park in front of the house on the right.

Andy was a little shocked at the neighborhood they

were in. A lot of the houses were boarded up and young men stood on the streets just watching the traffic. Casey seemed familiar with the area though, so he tried to relax.

Walking a couple steps ahead of Andy, she reached out and pressed the doorbell as he stepped onto the front porch. The house was in much nicer condition than most of the houses he could see. He heard shuffling and locks clicking before the door was pulled open. Ruth Simmons stood in the doorway.

"Casey, it's so good to see you and look who you have with you. How did you meet Andrew already? Come in, come in. Where are my manners?" Ruth moved back from the door as Andy looked at Casey. She took his hand, and they walked into the living room as the older woman offered them a seat.

"Ms. Ruth, when you called me the other night and told me you had met the most charming man on the plane, I had met that charming man in person. From the things you said, I felt sure we were talking about Andy. I wanted to surprise both of you. Besides, if he wasn't the one you were talking about, nobody would have known I was mistaken." Casey chuckled. "Andy, you never mentioned the lady's name you visited with on the plane, but I recognized the things you told me she said about Harold. It's a small world, isn't it?"

Andy had not said anything until now. "I have had the privilege of meeting two beautiful women in less than a week. Who would have ever guessed they knew each other?"

"See, I told you he was a charmer." Ruth cackled as the two women smiled at each other.

"Just how do you two know each other?" Andy finally asked.

"We became acquainted through Meals on Wheels. Have you heard of it, Andy?" Casey asked him.

"I have. Did you start bringing meals to Ms. Ruth?"

"Hardly. Ms. Ruth started the Meals on Wheels chapter

in this part of town. It has grown to serve more than one thousand people every day. Without her persistence, there would be no meals for all of those citizens," Casey told him proudly.

"Now, child, you know someone would have started it sooner or later. I was just tired of seeing my neighbors go hungry, and I was getting too old to feed them by myself every day. Casey was one of my best drivers. During the summers, she delivered over three hundred meals each day by herself. She worked her classes around the noon schedule so she could deliver as many lunches as possible. She volunteered until she had to leave two years ago to take a teaching job in that little town. What is the name of the place again?"

"It's Lincks, Ms. Ruth. That's where I met Andy. His family built the bed and breakfast I told you about. Hope is his sister. Hope has been over here a time or two to meet Ms. Ruth, Andy."

"What did you do while you were raising Jerome, Ms. Ruth? No, let me guess. You were a school teacher, weren't you?"

Ms. Ruth cackled. "How did you know that, Andrew? I never mentioned what I did for a living."

Andy laughed as well. "I can just see you, in that firm teacher voice I have already had Casey use on me, telling the city council how they need to get things arranged, and what they need to do. I'm surprised you aren't the mayor of St. Louis." Ruth and Casey both looked at him with straight faces.

"And what voice would that be?" both of the ladies said at the same time. They looked at each other, and all three of them burst into laughter.

"Casey, is Ms. Ruth the reason you are a school teacher?" Andy figured he already knew the answer. He had seen and heard the admiration she had for this woman.

"She's certainly a large part of it. I try to be like her every day. She has always been one of my heroes."

"We are all someone's hero, if we can make a change in their life. Remember what I told you, Casey? You should strive to put one hundred percent into everything you do, even though your one hundred percent might be different than my one hundred percent. As long as we each give all we can, we can make a difference. You are a much better teacher in so many ways. I could never work with those little preschool imps like you do."

The ladies changed the subject when Ms. Ruth asked, "Did I tell you Mrs. Johnson on Eighth Street passed away?" Ruth and Casey talked about different people Casey had delivered meals to for the next fifteen to twenty minutes.

Andy sat back and listened. He admired both of these ladies. There were so many things he wanted to know about them both, but he knew he would seldom meet two people more dedicated to serving others. He was proud to be their friend. There were areas of his life he wasn't giving the one hundred percent Ms. Ruth talked about. He needed to find ways to serve others better. Maybe that was God's way of telling him to take the deputy position Garrett offered him.

A bell rang a few minutes later, and Ms. Ruth excused herself to see about dinner. "Andrew, I hope you like chicken and dumplings. I always make it for Casey to get her to come visit me," she called from the kitchen. Casey and Andy stood to walk into the kitchen with the woman.

"Chicken and dumplings is one of my favorite dishes. I haven't had them in several years though. It smells delicious." Andy commented. "My stomach has been appreciating the aroma since we arrived."

"Well, Casey, you set the table, and Andrew, you toss the salad. We'll be ready to eat in a jiffy." The two worked to get everything on the table as Ms. Ruth dished up the food.

Andy carried the big bowl to the table as the ladies followed. He held the chair for Ms. Ruth and pulled Casey's chair out for her before seating himself. Ms. Ruth reached for each of their hands as she bowed her head in prayer.

Thirty minutes later Andy wondered if he would be able to drive home, he was so full. He had always thought his step-mom's dumplings were the best, but that was before Ms. Ruth's. He proceeded to tell her just that. The three visited for another hour or so before Andy and Casey needed to head back to Lincks.

"You must both promise to visit soon. I'm so happy you have found such a nice young man. It's time to let yourself trust again," Ms. Ruth said as she hugged Casey. "And Andrew, promise you will take good care of this special girl."

Andy heard the comment the woman whispered as she hugged Casey. He hoped she would explain the remark once they were in the car. "I certainly plan to, Ms. Ruth. I agree she is very special."

With a promise to return soon, the couple started toward Lincks. Casey kept the conversation going long enough for Andy to forget about the statement made by the older lady.

Chapter Seven

Pine Trees B and B was booked for the rest of the week. Andy had wanted to talk to his dad about the business the men had discussed, but Chuck was kept busy most every day. Finally, Andy remembered Casey telling him about Adam Reynolds. He decided to drive into town and see if he could meet the man. He had seen the strip mall project Casey told him about, and he headed in that direction, hoping the owner might be at the work trailer.

When Andy knocked on the office dooe, a man opened it and asked if he needed help.

"I'm looking for Adam Reynolds." Andy looked at the two men. One man sat behind a desk and the one who opened the door still stood beside it.

The man at the desk spook. "I'm Adam Reynolds. How can I help you?"

"My name is Andy Thomas," he said as he walked toward Mr. Reynolds, while extending his hand. "I was wondering if I could make an appointment with you to discuss a business venture a couple of guys and I are thinking about." Andy explained.

Adam shook the hand offered to him. "You must be Chuck Thomas' son. Dani told me you were in town. She can't say enough good things about you. Do you have time to talk now?" Adam had heard about the man all over town. He already knew Garrett had offered him a position.

"I would appreciate that if you have a couple of minutes."

Andy hadn't expected to be able to discuss the situation today, but he certainly was going to take the man up on his offer if he was willing to talk now. He hoped to have some better ideas when he sat down with Tom and Owen again. "This is my foreman, Bud Rutledge." The men shook hands, and Bud told Adam he would get the crew on the area they had been discussing. Then he left the trailer.

"Sit down, Andy. Can I offer you some coffee? It tastes like it's boiled with tar, but Bud makes it, so I can't complain." Adam grinned at him.

"I'm fine, thanks."

"What's on your mind?" Adam figured they were both busy men and there was no reason to make idle chit-chat.

"I have been talking to a couple of men about starting a renovation company here in town. We haven't decided if we want to purchase homes and remodel them or just look for projects to renovate. The reason I came to you is the lumber and materials. Tom said it just isn't available around here. I was hoping you might know of sources closer than St. Louis that we could contact instead of ordering from the hardware store."

"Well, there's certainly a market in Lincks for quality craftsmen. Are you as good as your dad?" Adam asked.

Andy laughed. "My dad taught me everything I know about wood and building. I don't know how well you know the man, but I can tell you I wasn't given a break being the boss' son. He would have fired me as fast as any other man working for him if I messed up. I've seen the work Tom Wallace does. We're thinking about this venture together with Owen Jones and Cody somebody. We haven't met yet."

"Those are some of the finest men in town. Tom does excellent work. I have tried to hire him a couple of times. Cody is coming right along, as well. Owen is a hard worker, but he hasn't done much with his hands yet. I know a couple of different lumber yards I can get you in touch with. I get shipments from them probably twice a week most weeks. They are both full service and should have about any type and grade of lumber you would need. I'm sure we could get your order placed on the truck with my wood. Let me know when you men are ready to get started, and we'll talk to the owners to see what we can do." Adam knew they would be able to keep busy especially working around their shifts at the police station.

"Are you going to work for Garrett? I heard he offered you Dan's position."

Andy looked at him and grinned. "I'm thinking about it. I've never lived in a place as small as Lincks. I just want to make sure it's a good fit before I commit to the work." He decided not to comment on the fact that Adam already knew about the job offer.

"Lincks has a way of grabbing onto you and lulling you into staying. I don't think you can find any better people anywhere around. I know you would be a great asset to our town. Casey says a lot of good things about you." Adam smiled at the grin on Andy's face.

"I suppose Casey is a friend of yours."

"My wife, Grace, is the principal at the early childhood center where Casey teaches. They're very close. You and Casey will have to come to dinner soon and meet my family. We can discuss your business venture some more."

"Adam, I really do appreciate your help. It's good to know we can find a source for the materials. All of us are working with little capital, so we can use all the breaks we can find. Thanks so much for your time. I'm anxious to talk to the others." He stood, and the men shook hands as Andy turned to leave.

"I'll have Grace give Casey a call." Adam told him as he started out the door.

"We'll look forward to that. Thanks again." Andy was anxious to see if Tom was on duty today or not. He headed toward the police station.

———⚜———

"We have to change our tactics somehow, Garrett. I tell you these guys know we are the cops, and they're watching us watch them." Owen was pacing in the front office of the police station as he spoke to Garrett and Tom.

"Okay. And just what do you suggest?" Garrett felt their frustration.

All three of the men looked at Andy as he walked through the door. Owen smiled, Tom nodded his head, and Garrett scowled.

"Am I interrupting something, fellas?" Andy felt like he was either the big winner or the loser. He just wasn't sure which.

"Andy is just the man we need." Tom took matters into his own hands. He wasn't waiting for Owen to make the same statement. "They won't know anything about him. Even if they checked, he's straight out of the service. He has a great alibi."

"My thoughts exactly. Garrett, he would be perfect." Owen agreed with Tom.

"What are you men talking about? What would I be perfect for?" Andy was confused.

"Just ignore them, Andy. You aren't even on the force. You couldn't help if you wanted to." Garrett frowned at the two officers. "We need to find a different angle."

"Is this about the drug dealers you're trying to arrest?" Andy was beginning to see where the conversation was going if Tom and Owen had their way. He was interested in knowing more.

"What do you know about drug dealers, Andy?" Garrett wondered how he knew anything about the investigation.

49

"Only that Owen mentioned you had the place under surveillance, but figured the men knew they were being watched. Sounds like you need someone undercover to bring them out in the open. I was pretty good at getting information while I was in the service. I could usually get someone to talk about sniper locations when we needed it. I think it's my honest face." Andy grinned. The tension broke when all of the men started chuckling.

"Andy, I can't let you do this unless you are taking the deputy position, and I don't want you to feel pressured to do that. I can bring in someone from another county or even the state if we need to. Problem is we don't have enough proof yet." Garrett was feeling the same frustrations as his deputies.

"How bad are these dealers, Garrett?"

"We know a few of our youth have been buying, everything from marijuana to meth to heroin. We have caught them with the stuff, but none of them will turn on the dealers. We don't need this in our town. We've noticed a lot of out-of-towners coming through lately too. We can track them to the house and arrest them with possession, but we can't prove they bought it there. We need to get the men dealing the stuff." Garrett hadn't had a problem this bad, this long in his town before now, and he didn't like it.

"Then we need to shut them down. I'm ready to help with this in any way I can." Andy had seen buddies get hooked on drugs, knew they were being sold under the noses of the officers, and it made him sick. He had helped with an investigation once while he was overseas. He felt comfortable getting close to the dealers. He told Garrett what he had done to help in the past.

"Andy, are you sure? You don't want to think about this?" Garrett didn't want him to take the position just because he was caught up in the heat of the moment.

"Garrett, I want to help get this out of Lincks. I don't want this town to attract that type of people, and I don't want the people of Lincks subjected to this kind of trash. If I'm going to live here, I want to do my part to make sure this is a clean town." Andy knew he had just committed his future to this place, but he felt it was what God intended for him to do. He was ready to go to work.

"Then let's get you sworn in. No one will know you are working for the police, though. Can you keep this from your family and Casey? The fewer people to know the truth, the better off we'll be. People don't know what you have been doing while you were in the service. I think we should go in with the plan that you need a new supplier for your buddies. We need to make sure we get as high up the ladder as we can, or they will just replace the men and keep on dealing. We're centrally located enough to be a good place for distribution, as well as recreational sales. What do you guys think?" Garrett had been considering a plan like this since he met Andy. He felt like he could create a cover that would be solid enough to work as long as Andy could deliver it.

The idea of keeping his activities secret from his family and Casey wouldn't be easy. Casey didn't know him well enough to trust him yet. But that would be the only way to keep them safe. The men headed back to Garrett's office to hash out the plan.

As they talked, Bethany came back to the room in a hurry. "Cody just called in. The house under surveillance has blown up. I dispatched the fire department."

Garrett and the men were down the hallway ahead of the dispatcher. "Andy ride with me. We'll meet you two there," the sheriff stated as he ran for his vehicle.

By the time they reached the house, it was fully engulfed in flames. Cody could only watch and try to keep people away from the scene. The fire department had pulled up and were attaching hoses as the men jumped out of their patrol cars. Owen, Tom, and Andy helped the fire department while Garrett checked in with Cody.

"What happened?"

"I saw all three of the men we've been watching go into the house. Five minutes later the whole thing exploded. I would bet they were cooking meth and something went wrong. Garrett, Truman Vaughn had been in the house for the last thirty minutes or so. None of the men made it out of the building."

Cody gave him all of the details he had recorded. Truman was only twenty-one years old, but he had been in trouble around town before. Garrett hated to see him lose his life over something like this.

The fire department was mostly volunteers, so it took a little more time for others on the team to reach the location. They had the fire under control within minutes, but there wasn't anything left of the place. Between the explosion and the fire, the building fell in on itself. *Recovering bodies won't be easy.* Garrett looked at the blaze as he called the county medical examiner and explained the situation. He would take him a while to get to the scene. *Not much he can do anyway right now.* Garrett walked toward the fire chief.

The deputies had done all they could to help with the fire. Mike Guthrie, the fire chief, wet down the hot spots before talking to Garrett.

"How many bodies are we going to be looking for?" Mike asked his good friend.

"We know for sure there were four inside. Hopefully, that's all. We've been watching the place closely for the last two weeks. We were tracking all of the comings and goings of the occupants."

"Give me a few more minutes to make sure the fire is out, and you can go in. Your men will need their suits though.

I assume this was a meth fire from the way it blew?"

"It looks that way. Just let us know when we can start our investigation. I'll issue the protective gear." Garrett motioned for the deputies to follow him. He led them to his car. "Owen, do you have your hazard gear in your vehicle?" He looked at the deputy.

"Yeah, I'm ready to suit up. I have one extra suit with me." Owen looked at Tom and then Andy.

"I have two suits in my trunk. Tom, you and Owen get dressed. Andy, I'll give you the extra suit I'm carrying. I need Cody to keep eyes on the crowd. We need to make sure we don't recognize any others from the ring."

They all got ready to slip into the protective gear needed for the investigation. Garrett went over what he wanted Andy to be looking for and what to bag as evidence. Tom and Owen would be working with the M.E. office.

Chapter Eight

Andy was due to report for duty later in the day. It had been after eleven o'clock when he finally headed home. Dan and Tom stayed at the crime site overnight to make sure nothing was disturbed. Even though he came in late and then spent over an hour talking with his dad, Andy was up by five, and decided he needed to run to clear his head. He was thankful he wasn't needed undercover, but knew the next few days would be anything, but ordinary.

Just as he reached Garrett's home, he saw the two men heading for the road.

"You couldn't sleep either, huh?" Owen teased Andy.

"Figured a run would clear my thoughts before I started today," he told the men.

"You started yesterday, Andy, and you did a great job. You were thorough and efficient. It'll be good to have you on the team." Garrett patted his shoulder.

"Thanks, Garrett."

"What made you come by the station in the first place yesterday? Were you ready to accept the job?" Owen hadn't thought about him being there when they needed him until now.

"Actually I came by to talk to you and Tom about lumber. I met with Adam Reynolds yesterday. He's going to help us get a better price on shipments of wood if we decide to go into business. I still haven't had the opportunity to talk with my dad, but I'm excited about this venture," Andy told Owen.

"I don't know why we didn't think to talk to Adam before. That's a great idea." Owen was feeling more excited about the idea all the time. He never had that much to do on his days off. With their daughter, he wasn't able to take off and go like he used to do before he got married, so earning some extra money sounded like a good idea to him.

"Adam said he would help us if we wanted to pursue the business. He thinks there are plenty of jobs in town to keep us busy."

"I don't want you men to decide you like this work better, and all quit on me." Garrett teased them.

"I think we're pretty secure in our positions, Garrett." Owen grinned at them.

"Garrett, do you feel like the fire yesterday took care of the drug ring in Lincks?" Andy had been thinking about it last night and again this morning.

"If there were any others involved, maybe they'll go looking for a different town, now. They all knew we were watching and closing in more every day. I can't imagine them sticking around. It would be much easier to start over someplace else. At least, that is what I hope they'll be doing. Time will tell, I guess." Garrett had already asked himself the same questions Andy did.

"One good thing, even with me on the force, I'm still the new guy in town. I could always use the cover we talked about. It would be pretty brazen to sell drugs in a police uniform, but it certainly wouldn't be the first time it has happened." Andy commented. It might take a few weeks for the men to regroup, but if their traffic was good enough in town, they could come back, assuming there were men still alive that knew the trade here.

The men finished their run and went to their homes to get ready for work. Andy was to pick up his uniforms today. He had some training to go through and would be riding with one of the men for the next few days. They would be at yesterday's crime scene most of the day, again, checking for things they had missed. They had located the four bodies and no others so they were comfortable with the total death count.

After his shift today, he hoped to be able to talk to his dad about the other business, as well. It was going to be a full day, and he was excited about getting started.

Walking into the police station an hour later, he saw Garrett talking to a deputy he had not met yet. He knew it was Cody from the fire yesterday. They just hadn't had a chance to be introduced.

"Andy, this is Cody McGuire. I want you two to start out together today. I need both of you to relieve Dan and Tom at the crime scene. I'll be over there after I check with the M.E.'s office. Make sure we didn't miss anything. Cody, you need to look again at the photos that have been taken over the last few weeks to make sure the three who went in yesterday are the only dealers we've seen there. I don't want someone else relocating in Lincks. Andy, I have your uniforms in the back room." Garrett turned to head that direction while the two men followed him.

Fifteen minutes later, Andy had been issued his uniforms, badge and gun. Andy and Cody drove to the scene and got out of the cruiser. Tom and Dan were waiting for them, looking toward the burned down house as they approached.

Tom introduced Dan and Andy before the older officer left for the station. Tom decided to hang around for a few minutes. Maria was at the bakery already, so there was no hurry. He would go by to see her in a while.

Cody asked Tom how the night had gone. "We had a few vehicles drive by. After they saw us taking pictures of their cars and their license tags, they took off pretty fast. We noticed a few we had seen before, but a lot of them might have just been gawkers too. This was a pretty big deal in Lincks." Tom told the men the other facts he knew.

"This investigation is far from over, isn't it?" Andy knew there would be a lot of paperwork involved trying to place all of the traffic and the people coming and going. "Are you all pretty comfortable thinking the fire killed all of the men involved?"

"I don't think we've seen anyone besides the three men that we considered dealers. They had to be getting their supplies someplace, but judging by the length of time they were gone each time they left, we feel pretty good that their source was no place close to town. We tried tailing them, but they were pretty sophisticated. They knew how to lead us on a wild goose chase. We were just too short on manpower to follow all three of them when they would all leave at once." Cody shared with Andy.

The two officers spent the next few hours sifting through the debris looking for anything they missed yesterday. When they came across something, it was photographed and bagged as evidence. Both men knew to treat everything as if there would be someone going to trial.

By the end of his shift, Andy was ready for another shower. He pulled into the drive and saw Casey's car there. He was anxious to see her, but had hoped to change his uniform and shower first. *She doesn't even know I have accepted the position, yet unless someone in town told her of course. That's certainly a distinct possibility.*

He walked in to see his folks talking to her in the great room. She didn't look at all surprised to see him in uniform. "I guess you can't have any surprises in Lincks, can you?" he grinned at her.

"None whatsoever. You look very handsome under all that soot." She grinned back at him.

"I'm going to go up and get rid of all that soot and be back

57

in a few minutes. You are staying, aren't you?" He looked at her making sure she knew he wanted her to be here when he returned.

"I'll be here." She smiled back at him. For a second, they both forgot Andy's folks were in the room.

Casey was in the kitchen helping Nora with dinner. Chuck was still in the great room, when Andy came downstairs. "I was hoping we could talk for a minute, Dad. I've talked to some of the deputies, and we're considering forming a renovation company. We would all work part-time on our days off. We could use the extra money, but it would also be a way for me to keep my hand in the construction business. I miss working with wood, the way we used to do."

"I think that would be a great idea, Andy. I know the work Tom and Cody do. There is certainly a demand for renovation work around here. Are you thinking about redoing houses or just taking on odd jobs?"

They talked about the pros and cons of each aspect of the business. Andy told him about meeting Adam Reynolds and his willingness to help.

"There are some other things you would need to consider. There would be the insurance and the other legal work to form a company. You're going to need a location to work from and a vehicle to haul things." Some of the things his dad mentioned Andy had already thought about, but some were new issues they would need to discuss. Finding a time when all four men could sit down together was going to be difficult with at least two of them on duty at any one time. They were still discussing details when the ladies called them to dinner.

Chuck gave thanks and Andy asked about his sisters. They hadn't been home much at all since he had returned. His mom told him they both had another date.

"I saw Greg on the way into the house this afternoon." Casey brought up the subject casually.

"We need to invite him over for dinner one evening." Nora picked up the conversation. She had liked the man and thought he would be good for Hope. She wasn't too crazy about his schedule and the amount of time he was gone traveling. But she knew how Hope felt about him and wished they could have tried making a go of their relationship.

Chuck knew where Casey and his wife were going with their comments. He liked Greg Parsons, but he wasn't sure he approved of the age difference between Greg and Hope. Just as those thoughts crossed his mind, he thought about Andy and Casey. He knew she was the same age as Hope. Andy would be thirty-four in a couple of weeks, almost the same age as Greg. He decided his best bet would be to keep his mouth shut. He took another bite of dinner instead.

Andy had been thinking about the age difference between him and Casey as well. She seemed so mature, more mature than Hope. He hoped she didn't feel there was too much of a gap in their ages. He would talk to her about it tonight. He looked forward to spending some time alone with her.

After dinner, the two walked down to the lake. Andy wanted to explain about his new position, and why he hadn't talked to her about it. He told her why he accepted the job, but something stopped him from telling her the part about going undercover. He explained how it had happened so quickly, his parents didn't even know about it until last night.

"Andy, you don't owe me any explanations. I know you will be a valuable asset to the police force." Casey looked at him and smiled.

"Casey, I want to owe you explanations. I want to tell you what I'm thinking and hear your opinions. I value your thoughts more and more every day." He reached out and ran his hand down her cheek before pulling her into his arms. He lowered his mouth to capture hers applying the briefest pressure to the back of her head moving her closer to him. Casey moved willingly, wrapping her arms around his waist as Andy deepened the kiss. When he pulled away from her lips, he continued to hold her hugging her close to him.

"Grace Reynolds called me today to invite us to dinner Saturday night." Casey decided she had better bring their thoughts back to safer conversations. She was too comfortable in Andy's arms.

"When I met Adam the other day he said he would have Grace call you. I will be working Saturday morning, but will be off by three-thirty. I would like to meet her if you want to go."

"I'll call her tomorrow and see what time we should be there." She told Andy how Grace and Adam had adopted three siblings before having a daughter of their own.

They spent the next hour talking and enjoying each other's company. Andy asked her what she thought about the renovation plans. They talked in length about the things they would need and the best options. He appreciated her ideas. He knew he was thinking of Casey as a partner already, someone he could share his dreams and future with.

"Casey, I'll be thirty-four in a couple of weeks. I know you and Hope are close in age. Do you feel like there is too much of an age difference between us?" Andy looked at her to see what her first reaction would be.

"I never thought Greg and Hope were too far apart in age. I don't see that we are any different. You don't feel that way, do you, Andy?" She knew Andy hadn't had the opportunity to visit with Greg.

"I have to admit I was worried about it at first. But you seem so much more mature than Hope. I think of her as a girl, but you are definitely all woman, Casey." He grinned hoping she didn't take the statement wrong.

She laughed. "Andy, Hope is very mature. You just

haven't spent enough time with her to realize she is not your little sister anymore."

"You're probably right, but neither of them is ever around. Maybe we could get her and Greg together one evening, and the four of us go to dinner or something. I would like to get to know him better."

"I'll talk to him and see if he would be willing to join us. I'm sure Hope would be if he will come." They talked more about the idea until Casey yawned.

"You are the one getting up at five o'clock, and I'm the one falling asleep. I had better get home so both of us can get some rest." She stood to leave waiting for Andy to move beside her. They walked back to the house hand in hand.

Nora and Chuck were sitting in the kitchen talking when the two walked through. Casey told them goodbye, kissing Nora's cheek as she hugged her and then Chuck. She had treated them as she would her parents for more than a year now.

"Come over tomorrow, and we'll work on the plans for the birthday party," Nora told Casey.

"What birthday party? Mom, you aren't having another party, are you? Don't you think we are getting a little old for birthday parties?" Andy couldn't believe his mother was planning another event for them.

"You know we always have a Fourth of July party. The lake makes a beautiful place for a fireworks show. Besides, the girls like celebrating their birthdays, even if you think you're too old for one. We're having a party with birthday cake. That is the only mention of your birthdays, promise." Andy had complained about it the last time he was home as well. That was fine, Nora knew he would still enjoy it.

He walked Casey out to her car. "I'm going to count on you to keep Mom's party from getting out of control. She always gets carried away when she does these things."

"That's because she loves doing them. You know she will do as much as she wants no matter what anyone says. I won't be able to stop her." Casey knew Nora would listen to her ideas, but would do what she wanted. "I had better get going so you can get some sleep." She reached up to kiss his cheek, but Andy turned toward her mouth instead.

As Andy wrapped his arms around Casey, she laid her palms on his chest keeping a distance between them. "Andy, we need to talk but not tonight. I'm too tired, and I know you are getting up early. There's something I need to tell you."

"Casey, is there someone else?"

"No, Andy. But…"

"Okay, we'll talk tomorrow. Please be careful going home this evening." Andy kissed her cheek before stepping back to give her room to get into the car. He had only known her a couple of weeks, but it felt like they had been destined for each other. She was his other half, and he wanted to tell her how much he loved her. He didn't have anything to offer her yet. He would need to be patient, but he was determined to make this work.

Tears washed down Casey's cheeks before she packed out of the driveway. *I think I'm in love with Andy Thomas. Can a person fall in love that easily? I can't let these feelings grow any stronger before I tell him about Richard. God, please help me to know Your plan for my life. I don't want to hurt Andy. Please give me the words to tell him tomorrow.*

Chapter Nine

Andy knew something was wrong when he walked into the police station the next morning. He had run with Garrett and Owen earlier, and they were fine. Now both men were standing in the front office watching him as he walked through the doors.

Garrett grabbed him wrapping his arm around behind to his back, while Owen took his gun. "What's going on, Garrett?" Andy was shocked at the way they were treating him. They pulled his handcuffs off of his belt and placed them on him before they moved from the front window. Then they led him back into the office areas further.

"Sorry about that, Andy. We're being watched. After we got all of the photos spread out and starting comparing them, we noticed another person we hadn't paid much attention to before. He always came in heavy and left thinner. We should have caught onto him earlier. We just didn't see it until we laid the photos across the table. We figured he was a customer. He's hanging around town. It looks like he's checking out the area to set up shop somewhere else here. Are you willing to go undercover and see if you can get him to talk?" They had removed the handcuffs as soon as they brought him back to Garrett's office.

"Well, you were pretty convincing out there. I figured I was in trouble. What do you have in mind?"

The men discussed different scenarios trying to come up with the best option. Finally they had a plan in place. The

63

three of them would be the only ones who would know what was going on. Garrett wasn't going to tell the other deputies. They would all think he was dirty and had been kicked off of the force. Andy mentioned how hard he thought it would be to convince his family and Casey he was really a drug dealer.

"I know your family won't like hearing it and I don't think Casey would ever believe you if you said you were really guilty, Andy. You two seem pretty close already. She'll be the hardest one to fool. Think you can do it, if it comes to that?" Garrett had his doubts. He had seen the way the two looked at each other.

"I don't know. We talked about why I joined the force, but I didn't say anything about going undercover. Hopefully, she will trust her instincts and my family to know to truth. She already made the remark that she would never believe me capable of anything shady like that. We'll have to see how good of an actor I really am. Garrett, it can take months, even years to get enough information on drug leaders and to make it worth the surveillance. Are you interested in confiscating their money and possessions?"

"Lincks is a small town and our budget is tight, but I don't want this ring in business any longer than necessary. I want to give it enough time to make the drug lords aware we can hurt them, and then we'll close it down. Bigger cities can deal with the big bosses." Garrett knew Andy was concerned about how long he would be undercover as much as how long they would wait to catch as many as possible.

An hour after Andy reported for duty, he was walking out of the police station rubbing his wrists where the handcuffs had been. Owen followed him to the door. "Remember what we said. You are not to leave town," he hollered as Andy walked across the square toward the bar on the corner. Andy shot an inappropriate gesture into the air never turning back.

———❧———

"I'll have a beer on tap, and I don't care what brand it is."
Andy wasn't much of a beer drinker, but he figured he could
nurse one or two, hoping someone would approach him. He
had already noticed the man in question follow him into the
building.

"I'll have one of the same. Put them both on my tab."
The man took a seat one stool away from Andy. Andy looked
at him suspiciously.

"Why are you buying me a beer? I don't know you." Andy
almost spit the words.

"Happened to see you coming out of the sheriff's office
without the uniform you wore in. You're the new deputy they
just hired, right?" The guy asked swinging around on the
stool to face Andy.

"I'm the one they fired, you mean? Hick cops think they
can pin something on me. I was never convicted of any
charges. They're saying I was dealing drugs in the service,
but nothing ever stuck. They don't know how smart I am.
They never will get any charges to stick on me, either." Andy
took another swig of his beer trying not to grimace.

"Did you hear about the drug ring that had set up here in
town?" The man had turned once again to face the bar. He
tried to ask the question casually enough.

Andy snorted. "Crazy fools. It seems to me like they
would have had a good thing going, if they'd been smart.
Bringing in locals and letting them cook. They got what they
deserved. I imagine someone was pretty upset about the
whole thing. Those guys weren't smart enough to be the
leader. They had to be flunkies. But I guess I've already said
too much. Anyway, thanks for the beer." He set his glass
down and started to leave.

"Are you going to be looking for work?" The man laid a
hand on Andy's arm to stop him. Andy looked at the man's

hand, and then at the man. The stranger pulled his hand away.

"I might. Do you know of any place hiring around here?"

"Let's go over to that table in the corner and talk. I might have a proposition you would be interested in. Name's Alfonzo, by the way." He led Andy to a table where a person could see the door, but tucked in a corner away from the other tables.

An hour later, Alfonso took Andy with him for a ride. They drove out of town for a while until they reached another rundown neighborhood much like the one the drug house was located in at Lincks. They entered the place, where three other men were busy working at the table, packaging drugs. They talked for a few minutes before Alfonzo introduced Andy. One of the men stood and walked over to Andy, quickly patting him down.

Andy was shocked. These men were ready to set him up with a score. They just needed a place to work from. Andy told them he knew about a place he could deal from and have the perfect cover. He told them he would need three days to get everything in order. He promised to return when he was ready with a location.

Alfonzo dropped him back in town. Andy didn't want him knowing where his family lived, so he told him to leave him at the square. He walked out to the inn making sure no one followed him from town.

He would need his dad's help securing a loan since he no longer had a job he could list. He talked to him about one of the houses he had seen for sale two doors down and across the street from Tom's. Andy knew it needed a lot of work. Houses on both sides of it were also empty and for sale, so there would be fewer neighbors keeping track of things. He knew Tom would keep an eye on the place once he saw the traffic.

Chuck Thomas had lots of questions, but he knew Andy well enough to let his son come to him when he was ready. He was more than willing to cosign for a loan. They talked to the insurance agent and got coverage on the place. Andy knew he wanted his family to be protected in case something happened.

Two days later, Andy had the keys to the house he wanted to remodel. As soon as this was all over, he would get the rest of the men involved with the renovations. Until then, he would work on it himself, using that as a cover for the drug sales. Hopefully, it wouldn't take long to get them to sell him a shipment. He had told Garrett and Owen about the meet, when they met to run. Today, he planned to move into the house, telling his parents and Casey he had to be gone for a few days on business.

He drove to St. Louis and traded his mustang for a truck he could use to haul lumber, and his family wouldn't recognize. Parting with the car had been difficult, but that part of his life was over. He would need the pickup when they started a business, so it made sense to trade it now.

Since Andy planned to stay at the new house, he knew he would be needing some things. He stopped by a thrift store in the area where Ms. Ruth lived. There, he was able to purchase an air mattress, bedding, a microwave, coffee pot and a couple of place settings of dishes. Garrett had told him they had a small refrigerator not being used at the station. He picked it up from the back of the station where the sheriff had stashed it. He hated using the extra money he made from trading his car, but there was no way to get the things from the barn at the inn. His folks would be worried enough without thinking they had a burglary. It took the last dollar he had in his wallet to rent a trailer for carrying the lumber he purchased to start the renovation. *Hopefully, this undercover won't last long. This lumber won't make a dent in what we'll need for the renovation.* He didn't want to even think about what he was going to do when the food he purchased was gone.

Approaching Lincks, he called Alfonzo to set up the meet. He knew Garrett had tapped his phone so all calls would be recorded. He also had a very sophisticated bug planted on him most of the time. Garrett or Owen would hear and record every conversation he had.

Alfonzo set up the buy, driving Andy to the same location as before. An hour later, Andy had the drugs in his possession. Alfonzo told him he would get the word out that they were back in business.

Chapter Ten

Andy had worked most of the day ripping sheetrock off of the walls in two bedrooms. He decided to pile everything in one of the rooms for now. He figured Tom would get curious and come over to see what was going on if he saw a dumpster at the house. He planned to move as much of the debris into the pickup late that night. That way he could empty it the next day, hoping to keep it from being seen as much as possible.

As he pulled the last of the plasterboard from the closet wall in the smallest bedroom, he heard the doorbell ring. Smiling to himself, he said, "Show time."

Expecting to see Alfonzo at the door, he was surprised to see a woman grinning at him. She had once been beautiful with long blonde hair waving around her shoulders. Her makeup was a bit much for Andy's tastes, but he had a part to play. Most men would certainly appreciate the young woman standing in front of him. He allowed his eyes to roam over her from head to toe before looking back up into her brown eyes.

"If you're through staring, you could invite me in." She smiled and ran her finger down his cheek as she pushed past him.

Andy looked each way up and down the street. There were no cars around and no one with her. Shutting the door, he turned back to his visitor. "To what do I owe this pleasure?" he asked hoping he sounded enthusiastic enough.

"Alfonzo sent me. I'm Edie and I'm all yours." The woman laid the palm of her hand on Andy's chest before moving into the living room. "Love what you've done with the place." She turned and raised an eyebrow, apparently waiting for Andy to say something.

This was certainly a complication he could do without. "It's nice to meet you, Edie, but you aren't staying. I work alone. I don't need or want any company." Andy reached for the door knob.

"Sorry, Andy. It isn't a choice. It's my job to 'help sales along.'" She raised her hands quoting in the air. "You could certainly make my work much more pleasant." She had moved back to the front door as well. There she took Andy's hand and moved it to her waist while she stepped closer to him. Wrapping her arms around his neck, she pressed her lips against his.

Taking her shoulders, Andy pushed her away from him. "You tell Alfonzo, if he wants my business, we do things my way. I don't need a woman to help sales along as you put it."

Edie turned her back on Andy and walked back into the living room. Her shoulders sagged and she let out a long breath. "I can't leave, Andy. Alfonzo expects me to keep an eye on you. I'm to report to him how things are going. Did you really think they were going to trust you so easily?" She had turned toward the man once more to see his expression. She probably shouldn't have told him as much as she did, but she had to make sure Andy let her stay. She could hardly suppress the shudder thinking about the last time she hadn't followed Alfonzo's orders.

Something about the way Edie stood there watching him made Andy know there was more to this than simply making sure he was doing what he said he would do. This woman, probably no more than in her early twenties, was scared. He let out the breath he didn't realize he was holding.

"You can stay the night. We'll talk about things in the morning. But you need to know, I'm not interested in any benefits with this job. I'm here to make some good money period. Nothing personal, but...." He hoped he didn't need to say anything more. "I'm heading to the shower. You can use the air mattress tonight. That's the best I have to offer you." With that said, he turned and headed for the master bathroom. Thankfully, there was a lock. With the shower running, he told Owen they needed to meet. He was the one manning the transmissions this evening. Giving Owen a place and time, Andy undressed and stepped under the warm water.

Ten minutes later, he walked into the living room to see Edie kneeling in her underwear ready to climb onto the air mattress.

"There's plenty of room, Andy. Come keep me warm," she coaxed.

"I've got things to do tonight. I'll try to be as quiet as I can, but I have to load my truck with this debris in order to keep tearing out the other walls. Get some sleep. I'll see you in the morning." He walked into the smallest bedroom and picked up an armload of sheetrock before moving to the front door.

"I might as well get dressed and help you. I can't sleep with you going back and forth." Edie started to get off the mattress once more.

"You aren't going to help me. Pull the mattress into the back bedroom. It will be quiet back there." Andy had planned to do that before he went to bed tonight, anyway. He hadn't gotten around to it. *Since I wasn't expecting company yet, she can make herself useful.*

It took almost an hour to carry the last of the sheetrock to the truck. He had taken time to make sure none of it showed above the bed of the cab. Covering it with a tarp, he went back to lock the house.

Edie was dressed, standing in the living room. "Do you plan to dump that stuff tonight or in the morning? You know, most customers will want to buy later at night until they get comfortable with the set-up. They will need to trust you enough to stop during the day. You even chose a location across the street from not one but two cops. Alfonzo said you were going to be arrested before you got started. What were you thinking?" She was getting more and more agitated.

She's crashing. Alfonzo must have her addicted to get her to do the things she was suggesting. "How long since your last hit, Edie?" He watched her reaction.

First, the sharp inhale, like she wanted to protest, then her shoulders slumped again. "I guess you have been around the stuff long enough to know, haven't you? Alfonzo gave me half before he dropped me off. He told me I could earn the rest keeping you entertained. Andy, I'm hurting. I need something."

This wasn't what he wanted at all. Stopping the supply was the reason for this whole thing; not supporting the users. But he knew Edie could be a wealth of information, if she knew enough about Alfonzo and the operation. "Wait here." He walked into the master bedroom and the restroom attached. Removing the stash Alfonzo had sold him, he took a small bag and put some of the powder into another empty bag. He wanted to give her enough to get past the shakes, but not get that high she was wanting. Then he took the rest of the supply and put inside of his shirt. He would need another place to hide the stuff.

Walking into the room, he almost felt sorry for the girl. She was sitting on the floor with her arms wrapped around her knees, rocking back and forth. He had seen men in some of the platoons with the same problems when drugs were not readily available. He knelt down and lifted her chin with his finger. "This will be enough to get you by. When I get back, we are going to have a talk before you get any more. Understood?"

She was in no condition to argue by then. Edie nodded and grabbed for the bag, hoping Andy wasn't going to make her beg. Her thoughts turned to Alfonzo. He liked playing that game. He would hold the bag in front of her until she reached for it. Then he would slap her across the face. *Think you'll get this for nothing, babe? You gotta earn it if you want it.* She was surprised when Andy let go so quickly. Looking at him, she waited for the abuse or the curse words she always heard. What she saw in his eyes surprised her. It looked like compassion. Maybe he just felt sorry for her. Whatever the look, she quickly scooted back and tried to stand. Andy was there to steady her.

Andy released her as soon as she was able to move on her own. "I'll be back in about an hour. I have to dump that load in the truck. Don't destroy the place looking for the rest of the drugs. I'm taking them with me." He didn't wait for her to answer. He turned back at the door to see her dumping the powder in a line on the kitchen cabinet.

Chapter Eleven

"I wasn't sure if you got the message or not." Andy said quietly. He had finished dumping the load from his truck just as he heard the noise coming from beside him. "Noticed you waited for me to finish here." He grinned. He looked straight ahead as he heard Owen's voice in the bushes beside the truck.

"Guess that Army training is still in your blood. I thought I was pretty quiet." Owen chuckled softly.

"You didn't think about that after-shave you're wearing. Don't take a shower and expect to sneak up on someone. We have more important things to discuss though. What do you think I should do about this woman?" Andy wiped his forehead with the sleeve of his shirt and sat on the tailgate of his truck.

"Yeah, Alfonzo pulled a fast one on us there. Is she as young as she sounds?"

"I figure she is between twenty and twenty-two. Alfonzo must have been using her for a while. Her teeth are in pretty bad shape, and she's trying to hide a pretty bad complexion with heavy make-up." Andy shook his head. "She was once a beautiful girl, I'm sure. Still looks good until you look close."

"Do you think she has enough information to be of benefit?" Owen asked knowing Andy had already wondered the same thing.

"I hope so. I know by the time I get back she is going to be needing more stuff. I want to talk to her before she is begging for it. Owen, I think we need to bring Tom in on this. If I can get her outside, maybe he can figure out a way to bust her. I don't want her involved in this any more than Alfonzo already has."

"Have any ideas how you want to do that? I'm sure Alfonzo has someone watching the place," Owen said.

"Actually, I'm counting on that. If I can get her outside while she is under the influence, Tom can be coming out of the house to go to work. When he hears the ruckus, he'll need to investigate. I want Alfonzo to see I'm doing my best to be an outstanding citizen, staying clean and out of trouble."

"How do you plan to get her to cooperate without selling you out?" Owen wasn't seeing this plan working.

"I have a feeling Alfonzo has his clutches into Edie deep. As much as she needed that drug, she was scared when I held it in front of her. I figure Alfonzo must have a mean streak in him. Hopefully, I can talk some sense into her before I kick her out. I don't know, I guess I'll play it by ear. Let's see how willing she is to talk when I get back. It may be a day or two before I can get anything out of her. Talk to Garrett and see what he thinks. I hate for Tom to be stuck at the house for a couple of days, and the rest of you being short-handed."

Owen chuckled. "Yeah, Tom would hate to hang around the house and get paid for it. I'll call him as soon as you give me the signal. He'll need a couple of minutes notice before he comes out."

The men talked a few more minutes before Andy headed back to town. They had a plan and a code word in place when he needed to use it. Now he had to hope he could get Edie to talk without any hint that something wasn't right.

———⬥———

Casey glanced down each street as she slowly drove out of town. She wasn't convinced Andy was out-of-town on business. After talking to Dani and Mandy, she knew the deputies seldom if ever left the county on business. She thought about the phone call from Garrett last night. He told her he sent Andy to St. Louis for training. If that were true, surely he could have called. Even if he didn't call her, he would call his parents. Training didn't last twenty-four hours a day. He had been gone for four days without a word.

Once she reached the highway, Casey noticed a car behind her. She had seen it in town, but didn't think much about it. Even now, it didn't raise any red flags until she turned onto the lake road. Though she thought it curious, she kept driving until reaching the inn's drive. As she turned, she looked back at the car. A man with dark hair and a mustache stared at her passing the car slowly. Something didn't feel right. Instead of pulling on down to the building, Casey waited for the car to go by. As soon as he cleared the drive, she backed out and headed back to town. Within a minute, the car was behind her again. She decided to drive to the sheriff's office. If the man was up to no good, he had chosen the wrong victim. If it was just a coincidence, there would be no problem.

Parking in front of the building, Casey checked her rearview mirror. The car stopped at the corner and made a right turn. She watched him for a few seconds before going into the office. Owen was on his way out.

"Hi, Casey. What brings you here?" Owen had heard about her questioning why no one had heard from Andy.

"I may be paranoid, but I think a man may be following me." Casey turned back to watch the car through the large window. The car was still driving slowly around the square. The side windows were dark enough she couldn't tell if he was watching her or not.

Owen came to stand beside her. "What makes you think he's following you?" His eyes never left the car.

After telling the deputy about the trip to the inn and

back, Casey felt a little foolish. "I'm sorry, Owen. I guess not knowing where Andy is has me jumpy. I'm sure it was just a coincidence. I had better let you get on with your day." She started toward the door.

Reaching for her arm, Owen said, "Wait. Let's see where he goes. I haven't seen that car in town before. Did you get a look at him? Can you describe him?" He moved them back into the office further where they could not be seen from the window.

The deputy was beginning to scare her. "No, I didn't recognize him. He looked to be around forty. He has longer, dark hair with a mustache. I wouldn't have thought too much about it since there are so many houses on that road. But he almost slowed to a stop while he stared at me."

"When did you first notice him?" Owen tried to be nonchalant about the questions, but his heart was racing. It was the same car Andy had described to him. He was parked down the road from the drug house.

"I'm not sure. I think maybe while I was driving down First Street. I dropped some papers off with a friend at the elementary school and was heading toward the highway. A house caught my eye as I passed it. It looks like someone has purchased the one across from Tom and Cody's places. There was lumber in the drive and a pickup out front. Andy had talked about doing that. I stopped in front of the place, thinking about him. It's a place like he would want to renovate. It made me miss him." Casey wiped across her cheeks hoping Owen wouldn't notice the tears.

He wrapped his arm around her shoulder giving her a hug. "He's okay, Casey. He knows what he's doing."

Casey turned to Owen with tears shimmering in her eyes. "Will you tell him we sent our love and to please be careful?" She wondered how long it would be before she saw him again.

"I'll tell him. Right now I want you to come back into the office and wait for me. I'm going to drive around a bit to make sure the man has taken off. I'm sure it was a coincidence, but we'll see. Okay?"

She nodded and allowed her friend to lead her into an empty office.

"Can I get you anything before I leave?" Owen asked. He had compromised Andy's cover by saying the things he did to Casey. Somehow they had to make sure this Alfonzo didn't associate Casey and Andy's family with him. Undercover was bad enough without the worry of someone getting to those you cared about.

By the time Owen had driven around the town and down the block a few times, he was convinced the man had taken off. He didn't doubt that there were or would be others keeping an eye out. Andy had yet to make a sale. He hadn't proven himself to be reliable. Owen called the station and asked Bethany to tell Casey it was safe to go home. He waited down the block and followed to make sure no one would know where she lived.

Chapter Twelve

When Andy came home after dumping the sheetrock and talking to Owen, he found Edie giggling as she stared at the wall. Occasionally, she swished her hand as if trying to catch something. It surprised him how the drug had affected her. Maybe she wasn't as addicted as he first thought. He quietly stood her up and moved her to the master bedroom after he had put the air-mattress in there. He took the camp chair from the living room and placed it in the hallway. It didn't take long for him to fall asleep even as uncomfortable as the chair was.

Andy woke with a start. According to his watch, it was already seven o'clock. His next thought went to the woman. Where was she and what was she doing? Moving from the camp chair where he slept last night, he looked through the open door of the room before heading to the hall bathroom. She was still sprawled out sound asleep. After finishing his morning routine, Andy walked into the kitchen to start the coffee. The empty baggie from last night was still on the cabinet. He grabbed an evidence bag and placed the smaller bag inside of it. Then he marked it before stowing it behind the refrigerator in a bag attached to the appliance. He had just stepped back to the coffee pot when Edie stumbled through the door.

"Hey. Can I have a cup of that coffee?" She smiled as she moved further into the room. She watched as Andy poured both of them a cup and reached for hers when he extended it to her. "Have any sugar and creamer? I like that hazelnut flavor."

"Sorry. I drink it black. Guess you'll have to drink it that way this morning. You can pick up a cup fixed the way you like it on your way out of town." Andy watched her over the rim of his mug before taking a sip.

"I can't leave. I told you last night Alfonzo gave me instructions to watch you and report to him each day." Edie took a little sip and shuddered before setting the mug back on the cabinet. "Think I'll just have water."

Andy watched her move to the cabinet door where he had put the two glasses he purchased at the thrift store. He figured she must have gone through the house waiting for her drugs to kick in last night.

"How did you got hooked up with Alfonzo?" Andy asked.

She didn't say anything until she filled a glass with water. Then she turned toward him resting her hip against the cabinet. "My mom sold me to the man for drugs. Nice story, huh?" She turned back to the sink and stared out the kitchen window. "I was twenty, a sophomore in college. I came home one weekend and found my mother entertaining a group of men. All of them were higher than kites."

After a deep breath, Edie continued. "I had come home that weekend to spend some time with my mother. I dropped my bags in my room and went looking for Mom. I heard music playing in the basement. My dad had made it into a nice den and Mom liked to hang out down there. That's when I saw what was going on. I turned to go back up the stairs, but someone grabbed me. It was a week, I think, before anything started to make sense. By then, I was at Alfonzo's. The rest you can guess." She quickly wiped the tears from her cheeks.

Andy waited a minute before asking anything else.

"Where was your dad during this time?"

"He was killed just before I was supposed to go to college. A drunk driver hit their car. Dad died at the scene. Mom sustained a broken back along with a broken leg. She was never very strong; she got addicted to painkillers. When the doctor started weaning her off, she couldn't take it. Said she couldn't live with the pain, and I guess she turned to dealers. By then, I had done all I could for her. I was able to get in school the second semester and I left. We were never close. It was always Dad and me. I know Mom was jealous. I didn't realize just how jealous until that day." By this time, tears were streaming down faster than she could wipe them off.

His mind was working furiously. *What are my options here? If I have her arrested, there's no guarantee Alfonzo or one of his men won't get to her. But can I trust her? She could be the key to the whole set-up depending on how much she knows.* He took a deep breath before walking toward her. With a foot separating them, Andy put a finger under her chin, lifting her face until he could look into her face.

"This isn't a life you chose, is it, Edie?" He asked watching her eyes. He felt her shudder before she answered.

"I wouldn't wish this on my worst enemy. I think about suicide, maybe overdosing, but Alfonzo makes sure I don't get enough stuff to do that." She moved away from Andy, once again looking out the window. "You know he's watching the place, don't you? If I can't give him a detailed report of your activities, he'll beat me."

Andy felt like his choices were limited now more than ever. He had to trust her. "How are you supposed to report to him?"

"He'll be coming by a little later today. After he scans the house for bugs, he'll take me with him for a while. Then he'll drop me back off before dark. Since nobody showed up to buy drugs last night, he must have held off putting the word out. He won't wait another day. If he thinks he can trust you, there will by buyers coming tonight. I don't know what I'm supposed to tell him. You aren't like the others, Andy. Something's different."

"If I can help you get out of this, will you trust me?"

Edie looked at him then. "Why would you do that? How do you know I won't tell Alfonzo everything you've asked me; all we've talked about?"

"Honestly, I don't know. I guess I have to trust *you* and hope you were sincere with everything you've told me. Can I trust you, Edie? Do you want out of this life?"

Before she could answer, the doorbell rang. Andy saw her eyes enlarge and her body start shaking. "It'll be okay, Edie. I'll handle this." He walked to the front door.

"Alfonzo, I'm surprised to see you here already. Thanks for the gift by the way. She kept this dump warm last night." Andy stood in the opening.

"Aren't you going to invite me in? I would like to check on my merchandise, make sure she's happy." The smile on his face made Andy want to punch him or puke or both.

"She's asleep. Think I must have worn her out, ya know."

"Well, you wouldn't mind if I just looked in, now would you?" Alfonzo pushed on the door.

"Yeah, I would. When you give a gift, you don't have to keep track of it. You just need to know the one receiving it will make good use of it. It's not too smart of you to be coming to the house, anyway. You know there are two cops that live on this street. I spotted your car last night watching the place. If I can, you better believe they will see you sooner or later. These small towns are nothing but gossip mills. Someone is going to report a car in front of their house. Now you need to leave and let me get on with my business. I'll let you know when I need to buy more stuff. You've already run off one customer." Andy had noticed a car driving slowly down the street while they talked. He hoped it wasn't who he thought it was. Surely, Casey hadn't found him.

Alfonzo moved to within inches of Andy's face. "I'll let things be for now. Don't worry about who's watching who. You just handle what we set you up to do. This town is too convenient to lose. Tell Edie I'll see her later." He reached up and patted Andy's face a couple of times before he turned and walked back to the car parked a house down from him.

"That didn't make him happy. I hope you don't wake the dragon." Edie stepped out of the kitchen.

"What do you mean, wake the dragon?" Andy asked after closing the door.

"Alfonzo is the nephew of one of the biggest drug dealers in the United States. He messed up while living in Chicago, and the uncle sent him west to try to redeem himself. If he loses this business, Alfonzo is in big trouble." Edie ran her hands through her hair. "Since I worked so hard last night, I think I'll go take a shower. Thanks for keeping him away just now. I know I'll pay for it later but..." She smiled a sad little grin and walked toward the back of the house.

Andy reached in his pocket for his cell. "Tell me I'm doing the right thing. Should I be trusting her?"

Garrett had answered the call. "You've prayed about it?"

"All night."

"We have, too. Owen and I both think she is the key to information. We are talking to the Chicago drug task force as we speak. Find out everything you can. I'll see you tonight same place. Be careful." Garrett disconnected the call and turned to his best friend. "We can't let this go on too long. Andy is going to want to protect the woman more than eliminating the drug ring, I'm afraid. I can't blame him, but we need to do both."

"I know. Casey is going to give us problems too. She drove by the house again just a few minutes ago. She's either going to get herself in trouble or blow the operation. Undercover isn't what we do best, is it?" Owen grinned at his friend.

"I'll certainly be glad when this is all over and everyone is safe. Let's see what Chicago has to tell us."

Casey knew she had to stay away from the house, but she couldn't stop herself from driving by in hopes of seeing Andy. She had to know he was safe. The man she saw standing in the doorway had the same build and coloring as Andy, but he had scruff on his face and his hair was longer than Andy's military cut. If he was working undercover, he would have let his hair grow. His eyes never moved when she drove by though. Maybe it was a coincidence, but in her heart, she didn't think so. She drove to the Pine Trees B & B wondering what, if anything, she wanted to tell the Thomas'.

Chapter Thirteen

Edie found Andy pulling sheetrock off the hallway walls. The house looked more like a skeleton every hour. She walked to where he worked and ripped on a corner of the board as his eyes looked into hers.

He took her arm and led her to one of the two chairs in the kitchen area. "You need to talk. Tell me everything you know about Alfonzo and his uncle." His voice was gruffer than he intended, but maybe she would be worried enough about him, she would tell them what they needed to arrest the men and shut the operation down.

It took an hour to get Edie to tell him all she knew. She looked haunted by the time Andy stopped pressing her for more information. Finally, he said, "I'm going to get you out of here tonight. We'll get you to a rehab center to get your system clean. Then you'll go into witness protection until you can testify against Alfonzo and the others."

"They'll find me, Andy. You can't take on the whole mob. They're in cities across the north-east. You can't arrest them all." She shook almost uncontrollably.

"Let me worry about all of that. Promise me you'll testify, and I'll handle the rest." Andy knew she would be crashing soon. He couldn't give her any more drugs. It would make the rehab easier the longer she was without anything in her system. Garrett and Owen had heard the conversation and would already be getting things into place. "I'll pull more of the plasterboard from the hallway and then load the pickup. Why don't you make us something to eat. In an hour or so, we'll get out of here." He watched her face as she tried calming herself enough to stand.

"Do you have someone special in your life, Andy?" Edie asked as she moved toward the refrigerator.

"Not now. I don't want to talk about me. I'll be ready to eat in thirty minutes. There's hamburger in there. Can you cook? I have the stuff for spaghetti." He didn't wait for an answer, just turned toward the living room and headed for the hallway not stopping until he reached the bathroom. He waited for one of the men to answer the phone. "Do you think there is enough evidence to build a case?"

"Chicago is ready to move when we are. Finish eating and give us the go sign. When you both step out the door, we'll be ready. The men are watching. We'll arrest you, Alfonzo, and Edie at the same time." Garrett tried to stay as calm as possible. They had covered all scenarios earlier that day. They were as ready as they would be. He disconnected the call.

"Hey, this is pretty good spaghetti." Andy stuffed another big bite into his mouth. He tried to ignore the twitching coming from the woman across from him. "I didn't know canned sauce could taste this good."

Edie shrugged trying to keep a small bite down. She needed a fix, but knew it wouldn't do any good to ask Andy for more drugs. She was going to jail soon. As much as she wanted to believe he could keep her safe, Edie felt sure this was her last meal. She had thought about killing herself so often. Now being faced with possible death, she wasn't sure she was ready.

"Are you a Christian, Edie?" The question surprised Andy almost as much as it did her.

"My parents never talked about religion, never took me

to church. Alfonzo didn't seem to find time for that either."
Her words were more sarcastic than she really intended.
*What is it with Andy? He's not like any man I've ever been
around.* She knew in her heart he had to be an undercover
cop. Somehow it made her feel safer.

"Before anything happens, I want you to meet a personal
friend of mine." Andy picked up their discarded plates and
took them to the sink before he turned back to the woman.
"I want you to know Jesus, Edie. You need a personal
relationship with God. It has nothing to do with religion or
going to church. It's a one-on-one with Jesus, your Savior.

Andy spent the next hour telling her about salvation and
answering questions. Before he gave Garrett the signal to
set the plan in motion, Edie had dropped to her knees and
asked Jesus into her heart. Andy told her no matter what
happened after that night, she had a forever home waiting
for her.

It was twelve-thirty the next afternoon before Andy
walked out of the sheriff's office with his gun and badge.
Alfonzo had been caught unaware when Owen walked up
behind him. He was too intent in the arrest of Edie and Andy.

Edie had spent almost eight hours telling Garrett and
a DEA agent everything she knew about the drug ring. The
agents from the Drug Enforcement Administration had been
brought in to handle the arrest of the men in Rachelle as well
as several other cities between Lincks and Chicago.

Garrett had told Andy Alfonzo was hollering for a deal
and wanted protection. "He's not even asked for a lawyer
yet." Both men shook their heads.

"Where is Edie?" Andy was more concerned about her
than the drug bust.

"Tom and Maria have taken her to a rehab center. She'll
go through the drying-out process and then DEA will move

her to an undisclosed location until she can testify just like you told her. They'll keep her safe. She has more than men watching over her now. It was a moving experience to hear her accept the Lord. Hopefully, she will find good people to help her along the way. That's the reason I sent Maria with Tom. He asked, and I knew Maria would share her story with Edie. Their lives were a lot alike in many ways."

Andy had only met Maria a time or two and didn't know anything about her background. He hoped it wouldn't be long before he could sit down with her and Tom. He wanted to know them better.

Garrett had given him the keys to a squad car when he returned his badge and gun. "You did a great job, Andy. We were fortunate Alfonzo brought Edie in to cover you. It would have taken much longer to get enough evidence on him without her. Now you need to go see your family. There have been a lot of rumors going around town about you. Chuck has called several times madder than an angry bear. He didn't know what to tell people. Casey was starting an investigation all on her own. They'll all be glad to see you back in uniform." Garrett shook his hand before Andy headed out the door to his new vehicle.

He was more than ready to get back to being Andy Thomas, deputy sheriff. He hoped he was never asked to go undercover again. Before going to see his folks and Casey, he headed back to the house to shower and shave.

The first person Andy wanted to see was Casey. He got in the patrol car and headed toward her apartment. He was disappointed to see her car wasn't in the parking lot. Driving toward the lake, he expected she would at the house. It would probably be easier to tell everyone as much as he could at the same time.

After a hug from each family member, Andy asked about

Casey.

"We aren't really sure, Andy," Hope said. "She came by yesterday and acted different, like she wanted to say something but didn't. I tried calling her several times today, but her phone goes straight to voicemail. She's not at her apartment. I even checked inside. It's not like her to take off, but maybe she was upset enough about you she decided to go visit her parents. I didn't seen any clothes or suitcases missing though."

"Do you have their phone numbers?" Andy was scared. It was too coincidental her disappearing just as they broke up the drug ring.

"I think I might. Let me check my phone." Hope stood and pulled her phone from her pocket. "Do you think something is wrong, Andy?"

"I've missed her. I just want to talk to her." He didn't want to let his family know his undercover work may have caused Casey harm. He punched in the numbers for her parents as Hope read them off. "I need to head back into town. I'll let you know if I reach her. Love you all." Andy was gone before anyone could reply.

Andy prayed the entire trip back to the sheriff's office. He couldn't lose her. Someone had to have information about what had happened. He walked straight back to Garrett's office, not seeing Owen as he walked past the man.

"Casey is missing. She was at the inn last night, but they haven't heard from her since. She drove by the house late yesterday afternoon while I was talking to Alfonzo. Garrett, I have to talk to him. If he has taken her—"

"Hey, calm down, Andy. We'll find her. Are you sure this is connected with the drug bust?" Garrett had to keep his emotions under control if he was going to be any help to Andy.

"It has to be. She disappeared within an hour or so of the

bust. Someone had to be watching her." Andy ran his hand through his hair as he paced inside the office.

Owen had followed Andy into the office. "Andy, we've been watching Casey's place. The day after you set up shop a man followed her after she drove by the house so slowly. She was smart though, she led him right back here. I checked for the car, and then followed her home to make sure she didn't have a tail. We've patrolled the apartments ever since. I don't know how they would have tied her in with you."

"I need to see Alfonzo. Garrett, will you get him into interrogation?" Andy acted like he didn't hear anything Owen had said.

"We aren't supposed to have any contact with the prisoners now, Andy. Let me talk to the agent in charge. I'll see what I can do. Meanwhile, have you checked her apartment? Anything look out of place? Did she pack anything, like she was going on a trip?" Garrett asked.

"Hope checked earlier this morning. Nothing seems to be missing. I'm going to call her parents while you talk to that agent." Andy walked out of the room with his phone already searching for numbers.

"Casey, what a pleasant surprise. And Richard, I haven't seen you in quite a while." Ruth Simmons looked from Richard to the look of terror on her young friend's face. "It's good to see the two of you again. Please come in."

"We've come to show you Casey's engagement ring. She's finally going to marry me." The man pulled her toward the older woman holding Casey's hand for Ms. Ruth to see the ring.

"Well, my goodness. Sit down and tell me all about how this happened."

An hour later, Richard told Casey they had to leave. He had told her friend how he had won her heart after a long talk.

"Richard, are you still living in those apartments on Phoenix street?" Ms. Ruth asked as she hugged the man.

"Yeah, that's where we're staying right now. After we get married, I'm buying Casey that big house she always wanted. I'll make her happy."

"I'm sure you will, dear." Mr. Ruth moved to take Casey in her arms. "I'll call Andy," she whispered as she laid her cheek close to Casey's ear.

"Thank you." Then, louder she said, "I love you, Ms. Ruth. If you get a chance to visit, remember the apartment number is 216. You be safe now." Casey worked hard to keep the tears from falling. Her friend knew the situation with Richard and had played along. Hopefully, Andy would find her in time.

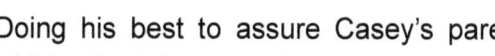

Doing his best to assure Casey's parents everything was alright, Andy hung up the phone and did the only thing he knew to do at that minute. He was still praying when his cell phone started ringing.

"Ms. Ruth—" Andy started to say.

"No time to talk, Andrew. Casey needs you." She told him everything about Casey's visit.

"I love you, Ms. Ruth. I'll find her. Thank you." Andy disconnected the call and headed back into Garrett's office.

"Andy, they won't let us talk to Alfonzo. They don't think there was any kidnapping." Garrett watched his deputy's face.

"A man she knew in St. Louis kidnapped her and took her back to his place. He's under the delusion that they're getting married. He brought Casey to show Ms. Ruth, a friend of ours, the engagement ring. He's holding her in his apartment in St. Louis, Garrett. I'm going to get her."

"Whoa, Andy. You can't just go into an unfamiliar city

91

and expect to get Casey back. The police will arrest you faster than him. Owen, call Dani and Chuck. Tell them where we're going. You're in charge until we get back. Andy, you drive while I talk to the police in St. Louis. Just make sure the wheels stay on the ground." He smiled at his deputy as they rushed through the office doors.

Officers from the local St. Louis precinct were waiting at the apartment door when Garrett and Andy walked up just as Garrett had requested. Andy showed them his badge since he was in civilian clothes. He had talked to Ms. Ruth on the way to the city and understood more about the situation. He told the two officers what he knew.

"We haven't tried to get anyone to answer the door. The man's pretty unstable. We've dealt with him before," the lead officer said to them.

"I know you don't know me, but I feel like God is telling me to be the one to talk to this man. That's my girlfriend he's holding hostage in there." Andy wasn't even sure what he was going to say. It just felt like the thing he was supposed to do. "I understand what he went through. I just left the service about a month ago."

The two officers looked at each other. It certainly wasn't protocol.

"I'll take responsibility if that would help," Garrett told the men. He had been praying about the situation as well. "If you two want to walk back down the hall, we'll be the first ones to arrive."

One man nodded to the other, and they both walked away with one saying, "Good luck."

"You sure, Andy?" Garrett asked.

"I think God is." Andy saw the sheriff's nod before he knocked on the door.

"Hey, Richard, its Andy, remember me from the service?"

It took ten minutes before the man opened the door and another twenty minutes before Andy was able to convince Richard Casey wasn't ready to marry him.

The two officers, standing outside the door with Garrett, took Richard into custody. They would see he got the help he needed. "Hey, man. You did great in there. If you're ever looking for a new position, St. Louis could use a man like you," one officer said. The other agreed with him.

"Fellas, he's just fine where he is. We'll meet you at the precinct." Garrett gave Casey and Andy time as he walked the officers out of the apartment.

Chapter Fourteen

Casey gave her statement to the police explaining how Richard had somehow found her and forced her to drive them back to St. Louis. Andy was thankful they had taken Richard to the hospital for evaluation. He wasn't sure he could have let the man go if he got his hands on him again.

Garrett and Andy had to tell their involvement in the situation before they were free to head back to Lincks. Andy drove Casey's car followed by Garrett in the patrol car. They weren't on the road more than ten minutes before Casey had fallen asleep. Andy didn't ask where she wanted to go, but headed straight to the inn. He couldn't wait until the morning to hold her. He was at her side of the car before she released her seatbelt.

"I missed you," he whispered next to her ear as he held her in his arms. Casey felt the warmth of his breath as much as she heard the words. In spite of the talking she'd had given herself earlier in the day, tears formed in her eyes and made their way down her cheeks.

Andy pulled back looking into her eyes. "What is this all about?" He wiped them away with his thumbs as best he could holding her face in his hands.

"I promised myself I wouldn't cry when you found me. I knew you would come if you could. I hadn't even told you about Richard, but you knew just what to say to him. You were a true hero back there, Andrew Thomas."

"Casey, you wouldn't think much of me if you knew what

I wanted to do to that man. God took control of this situation. I wasn't a hero, I was scared to pieces for you."

"You couldn't have been any more afraid than we were when you disappeared. I'm not so sure I'm cut out to be an undercover officer's woman. None of us knew what to do."

"I think I like the sound of that," he said, placing a kiss beside her ear.

"What, that we were afraid for you?" Casey pushed back from his hold to look at his face.

"Not that, the part about being an undercover officer's woman. Are you my woman, Casey Newton?" Andy asked.

"Um, I think I may be heading in that direction, Deputy Thomas." Casey stretched up to brush her lips across his before laying her head on his chest again.

———⸙———

The next morning Andy spent time in prayer about the relationship between Casey and him. He loved her and making the comment she did last night, he thought she was feeling much the same way. As he prayed, a plan began to form in his mind. With God's leading and help from friends, he knew it would be possible.

He was early for the run, circling in front of Garrett's a couple of times before the men came out. Owen asked Andy about the house before he had a chance to mention it. He would have liked to talk to all of them together, but maybe it would be best to see what one man thought before telling the others.

"I'm glad you mentioned that, Owen. I wanted to talk to all of you before I did anything more. After praying about it, I think I'm supposed to keep this house for my own. I want to ask Casey to marry me, and I really feel like this is where we are to live. I still want to start the company, but I need to do some work on this house first. I tore out most of the walls while I was staying there. I'm going to talk to Dad about helping me get it back together, so we can work on another house faster."

"Andy, that's wonderful. Casey is a great gal. I assume you haven't asked her yet?"

"No. I want to get the house ready first. I don't have anything to offer her yet."

"I'm not sure Casey would think that, but that's your business. As far as the house is concerned, I'll be happy to work on it if you will let me. First of all, I would do that for any friend and secondly, I need the experience." Owen grinned big as he patted Andy on the back.

"Andy, all of us would be honored to help you, as much as possible. You are a great asset to the force and like Owen said, that's what friends do for each other. I can hammer a straight nail and follow directions pretty well. Just ask Dani about that." Garrett laughed and the other two joined him.

"Thanks, both of you. I appreciate it. I'll talk to Dad as soon as I can and let you know when we are ready to start reconstructing the place." Andy was excited about the plans. He thought about the rooms while they ran and was anxious to talk to his dad about the remodel. He hoped Tom and Cody would be as understanding.

Garrett had already told him to take today and tomorrow off before he went back on duty. He looked forward to the time to work on the house. Andy found his dad cutting the lawn when he finished his run. He picked up the edger to work around the flower beds as Chuck finished mowing. Nora stepped out onto the front porch to let them know breakfast was ready just about the time they completed the job.

Hope and Faith had taken a group of teens to St. Louis for a few days retreat so the three of them had the house to themselves. The next booking would not be there until late that afternoon. Andy took the time to tell his parents about his plans.

"Mom, I don't want you to go planning any wedding yet. I haven't even asked Casey to be my wife. I need to know she feels the same way I do. We haven't known each other very long, but I'm certain she is the woman God intends for me to marry. I want to finish the house for her." Andy saw the glow in his mother's face when he mentioned asking Casey to marry him.

"Well, you and your friends get the house finished. If Casey is God's choice for you, I know it will work out just fine." Nora knew Casey loved Andy. They had already talked about it. With Casey's family so far away, the two of them were as close as she was to her own daughters, sometimes closer. But it wasn't her place to say anything to Andy. She knew they would work things out.

Chuck and Andy spent the rest of the morning at the house drawing up plans for the reconstruction. Tom and Cody had stopped by on their way to work. Both of the men were just as supportive as Owen had been and were anxious to work with them on the place. Andy made a materials list and headed for St. Louis after lunch.

Getting into St. Louis a little earlier than he expected, Andy decided to go by and see if Ms. Ruth was home. Casey talked to her regularly on the phone, but they hadn't been back to see her since the kidnapping.

He waited at the door hearing the shuffling of feet and then the locks turning. The elderly lady opened the door with a grin from ear to ear reaching out for Andy as she swung the door open.

"Andrew, what a pleasant surprise. Come in here." She looked out the door before closing it. "You didn't bring Casey with you?"

Smiling, Andy told his friend why he was in town. "I want to remodel the house I bought, and then ask Casey to marry me. Do you think she might be interested?" He knew they were close, and he figured Ms. Ruth would know how she felt as well as anybody.

"I know you had better work your magic quickly before she is over there helping you. I knew when you two first visited me there would be a wedding soon. You are both special people and will be good for each other." She cackled as she gazed at Andy.

"I will expect an invitation to the wedding. Jerome will be happy to bring me." Ms. Ruth stood. "Now, what would you like to drink with this blackberry cobbler I just made?"

He had smelled something freshly baked when he came into the house.

An hour later, Andy was at one of the lumber yards Adam Reynolds had told him about. They loaded Andy's pickup and the trailer he had rented with the materials he hoped would make a good start on renovating the house. It was dark before he got back to town.

Backing the trailer into the drive, he ate the hamburger he had picked up on the way into town and reached for his phone to call Casey. He told her he still planned to stay at the house like he had been doing. They had only been on the phone for a few minutes when the doorbell rang. Still talking, he walked to the door to see who would be stopping by at this time of the evening. Casey stood on the other side with her phone still at her ear. They both hung up as she grinned at him. Stepping aside, Andy made way for her to enter the room.

"I had been to the grocery store when you called. I was only a block or two from the house and wanted to stop by. I hope you don't mind." She smiled hesitantly.

Andy pulled her into his arms and kissed her briefly before running his hand down her cheek to her neck. "You are the best surprise I've had all day." He took her hand and led her further into the room.

"Are you going to show me what you have done so far?" Casey didn't wait for an answer as she started to pull Andy into the open spaces of the house. They walked around supports from one area to the next. "Tell me what you plan for the place." Her eyes sparkled as she moved through the spaces.

Andy knew he wouldn't be able to keep the house a secret. She would be involved with every phase of the remodeling. It would be better that way. He wanted her to feel like the place was theirs. He began describing what he had in mind. Casey added suggestions here and there, but overall thought the plan sounded just about right. "I want to use as many environmentally safe products as I can. It's not easy finding the things I would like even in St. Louis." He had been disappointed there were so few options. The selection was much better in Chicago.

"I love that idea. I'm so excited about the whole thing. What can I do to help?" Even with the workshops she planned to take during the summer, she still had almost two months before she would report back to school. They weren't nearly as important as working with Andy would be. They talked about the plans until late into the night.

Chapter Fifteen

Casey stopped by the hardware store on her way to Andy's house. She picked up a pair of heavy gloves and safety glasses. Andy had told her she could not help without those things. He had planned to pick them up himself, but she decided it would be easier if she did that on the way to the house. She also stopped by the bakery and bought apple fritters and coffee.

Pulling up in front of the house, Casey looked at the house in the daylight. She could imagine the house painted in warm earth tone colors. Right now the trim was black and white. It wasn't at all attractive. She envisioned a swing hanging from the rafters of the large covered porch with the flower beds blooming with a plethora of brightly colored flowers. She sat in the car thinking about the home until Andy opened the door and stepped out. Grinning, he asked her if she planned on working from the car, or if she wanted to come inside.

He helped her carry her purchases inside and then asked her what she was staring at so intently before he came outside. She told him what she had been thinking. Together they walked back outside to look at the exterior. "I really hadn't given much thought to the outside of the house. Would you be interested in painting while we work on the reconstruction on the inside?" Without waiting for an answer, Andy reached into his wallet and handed her his credit card.

She was thrilled with the idea. "I told you Mom and Dad

always let me do the painting anytime we worked on the house. I love doing that kind of thing." She slid the credit card into the back pocket of her shorts. "Are you going to trust me to purchase the paints?" She already knew what color palette she wanted. "I'm turning that all over to you. I trust your judgment completely."

Casey finished the last bite of her fritter, kissed Andy quickly on the cheek and hurried to her car. Within an hour, she was back with all of the tools and paint she thought would be needed to complete the exterior of the house. She got to work scraping before priming the wood.

Andy smiled as he thought about how excited she seemed to be. He was thankful she looked forward to the work. She had tied her hair back with an old rag he had found and was scraping away when he checked on her. He had hauled most all of the debris from the house by late morning. About eleven-thirty, she walked into the house removing the rag from her hair, washed her hands and grabbed her purse. Before walking out the door, she walked over to Andy. She gave him another kiss and left, not saying a word. Andy watched her leave not saying anything either. Within minutes, the woman walked back in the door with a bag and two drinks.

"I brought lunch." She announced in a satisfied voice. Andy washed his hands and face before joining her.

"I thought maybe you had already had enough and left." He teased as they took their first bite of sandwich.

"Why would I quit? I'm having a ball. I can't wait to start painting. I bought the prettiest shades of pinks and lavenders." She tried hard to keep her face straight especially when Andy's eyes got big and his mouth opened. "You did say you would trust me with the colors," she proclaimed innocently.

"I did at that." He gulped before taking another bite of

101

his sandwich.

"Is that all you have to say? You would let me paint this beautiful house to look like a Barbie playhouse? Shame on you, Andrew Thomas." Casey slugged him playfully on the arm.

"That was cruel. I was afraid you were serious. I didn't know what to say." He grinned sheepishly. "Want to tell me what colors you did buy?"

"You just have to wait and see now. I should be ready to paint the front tomorrow." They discussed his next steps and quickly got back to work.

When Andy's phone rang, he knew it was his dad. "Hey."

"Are you coming out for supper? We've fed all of the guests, and you're stuck with leftovers." Chuck told him. Andy hadn't realized it was so late.

"Casey and I will be there in thirty minutes or so." He disconnected the call and dropped the phone back into his pocket before going to the front door.

She had started painting earlier in the afternoon. When she turned around to smile at Andy, he grinned. "You have paint on your face, beautiful." He walked over to her kissing her nose spotted with a warm butterscotch color. She had painted a moss green around the windows and the butterscotch was going on the siding. It had already changed the look of the house considerably.

"Much better than pinks and purples, I must say." He stood admiring the colors as she walked over to stand with him.

"I don't know. I could still change the colors."

Andy growled and tossed her over his shoulder carrying her into the house. She was laughing when he lowered her to her feet before him. His look sobered as he gazed into her eyes, and then to her mouth just before he caught her lips with his. Casey wrapped her arms around his neck standing on tiptoes to get closer to him. Andy deepened the kiss coaxing her closer. Casey moved back first, gasping for air. "You have paint on your face now." She reached up and swiped the spot on his cheek only spreading it more. She giggled slightly as Andy once again sought her mouth. By the time they separated, both adults were breathing heavy.

"Mom and Dad have leftovers at the house for us. I think it might be a good idea if we go eat something." He watched her face as she struggled with her feelings. She was just as affected by the kisses as he was. It wasn't a good idea to stay here any longer.

"I need to get cleaned up." Casey said absently. She was in no hurry to leave Andy's arms.

He reached for the cloth she had tied her hair with and stepped away from her. "Come here. I'll get the paint off your face." He wet the cloth and began to tenderly wipe the spots, placing a kiss on each area as it turned red from rubbing it. By the time he had the paint off of her face, they were both breathing heavy again. She took the rag from his hands and rinsed it out before cleaning his cheek. He also got a kiss. Then she wiped her arms until she could find no more paint.

"Are you ready?" she asked sidestepping him, when he reached for her once again.

"I'm ready, but before we head to the inn, I want you to tell me about Richard. Are you willing to do that?" Andy had taken her hand in his and was rubbing his thumb across her palm.

She moved them to chairs never breaking the connection between them. She didn't say anything for a couple of minutes. "I met Richard when I was delivering Meals on Wheels. He had been discharged from the service six months earlier and was struggling with life. I knew enough to know he suffered with PTSD, but he never wanted to talk about how he felt.

He always wanted to talk about other things as long as I would talk to him. He was my last delivery each day so I had more time to spend with him than I usually had for the others. Soon, he started asking me for a date." Casey dropped Andy's hand at that point and stood to pace the room.

"He couldn't understand that I wouldn't go out with him. Finally, I felt so bad one afternoon I told him I would take a walk with him. We met at his apartment, and I told him we could walk to the lake behind his building to talk. We both were wearing short and flip-flops. He kicked his shoes off and pulled me toward the water. I tried telling him I didn't like the water. I had never learned to swim. But he was much stronger than I was and when he pulled me, my foot stuck in the mud causing me to lose my balance. I would have fallen into the water if he hadn't caught me. He pulled me up against him just as a string of firecrackers went off. It set off his PTSD, I guess." Casey wiped tears as the fell down her cheeks. She held her hand up to stop Andy as he came toward her. She had to finish.

"I don't know if he thought I was the enemy or he was protecting me, but he grabbed me by the shoulders and pushed me under the water. The next thing I knew I was in the hospital. The doctor said I almost drowned." She wrapped her arms around herself rocking slightly back and forth.

Andy pulled her as close as she would let him. "That's why you reacted the way you did when I dropped you in the water. I'm so, so sorry, Casey. I would give anything if I could take that moment back."

"No, Andy. That made me realize I have to face my fears. I have to learn to swim. I can't be afraid of the water the rest of my life."

"I'm a pretty good teacher, and I promise it won't be by dropping you in to sink or swim." Andy grinned at her.

"I would love that. Now let's go to your folks before they

come looking for us." She kissed his cheek before moving out of his arms.

Casey asked Andy if they wanted to take her car since his truck was still attached to the trailer. She handed him the keys and walked to the passenger side of the car. Andy was there before her, holding the door open. He placed a brief kiss on her lips before shutting the door.

"Andy, is your Mustang still at the house?"

He wondered when she would ask him about the car.

"I traded the car for the truck. I needed something to haul lumber, and I didn't want you or the family to see the Mustang in town. I was able to stay low profile with the truck." He told her.

"Oh, Andy, I'm so sorry. You loved that car."

"You know, I don't really miss it. I think that phase of my life is over. I have different needs now." He meant what he said. They talked about the house, and things he wanted to do with it until they reached the lake house.

Casey told Chuck and Nora about the paint colors between bites of lasagna and salad. She and Andy had worked up quite an appetite. After cleaning the kitchen, the four of them moved to the private living quarters the Thomas family had. There were guests tonight, and they usually used the great room.

"What colors have you chosen for the interior of the house?" his mother asked the younger woman. Quickly, she looked at Andy who only grinned. She smiled back and pulled color strips from her back pocket.

Nora and Casey got so involved in talking about the house, they didn't notice how quiet the men had become until they heard snoring. Chuck had fallen asleep in his recliner, and Andy was sprawled out on the sofa.

"I think I had better get home. I didn't realize how late it was. Will you tell Andy I'll pick him up in the morning?" Casey picked up her purse looking for the keys.

"Why don't you sleep here tonight? You can use Hope's room with the girls gone. That way you can shower and have something to wear in the morning." The older woman was already waking her husband.

"Thanks, Nora. I think I'll do that. I'm beat, myself. Should I wake Andy, or let him sleep on the couch?"

"Let's just let him sleep. He will come upstairs if he wakes up." Nora turned on the upstairs lights while Chuck checked to make sure the house was locked up with all of the guests in their rooms. The couple would be up early to start breakfast for everyone.

As the three of them headed up the stairs, Casey took one more look at the man sleeping in the room below. She wished she had the right to curl up beside him.

Chapter Sixteen

Casey worked at the house most days painting or cleaning flower beds or mowing the lawn. She had the yard looking as pleasing as any in the neighborhood according to Tom and Cody. She was happy that the house was coming along so nicely. The outside was completely painted, except for the gables. Andy made her promise she wouldn't try to paint from the extension ladder. As much as he disliked painting, he felt much safer doing that himself than having Casey climbing that high.

As the men finished the drywall in the bedrooms, she moved her supplies in to paint behind them. The kitchen and living rooms were the only two rooms yet to finish, but they had nearly everything left to do in there. She and Andy had picked out cabinets for the kitchen and baths a few days ago. The bathroom cabinets were in stock so they were able to bring those back with them. The kitchen cabinets wouldn't be delivered for another week at least.

All of the men had been working as much as possible on the house, when they were not on patrol. Chuck had been at the house some, but the B and B had been so busy Nora needed him most days. They all decided to take a day to enjoy the party Nora and Chuck had planned.

The Thomas children all celebrated their birthdays on the fourth of July. Casey had purchased a gift for Hope and Faith months before, but she didn't know what to buy for Andy. She wanted something special for him. She had even talked to Nora about an idea. She finally settled on her first thought and went by to see if it could be delivered while they were at the party that afternoon. She had known the store owner since she moved to town and trusted him to make sure the gift was ready for Andy after the party. A lot of the townspeople were invited to the Thomas place for the birthday slash Independence Day celebration.

Casey stopped by the house and picked Andy up early. They wanted to be as much help as possible for the big event. Nora had been cooking for the last week making sure there was plenty of food for everyone. Andy had complained about the large amounts of paper products they would be using, so Nora made sure everything was biodegradable and made from recyclable products. It thrilled him that his mother went to so much extra work. Casey, Hope, and Faith helped Nora in the kitchen while the men watered the lawn for the fireworks. Andy had just moved one of the sprinklers when Sherman came bounding across the lawn with Greg hollering right behind him.

"I swear that dog never listens to me. How are you doing, Andy?" The men shook hands when Greg walked up to him.

"Good, thanks. Mom and Dad are getting ready for their big Fourth of July party. You are coming over, aren't you?" Andy asked.

"Usually, I'm out of town for the Fourth. I would enjoy coming if you are sure it's okay. I don't want to make the family uncomfortable."

Andy knew he was talking about Hope more than his parents. "I'm sure everyone will enjoy seeing you, Greg." He grinned at the man.

"In that case, can I bring anything?" Greg looked forward to the evening and to seeing Hope again. He had seen her coming and going from the house quite a bit since he had been home this time, and wondered if there was someone special in her life. There were different men picking her up in the evenings quite often. He should have felt guilty for spying on her, but the only feeling he felt was sorrow. He would have liked things to have been different between them.

"Mom and Dad have everything under control. People will start arriving between six and six-thirty. Come on over when you're ready. I'm glad you're coming." Andy hadn't had the opportunity to talk with Greg like he had wanted. Maybe there would be time to visit at the party.

By six-thirty, the backyard and deck was packed with people. Games were set up throughout the yard for families to play. Explosives were going to be shot off by the lake, so all sorts of fireworks were on the dock ready for later. Chuck and Andy manned the grill while Nora and the girls kept the bowls filled with all sorts of food. Everyone was enjoying themselves.

Greg walked across the yard moving toward the area where Hope was talking to some friends. She saw him coming and excused herself going to meet him. Her eyes sparkled as they approached each other.

"Hi, stranger." Her gaze never left his face. She waited for him to say more.

"You look more beautiful than ever, Hope." He leaned forward and kissed her cheek. "Happy birthday."

Her stomach somersaulted from the feel of his lips, and she wanted to reach out to touch him, but refrained. They stood, sharing polite conversation until others joined them. Hope was drawn away from his side, but frequently glanced back in his direction. Each time she looked his eyes were on her. She longed to share more than the few stilted words with him, but she decided the next move would have to come from him. Hope had already told him how she felt, and she was determined she was not going to beg.

Andy saw the way the two of them kept watching the

other one. It was obvious both of them were attracted to one another. He decided now would be a good time to talk to Greg. Just as he started toward the man, his dad let out a sharp whistle. His mother was pushing a huge birthday cake on a cart out of the door onto the deck. Chuck motioned for his children to join them. Talking to his neighbor would have to wait.

Chuck told the crowd they weren't going to embarrass the three of them by singing. He and Nora just wanted to wish them a happy birthday, and to tell them how very proud they were of each of them. He shook hands with Andy, patting him on the back and hugged each of the girls before telling everyone to come have a piece of cake. Thirty minutes later everyone had been well fed and was ready for the pyrotechnics display.

Fire Chief, Mike Guthrie, had been appointed the 'fuse man,' the one in charge of lighting all of the different fireworks. He and a couple of the volunteer firemen had taken the time to connect each explosive with a wick going from one to the next. Mike would light the first of the chain. Then he could sit back and enjoy the display with his family.

Andy found Casey to share a blanket he had brought from the car. He had invited Greg to sit with them, making sure Hope joined them as well. Andy sat down and cradled Casey in front of him, while Greg and Hope sat close, but not quite touching. The four of them sat in a comfortable silence ready to enjoy the show.

As the finale took place, Andy couldn't stand it any longer. He leaned down and nuzzled Casey's neck brushing light kisses from her neck to her cheek. He felt her moan, even though it was too loud to hear it. She turned her head slightly for him to kiss her lips which he gladly did. Turning in his arms, Casey wrapped her arms around his waist and returned the kiss he started.

Hope noticed the couple and turned toward Greg. "I think those two are headed toward the altar. They are together all of the time. I couldn't be happier for them."

"What about you, Hope? Are you happy?" Greg laid his hand on Hope's where it rested on the blanket.

"Happy, like them? No." She had to be honest. She had not been happy since she and Greg stopped seeing each other. "What about you? Are you happy with your life?"

Greg looked at the woman facing him. He hadn't been happy since they stopped dating either. But he wasn't sure it would be wise to tell her that. He wasn't certain he could start another relationship with the woman and not want to marry her. He didn't know if he was ready for that or not. Being gone so much would be hard on a couple. It would mean choosing his work or Hope. Right now as much as he ached to hold her in his arms, he thought he might be ready to make that sacrifice.

"Content maybe, but not happy."

"Is that enough for you?"

"With you sitting within arm's length of me, no it's not enough. I'm aching to hold you, to kiss you again. I miss you, Hope."

"You know, I didn't want to walk away. You made the decision for us."

"I know. Ten years is a big difference in our ages, Hope." He ran his fingers through his hair in frustration looking out at nothing not knowing what he wanted.

"Well, now we are only nine years and seven months apart. There is nine years between Casey and Andy. My parents don't think there is anything wrong with that. Besides I'm old enough to make my own decisions, Greg. I know what I want. It's you who needs to decide." She stood and walked back toward the house, leaving him sitting there with the other couple.

"You know she's right, Greg. You two love each other. Your age has nothing to do with it. Don't let her get away this time. She won't wait for a third chance. Two men have asked her to marry them already." Casey knew she shouldn't be sharing things Hope had told her, but she didn't want to see the two make another mistake.

The three of them stood, and Casey hugged Greg before taking Andy's hand. They walked back toward the house ready to tell the guests goodbye. Many were getting ready to leave. She knew Andy had to get up early tomorrow, and she still hadn't given him his birthday present.

Greg made his way across the lawn feeling more frustrated than ever. He couldn't get Hope out of his thoughts. He had some praying to do. That might have been the problem before. He hadn't really talked to God about Hope. He had just listened to friends and to Chuck. He thought they were too old for each other, but Greg wasn't so sure any more. Hopefully, God would help him to see the path more clearly.

Casey and Andy told his parents good night and headed toward town. Casey had told him his birthday present was at the house, so he knew she would come in with him. They parked the car and went inside. Casey took his hand and headed toward the master bedroom. It had been finished the week before.

"You are working too hard and not getting any rest." She opened the door and stepped aside. Set up along the long side of the wall was a king size bed complete with bedding.

"Casey, this is too much. Oh, wow, how nice it'll be to not sleep on that air mattress anymore." Andy walked over to the bed and lay back onto it. "But really, this is way too much. I can't let you pay for this."

"Hush, I wanted to do this for you. You need rest. Besides, you're going to need furniture to sell this place properly. This is just one piece early. I have to get home, so you can enjoy it. Walk me out, okay?"

The couple walked to the front door and Andrew took her in his arms. "Thank you. You have made this an incredible day." He kissed her softly at first, arousing passion in both of them. He pulled her closer as he tugged her lower lip between his own.

"Andy, I have to leave *now.*" Casey knew her will was slipping, and she wanted to give in to the emotions they were feeling. But she also knew, she wasn't like that. She had made a promise to God. Waiting until her wedding night was important to her.

He laid his forehead against hers. "I know how you feel. I want you to stay, but I know that is not what God would want." They walked to the car, and he kissed her once more before closing the door behind her. Casey pulled off to go home, and Andrew went in to take a cold shower.

Chapter Seventeen

Andy started his morning as usual with Bible reading and prayer. Since he had the early shift he decided to stop by the bakery for a fritter. He walked into the office at six-fifty ready to go on patrol. Cody was just going off duty. After a few hours' sleep, he was going to be at the house working on the crown molding in the living room.

The house was coming along quickly, thanks to all of the help the men had given to the project. The kitchen cabinets were scheduled to be delivered tomorrow. Andy and his dad had already planned time to hang them after the officer finished his shift tomorrow evening. Tom was off that day and had planned to be there to help.

Andy started for his patrol car, when Bethany called out to him. "Andy, there is an accident on First Street and Main. A truck ran a stop sign and hit another car. Paramedics are on their way."

He hurried to his vehicle and headed in that direction. Mike Guthrie was probably on duty by now and should get there about the same time he did. He saw no reason for his siren with the traffic as light as it was. He was on the scene in less than a minute. Then he saw the vehicles involved. A pickup truck had run into the driver's door of a car that looked just like Casey's. His heart stopped as he ran to the collision. Casey slumped against the steering wheel, unconscious and bleeding from a head wound.

The fire department pulled up to the wreckage, just as

Andy reached the vehicle. He couldn't get into either of the driver or passenger doors, the car was twisted so badly. The pickup was wedged against the driver's door.

"Mike, we need the jaws over here." His voice shook slightly as he tried to remain calm. He wouldn't be any good to Casey if he lost control. He noticed the new paramedic, Drew, check on the truck driver as Mike came around Casey's car to the officer's side. He began to wedge the passenger door open with the big machine until it popped. Andy pulled it open and started to climb inside.

"No, Andy. Let me go in and check her out. Help Drew with the other driver and the gurney." He knew it made sense, but Andy needed to know how Casey was. He needed to be there for her. He did as the Fire Chief asked just as Garrett pulled into the intersection. He patted Andy on the back as he went to check on Casey for himself. Garrett knew Mike had ordered the deputy away from the car. The other driver was out of the vehicle and moving just fine. Drew checked him over while Mike worked on Casey.

"How is she, Mike?" Garrett asked his friend. He saw Andy and Drew pushing the gurney toward the car.

"Her pulse is good. She has a cut in her hairline and probably has a concussion. I don't feel any broken bones. We had better get her over to the hospital and have her checked out." Mike put the neck collar on the woman and released her seatbelt.

They decided to push the pickup away from the car to get the driver door open. With the gear shift in the console, lifting her across the seats would be risky if she had back injuries. It took a couple of minutes, but the four of them were able to move the mangled pickup out of the way to get the Jaws of Life into the driver door. Slowly, the door gave away, and they were able to get the backboard behind Casey.

Mike and Drew lifted the woman onto the gurney and

115

loaded her into the ambulance. The driver of the truck rode in the front seat while Mike stayed in the back with the patient. Drew drove them to the hospital, where Mike's wife, Cindy, was the attending ER physician. She was expecting them.

Andy watched the ambulance leave the scene. Being the first deputy on the scene, he knew he was responsible for the paperwork and getting the accident cleared up. Lester had already arrived. He backed up behind the car ready to pull it onto the bed of his tow truck when the police gave him permission to remove the vehicles. He would tow the pickup behind the wrecker.

Garrett wanted to tell Andy to go with Casey to the hospital, but he saw the deputy taking photos and measurements as quickly as possible. He knew the man realized he couldn't do anything for Casey until after the doctors finished examining her. Andy was doing the job he was hired to do as much as it bothered him. Garrett appreciated his dedication.

He did what he could to make the job go faster. Garrett had already talked to the other driver about what happened. He told the sheriff he took his eyes off of the road when he was looking for a radio station, and didn't see the car until it was too late. He signed for his ticket after giving the officer his insurance information and driver's license.

Andy took Casey's personal things out of the car, and told Lester he could pull the vehicles away. The pickup driver could retrieve his things from the truck when he claimed it at Lester's yard.

"Go check on her, Andy. Cindy should know something by now."

"Thanks, Garrett."

Praying the entire time Andy worked the accident, he hoped he hadn't missed anything important. He could think of nothing, but Casey. He reached the hospital as quickly as possible, walking inside just as they brought her out of the examining room.

Cindy Guthrie smiled as the deputy walked through the door. "Mike said you would be here shortly. Casey is doing as well as can be expected. She has a concussion. She needed five stitches in her scalp, but other than that I found no other injuries. She is going to x-ray now to make sure there was no damage to her spine. She is still unconscious, but that's not unusual. She had a pretty traumatic experience. We will keep her sedated part of the day to make sure she's stable. She should be ready for visitors by the time you're off duty." The doctor could tell he was anxious about the woman. Right now there was nothing he could do to help her, so there was no reason for him to pace the hospital room.

Andy thanked Cindy for taking care of Casey and walked out to his patrol car. Before leaving the parking lot, he thanked God the accident was no worse than it was, and then, he called his parents to tell them what had happened. He knew Hope or his mom would be there to sit with her until he got off work. He realized Cindy didn't want him to worry about Casey, but he wanted to make sure she had someone with her if she woke up. If it couldn't be him, Hope or Nora would be second best.

The rest of the day flew by as Andy finished his shift. The District Attorney had come by to take another statement from him concerning the drug ring. They had indicted the men for the drug trafficking in Lincks County more than two weeks ago. It turned out the men had more warrants for their arrest in other states and the DEA was looking at them for transporting drugs across state lines. One of the men had cut a deal with the federal government to give evidence against the others. Along with Edie's testimony, the men arrested were looking at several years in prison. Andy and the others knew it would never be enough time, but they were off of the streets for a while, anyway.

By three o'clock, all Andy wanted to do was get to the hospital. He finished the paperwork he had to do and left just as Owen came on duty. The other deputy had already heard about Casey and told Andy to give her his best. They had all become close working on the house.

Five minutes later, he was at the hospital. Casey was sitting up in bed with Hope sitting in the chair next to her bed. They were laughing about something Hope had been telling her when Andy walked in. Casey smiled at the intense look he gave her as he walked straight to her bed. He leaned down and kissed her, barely touching her lips. Then he deepened the kiss as he felt her respond.

"This has been the worst day of my life." He told her between kisses as he sat down on the bed to pull her into his arms.

Hope cleared her throat rather loudly. "Hello, brother. Yes, I'm fine thanks. I have enjoyed being with Casey until you could get here. No, I don't think I need to stay any longer. I'm sure you have things to talk about." She teased the two of them, as Andy took no notice of her being in the room.

Casey grinned against Andy's lips as he started to kiss her one more time. She pushed slightly against him, as she turned toward Hope. "Thanks for staying with me. I will call you tomorrow. Andy, tell you sister goodbye."

Andy turned his head slightly, as he grinned at Hope. "Thanks, sis. I owe you one." He winked as she stepped away.

"Oh, you owe me more than one, big brother," Hope stated, walking out of the room.

"How are you feeling?" Andy asked as he laid his hand on her cheek.

"A little breathless right now." She grinned pressing a swift kiss on his lips.

"Maybe you need a doctor?" He teased back kissing her

once more.

"I think I have the best medicine right here." She wrapped her arms around his neck returning his kiss ardently. She moaned softly as Andy started kissing her neck moving toward the neck of her hospital gown. Just then the hospital door opened. His parents stood on the other side of the room.

"Excuse us." His mother cleared her throat. Andy and Casey both turned their heads toward the door. Grinning, the older couple walked into the room. "Is this a bad time?" Nora asked innocently.

"Actually, it was probably perfect timing." Casey said as she heard Andy growl low in his chest. She laid her hand beside his face and grinned at him. He shuttered the passion he had allowed her to see before turning once again toward his parents. He moved away only slightly as his parents sat down in the chairs.

"How are you feeling, darling?" Nora asked Casey.

"I have a headache, but other than that I'm just a bit bruised. I'm hoping they will let me go home a little later. Doc Miller and Faith were by earlier this afternoon. Did you know he was talking about retiring?" They discussed the doctor a bit longer until a nurse brought in medication for Casey's headache.

"Angie, did the doctor say I could go home this evening?" Casey hoped she had some news about her release.

"Sorry, Casey. He wants you to stay tonight for observation. He should release you in the morning, I would think." She gave a sympathetic smile to her patient and left the room.

"Andy, how bad is my car?" She didn't remember anything about the accident other than seeing the pickup coming toward her, then waking up in the hospital bed with Hope sitting next to her bed.

"Your car is totaled, sweetheart. The man that hit you

had insurance. Luckily, it was not any worse. You scared me to pieces, lying in that car. I don't ever want to go through that again."

"Thank goodness, Casey was not seriously hurt. God was watching over her." Nora commented. The older couple visited with the patient and Andy for about an hour. Just as they got ready to leave, an aide brought dinner into the room and set it on the tray at the foot of her bed.

Andy lifted the lid and grinned. "Don't think this is Mom's cooking," he teased.

"I'm pretty sure it isn't either. You need to go with your parents and eat some of her good cooking. You could sneak me in a piece of dessert later." She told the man sitting on the bed next to her.

"Are you trying to get rid of me?" He didn't really want to leave the room.

"You need to eat. Then you can come back and keep me company for a while. I would like that. By the way, did you happen to get my purse from the car? I would like to have my cell phone. I need to let my parents know what happened. If they call the house and I don't answer, they'll worry about me."

"I'll bring it back with me in a little bit. Eat you dinner and rest. I'll be back soon with dessert." He kissed her once more before standing to join his parents. Nora moved to the bed and kissed Casey's cheek.

"We'll see you in the morning. I want you to come stay at the house for a few days, so I can spoil you." Nora told her.

"Nora, that's not necessary."

"I know, darling, but I want to do it anyway. Most of our guests are gone right now, and the girls enjoy your company as much as we do. No arguing. We will see you in the morning." She took her husband's hand and turned to walk out.

Andy winked at her before following his parents from the room.

———❀———

While Casey rested at Nora's and Chuck's, she called her insurance company to get the settlement started on her car. She gave them all of the information Andy had received from the other driver. The company told her they would be in touch in a day or so. It was later that afternoon when she received a call from her agent.

"Casey, this is Mike Lawson. Are you sure you gave me the correct information from the other driver?"

"That's the information Andy got from the driver. Is there a problem?" She began to worry about the call.

"I contacted the insurance company. They have no record of the man or any policy written in that name. The police might want to question him again." He hated to be the bearer of bad news. "In the meantime, we will settle on your car and then collect from his company when you are able to get everything straightened out."

"That sounds good, Mike. I'll call Andy right now and see what he can find out." Casey's head hurt worse just thinking about the situation.

"I'll drop by the Bed and Breakfast with a check for you in a day or two. Will that work?" He knew she was recovering there.

"That would be wonderful. Thanks so much. I'll see you later." Casey disconnected the call and immediately dialed Andy's cell phone, telling him what Mike had learned.

"We never had any reason to doubt the information. I'll pull his records and go by to get it straightened out. He probably changed companies and gave me the wrong card. I'll call you after I talk to him. You rest and don't worry about it." After a couple more minutes, Andy told her good-bye and headed for the office.

He pulled the accident report and the ticket. Since he wasn't that familiar with Lincks' streets, he walked into Garrett's office to ask him where the man's residence was located. After explaining to the sheriff about the insurance mix-up, Garrett looked at the report.

"I'm not so sure this was a mix-up, Andy. The address on this man's information was the house that blew up. The name on the deed wasn't this man either. Let's run his name through the system and see what we get. Something doesn't seem right about this." Garrett turned to his computer and started inputting information.

After an hour, the name came back as deceased. The man had lived in New York and died two years ago. Garrett and Andy both looked at each other with the same thoughts.

"Are you thinking the same thing I am, Garrett? This wasn't an accident, was it? Either this was a very shoddy cover-up or someone wanted us to find information relating to the drug ring," Andy said as he sat down in the chair.

"I'm afraid you're right, Andy. I'm so sorry. Instead of coming after you, it looks like they may have been trying to send you a message. Casey was the carrier. I'll get in touch with the agents handling the case now. They'll want the information. We do have one thing going for us. The guy had to give a blood test as standard procedure since he went to the hospital. We can send it in for DNA testing. Maybe something will show up in some file. If he works for a larger drug ring, he'll have a record somewhere."

"I won't say anything to Casey. As far as she's concerned, this guy just skipped town and gave us incorrect information. I'll let her know we're investigating. I wish we were married so I could protect her better." Andy ran his hand over his head in frustration.

"You know, I don't think they will do anything else at least for a while. In my gut, I think they are toying with us.

They'll slip up though, Andy. When they do, we'll get them. If they had planned to hurt Casey worse, there are a lot better ways than an auto accident. I'll let the others know what's going on. We'll keep an eye on her. She doesn't need to know anything is happening. We're around her enough she won't think a thing about it." Garrett hoped he reassured his deputy. He wasn't sure it would be enough if it had been Dani in the situation. The look on Andy's face told him he was thinking the same thing.

"Okay, I feel better while she's staying with Mom and Dad. I'll try to keep her there as long as possible. I'm going over to Lester's and see if the pickup might still be there. Maybe we can lift some fingerprints." Andy stood feeling like he was doing something useful.

"Great idea. If the guy did hit Casey deliberately, there was probably someone waiting to pick him up. I'll run the plates and see who the truck is registered to while you check for prints."

Two hours later, the men had some answers. There were fingerprints all over the truck. The driver's prints came back with a list of priors for several crimes including drug trafficking. Garrett had already contacted the other agencies working on the case. An APB was put out for the man.

The truck had been stolen in Oklahoma the day before the accident. They assumed it was taken with the purpose of using it to hit Casey. The tag was from a different vehicle. It had been reported totaled and was setting in a junkyard waiting to be crushed. Having more information made Andy feel better. He knew any member of his family could be a victim. All he could do for now was pray for each of them, and let God protect them.

Chapter Eighteen

Andy was off duty at seven after coming on duty at eleven the night before. He planned to sleep a few hours before heading to his parents to pick up Casey. His mother had finally decided she was well enough to stay by herself. It had been four days since the accident, and she was no longer having any headaches. He had tried to get her to stay longer, but she insisted she needed to get home. He couldn't push too much, or she would start asking questions.

It was after two when he headed toward the lake property. He had slept hard having worked every day on the house as many hours as possible. This was the first day he had given himself the time off, but the house was almost finished. The only thing needed was a final coat of paint in the living room and kitchen. Casey had made him promise not to do that without her. His day off was tomorrow, and he planned to take her to St. Louis to find a car and to see about the last few pieces of furniture. Most of the items they had already chosen from the dealer in town, but they still needed a sofa or a loveseat, and maybe a second chair. Those he could carry in the back of the pickup.

Of course, they would have to go by Ms. Ruth's while they were in the city. Since he had told her about his idea to marry Casey, he knew she would be expecting to hear an announcement soon. Andy had waited as long as he wanted to anyway. He was ready to know if Casey loved him as much as he loved her. That was another reason he was late getting to his parents. He had stopped by the jewelers to pick up the ring he had on layaway.

As he drove down the road toward the bed and breakfast, he came upon a SUV pulling a new ski boat. The driver signaled and pulled into Greg Parson's driveway. Andy saw the man climb out from behind the wheel as he parked his patrol car and walked across his neighbor's yard.

"Get yourself a new toy?" Andy grinned at the man.

"Yeah, I figured it didn't make much sense to live on the lake and not be able to take advantage of it. I haven't skied in a while, and thought I would give it a shot again."

"You know Hope loves to water ski, don't you?"

"I seem to remember her saying something about that last summer." Greg smiled at him.

"So you bought a boat to impress my sister?" Andy smirked.

"Like you bought a house to impress a teacher I know?" Greg retorted.

"Touché." Andy grinned.

"Why don't we take it out this afternoon and see how it runs? Are you off duty now?"

"I am. Let me check and see what the ladies are doing. What time do you want to go?"

"Let's leave in an hour if that works for them." Greg checked his watch as he made the statement.

"I'll get them to pack a meal. Garrett showed us a cove that is great for swimming and a picnic he said." Andy also looked at his watch. "Do you need any help getting it into the water?"

"Nope. I'll meet you at your folk's dock in one hour with or without the ladies."

"Sounds like a plan." Andy patted him on the shoulder and headed toward his parent's to find Casey and Hope. His folks had owned a boat while they were growing up and had talked about purchasing another one. Andy and his sisters had grown up skiing, and he looked forward to this afternoon even though he figured he wouldn't be skiing until Casey was more comfortable in the water.

Hope and Casey were in the kitchen, when Andy walked in. He could smell the cookies they were baking before he opened the door. They would be great for dessert.

Casey turned toward the great room when she heard him approaching. She grinned big and walked toward him with a cookie between her fingers. She held the cookie up for him to bite into. As he chewed, he pulled her into his arms.

"As good as the cookie tastes, I would rather taste you." He whispered in her ear as he turned toward her mouth. The woman moved her face toward his meeting him halfway. His lips tasted of chocolate as Casey licked across them. She heard the soft moan he made as he deepened the kiss, pulling her closer to his body.

"Umm, do you need some privacy?" They heard Hope giggling behind them. She had taken the last batch of cookies out of the oven and was watching them. She wished she was in Greg's arms like Casey was being held by Andy. She didn't know if he was ever going to come around or not. They had talked several times, and he had taken her for dinner twice. He still acted apprehensive about their relationship.

The couple separated, grinning at each other before turning toward Hope.

"I just saw Greg before I came in. He invited us to go skiing in his new boat." Andy saw Hope's eyes light up as he turned back toward the woman in his arms. "Do you feel like going out on the lake?"

Both of the women whooped like children at the prospect. They quickly got to work making sandwiches and cleaning up the kitchen while Andy changed clothes and hunted up the picnic hamper. With minutes to spare, they were at the dock as Greg pulled along the side.

The men helped the ladies into the boat and then Greg took the basket and cooler from Andy before he stepped aboard. Hope settled into the seat beside the driver, while Andy and Casey took the bench seat behind them making it easier for Greg to see. They all put on their lifejackets before he took off.

Andy knew Casey wouldn't be comfortable skiing yet. She was doing very well when they had a chance to work on swimming lessons. There hadn't been enough time for them to do much practicing though. He was content to watch the other couple ski today.

Greg and Hope hit the water together swimming toward the skis. Both were ready within seconds, and Andy pulled them out of the water quickly. As Hope got the feel of skiing again, she decided to have a bit more fun. She swung way out and back closer to Greg. He grinned big as she moved back on the other side of the wake. There were no other boaters on the water so she brought her foot out of one ski and moved the foot behind the boot standing on just one ski. Greg wasn't about to be outdone, so he did the same thing.

Casey laughed. "They're just showing off." Andy swung the boat around to stay close to the other skis. The pair dropped by the first one and Andy stopped to pick up the second ski before circling back for them.

Both Hope and Greg were laughing as they handed their skis to Casey before climbing into the boat. Greg came on board first and turned to take Hope's hand. As he pulled her into the boat, she lost her balance and fell against him. He wrapped his arm around her to keep them both from falling. Looking down into her eyes, his gaze shifted to her mouth. He looked up once more into her eyes before kissing her. He had waited long enough to taste her. Hope returned the passion as if she were starving.

"Hey. Are you two about ready for dinner?" Andy teased.

They sat down on the bench at the back of the boat, and the driver took off toward the cove. Andy stopped the motor and drifted onto shore. Greg jumped in to haul the food and drinks to the beach, while the others shed their lifejackets. He threw his jacket back into the boat, as he helped the women step out of the rig. Andy vaulted over the side wading onto the sand.

Casey and Hope had the food spread out in no time, while the men sat and talked. After everyone had their fill, Casey packed it all up again while Greg and Hope went back into the water to swim some more.

Andy had slipped his shirt back on and asked the woman with him to take a walk. They stopped at a large boulder close to the path.

"Casey, this is not exactly the way I planned our evening to be going."

"Andy, I'm having fun. Are you not enjoying yourself?"

"It's not that. I enjoy anything I do in your company. I had planned to take you to the new steakhouse for a romantic dinner tonight. I would have waited for this, but we are going to St. Louis in the morning, and I need to ask you something first."

"Okay. What do you want to ask?" She was getting a little nervous.

"Casey, I fell in love with you the moment I pulled you from the water that first time I saw you. I feel like God has provided you as my soul mate. I love you, Casey Norton. Will you marry me?" Andy pulled the small ring box from his pocket and opened it toward her.

"Oh, Andy. I love you so much. I knew that same moment that I would never love anybody else. Yes, I will marry you." She threw her arms around his neck as his mouth found hers. As he started to deepen the kiss, he heard Hope calling.

"Should we go tell them our news?" He took her hand as they walked back toward the cove.

Casey stopped suddenly as she looked at Hope. Her face was so radiant, she knew what Hope was going to say before she even said it. Both women held up their hands at the same time to show each other their rings before they hugged each other.

"You asked Hope to marry you?" Andy marveled.

"Looks like we had the same idea in mind. I had planned to take her to dinner, but I couldn't wait. I have wasted too much time already." Greg wrapped his arm around the woman wearing his ring.

"I think we had better get back to the house and prepare our parents for weddings in their future." Hope laughed. She looked at Casey and grinned.

"That's great with me. I love the idea." She said smiling with Hope.

"What's great?" Andy asked.

"A double wedding." Both of the women answered at once as they started laughing. They felt more like sisters than ever. The men looked at each other and shrugged.

Chapter Nineteen

Andy went out to his parents place to pick up Casey for their trip to St. Louis. The ladies had talked so long into the evening she decided to spend the night at the bed and breakfast. He drove his pickup into the drive waving at Greg as he started toward the house as well.

"Hope called and told me I was expected for breakfast. I haven't told her yet. I have an assignment in Africa at the end of the week. Think I am going to be in big trouble?" Greg walked into the house followed by Andy.

His fiancée met him at the front door. "What's this about big trouble?"

"I just received an assignment. I leave tomorrow night for Africa. I'll be gone ten days." Greg waited for Hope to say something, hoping she would not be angry.

"When you get back we need to sit down and talk about our future. What would you think about me staying at the house and taking care of Sherman?" she asked.

"I was going to suggest the same thing. I think it's a marvelous idea. That way you can rearrange the furniture, or buy new things if you want them. I'm sorry I have to leave so soon."

"Well then, you will just have to give me the entire day today to make up for it." She kissed him before taking his arm to lead him into the kitchen.

Andy had walked past the two as they discussed the trip, looking for Casey. She was in the kitchen helping Nora prepare breakfast. There was only one couple renting a room right now, and they had left early for a day trip. The family had the place to themselves. By tonight, the bed and breakfast would be full through the weekend.

After a nourishing breakfast and a quick discussion about wedding plans, the couple headed toward St. Louis. Although the pickup wasn't as comfortable, it was nice to have the bench seat, so Casey could sit closer to him. He motioned for her to slide over before she fastened her seatbelt, and she quickly complied. They talked about the plans the women had discussed last night.

"We would like to wait until October, so we can have the fall break for a few days off. Do you mind waiting that long, Andy?" Casey wished they were already married, but knew the few months would be more practical especially with the double wedding the girls were planning.

"I suppose we're having a big affair, since there will be two weddings at the same time?" He knew the grin Casey gave him wasn't the answer he wanted. Andy had hoped they would be married before the ladies started back to school, but that was in three weeks. His mother would never agree to a date that soon, and he suspected the women would be just as adamant about waiting.

Andy knew he was changing the subject, but there wasn't much more to discuss since the date was pretty much set already "I haven't told you yet. I'm not selling the house. It is going to be ours if you're happy with it."

"Andy, I love the house. I was hoping maybe we could afford to keep it. Will the guys be okay with not selling it? I know they spent a lot of time on it with you." She was thinking about the side business they had talked about starting.

"I talked to them about it before I ever did anything about the remodeling. They insisted on helping all they could. We're looking at the house next to us to purchase for renovation.

We need to get the paperwork drawn up for the business first. We want everything to be legal."

The discussion continued until they reached St. Louis. "Do you want to go by Ms. Ruth's before or after we look for furniture and a car?" Andy knew it was going to be a busy day if they were able to accomplish everything they needed to do.

"I can't wait to tell her the news. Let's go by there first, please." Casey hugged his arm.

"Okay, but I have to tell you, she already knows to expect a ring. I asked her opinion several weeks ago. I'm sure she's wondering what has taken so long." He looked at Casey sheepishly.

"You talked to her about it?"

"I did. I wanted to know what she thought your answer would be since she knows you so well. I hope you don't mind?" He worried she might not have appreciated the idea.

"I don't mind in the least. I feel as close to Ms. Ruth, as I do my own grandmother. Did she say I would say yes?" Casey teased him.

Andy glanced at her to make sure she was smiling. "She told me I had better get that house finished and ask you quick. I worked as fast as I could."

"I knew she was a smart lady," she stated as they pulled up in front of the house. Ms. Ruth was in the front yard pulling weeds in the flowerbed when they arrived. She dropped the weeds that were in her hand, and quickly brushed her hands on the apron she was wearing before hugging her visitors.

She took them inside for a glass of tea while Casey told her all about their plans. Andy told her he had finished the house, and they planned to live in it after the wedding. The three of them discussed the future for the next hour before Andy told her they had to be going.

"We're in town to purchase a couple pieces of furniture

and a car for Casey," Andy told her. The woman had called Ms. Ruth the day after the accident and told her the car was totaled. They each hugged her and walked out to the truck.

"We had better look for you a vehicle. We can always order a sofa or loveseat if we have to," Andy stated.

Ms. Ruth had told them about a car dealership where her son always bought his cars. Casey had decided she wanted a used one, since she didn't drive it that much. Andy was determined she was going to have a larger, heavier vehicle, where she would be better protected.

They quickly found the car lot their friend had recommended, and Casey told the salesman what she was interested in. Andy saw just the vehicle he had in mind and led her to it.

"We want to test drive this one." He told the man. It was a SUV known for good gas economy, and the car had low miles on it. The dealer went in to get the key.

"Is this the way our marriage is going to be? You always get your way?" She grinned at the man beside her.

"Only when I'm right." He smirked, kissing her briefly, bringing a sparkle to her eyes and a chuckle to her lips.

The man brought the keys and held them out. Andy told Casey to take them and get in the driver's seat. "You'll be driving it more than I will." He knew it would be a perfect family car when they married.

She drove it through the neighborhood and onto the highway before returning to the dealership.

"I love it. Do you want to drive it, Andy?" She handed him the keys. He drove down a couple of blocks and turned around.

"Are you happy with it, or do you want to look around some more? We need to see the vehicle history, though," he said.

"I'm happy with this one if you feel like it's a good deal."

Casey trusted his opinion.

An hour later they had negotiated a contract for the car. The dealership promised to fill the gas tank and clean it up if the couple wanted to come back. It gave them enough time to shop two or three furniture stores before they returned for the SUV.

With Casey in the vehicle ahead of him and the last of the furniture needed in the pickup, Andy thanked God for a good day. They had accomplished all they set out to do. He just had one more thing to do before they got home. He called Faith and asked her to make reservations in his name at the new steak house in town. He still hadn't taken his fiancée out for the romantic dinner he had planned. As they drove the highway toward town, he called her.

"I'm heading to the house. I'll meet you at your apartment in two hours. We have dinner reservations. I love you." He heard her reply "I love you, too" before he disconnected the call.

Epilogue

Andy and Tom had just finished lunch at Lucas' when they ran into Faith. There was a stranger with her. Both men noticed the California license tags on the vehicle they stepped from.

Faith spotted them and all but ran into Andy's arms acting especially glad to see him. He lifted her off of her feet with a huge hug. He had not seen her in a couple of weeks. She returned his hug just as enthusiastically.

As happy as he was to see his sister, he was equally curious to know about the man beside her, especially judging from her reaction when she saw them. He waited only seconds to see if she would introduce them on her own.

"Aren't you going to introduce us, sis?" Andy asked.

"Sorry. Dr. Miller, this is my brother, Deputy Andrew Thomas and our friend, Deputy Tom Wallace. Dr. Miller is taking over his uncle's practice at the end of the month."

"Rafe Miller. It's a pleasure to meet both of you." He shook the hand of each man.

"I see you have California tags on your jeep. Is that where you were living before deciding to relocate here?" Andy asked the question both of them were thinking.

"Yeah, I had a practice with another doctor in San Diego. My uncle has been after me for a couple of years to move here and take over his practice. I guess the timing was right to do it now."

"Well, welcome to Lincks. Enjoy your lunch. We'll see

you later, Faith." He kissed his sister's cheek before walking away. Tom waved not saying anything.

Andy jotted down the license tag as soon as they got in the patrol car. "Uh, oh, going all big brother on Faith, are you?" Tom chuckled

"Just need to know about the new citizens to our fair town. Faith has never acted like that with anyone she is dating, that's for sure. The sparks flying off of that girl could start a grass fire." Andy shook his head. He and Tom both laughed.

By the time, Andy finished his shift he knew a lot more about Dr. Rafe Miller than he did two hours ago. He drove to the house anxious to share with Casey, thinking about Faith and the doctor he had met earlier.

Casey was there when he got home. She had been measuring the windows for curtains and draperies. They had spent one whole day in St. Louis earlier in the week, looking for things to hang on the walls. That was on the agenda tonight, hanging everything they had bought. This would be the last evening Andy would have free to do much for a while.

The deputies had worked out all of the logistics of their part-time business, and they signed the papers purchasing the house next door to him yesterday. They planned to start demolition as quickly as possible. All of the men had looked at the place and quickly agreed on the plans they had in mind. It was nice to know how much they thought alike. It would make reconstruction so much easier. They had also agreed that they were great with Casey choosing the colors for the place. They were impressed with the way Andy's house had turned out, and knew she would want something that would compliment their place for the structure beside it.

Casey smiled as her fiancé walked into the house she would be sharing with him in a couple of months. She could tell he was distracted by something, but waited for him to share what was troubling him. She had learned quickly that he sometimes had things happen at work she couldn't know about. As long as he was safe, she accepted that.

She also wanted to talk to him about the visitor she had earlier this afternoon.

Andy took her into his arms and kissed her like they had been separated for a long period of time. "You seem distracted. Is everything okay?" The way he kissed her was not quite the same either. He kissed her once more before he grinned, letting her go.

"I love the fact that you can read me so well. We are content with each other, aren't we?"

"Yes, I suppose we are. What's on your mind, Andy?"

"I saw Faith in town this afternoon. She was with Doc Miller's nephew. He's taking over the practice, but I'm not sure that is all he's taking over. You know, Casey, I've never seen Faith like she was today. She is either going to be looking for another job or there just might be a third wedding in October." He grinned as he pulled his woman back into his arms.

"I hope it's a wedding. I want Faith to be as happy as Hope and I are. I have something I need to tell you as well."

Andy looked at the woman in his arms. Casey pushed slightly on his chest to break his hold and moved away from his arms. She walked over to the windows keeping her back to him as she spoke. "You had a visitor this afternoon. A young woman came to the door looking for you. She said her name was Edie." Casey turned to watch Andy's expression.

"Casey, I couldn't tell you about Edie. She shouldn't have been here. How did she get here anyway? She's supposed to be in protective custody." Andy worst fears became reality. He should have told Casey about the woman even though it went against protocol.

"There were two very official looking men waiting at the

137

car for her. She told me she wanted to thank you for her new life. Andy, she told me about her time here and how you led her to Jesus. We laughed and cried together until one of the men came to the door. He told her they had to leave. I guess she told the federal government she wasn't going to testify until she could come by and thank you for saving her. She asked me to give you this and to tell you that you would always be her hero." Casey walked up to Andy and kissed his cheek.

"Did she look alright?" Andy hoped Casey would understand why he asked.

"She's a beautiful woman. I don't know her story, but I could tell she has been through a lot. She said she owes you her life. She made me remember once again what a special man you are, Andrew Thomas. I'm so glad you're mine. I love you." Casey wrapped her arms around Andy and welcomed him home in their own special way.

Surfer Doc
Book Six of the Lincks Series

Carol Clay

Chapter One

"If I could get Doc to start using his tablet, my life would be so much simpler. Then again, I would probably have more luck teaching him how to write legibly," Faith Thomas said in frustration. She sat at the computer as her fingers raced across the keyboard, when she could decipher the handwriting. That was the problem, it took a couple of minutes to think back to the patient's symptoms, and then the diagnosis to determine just what Doc Miller had said in his notes. He refused to use the computer system he had installed before she came to work for him two years ago. The previous nurse had insisted they needed the computer system, just before she got pregnant and resigned.

The office was closed for the afternoon, and Faith had hoped to finish updating the patient files early. She wanted to enjoy an afternoon at home with her family. She worked feverishly letting the music playing through her ear buds relax her while she typed. She never heard the front door of the clinic open.

A man walked up to the reception desk and waited for the woman to notice him. He cleared his throat hoping a noise would penetrate the music he could hear playing in her ears. Still she kept her back to him bobbing to the music, not realizing he was in the room.

He walked to the security door. He wanted to find it locked, but it swung open as he turned the knob. He shook his head as he followed the music to stand behind her. He knew it would scare her, but he figured something needed to frighten her at this point. So, he laid a hand on her shoulder. Faith felt the hand as she smelled the clean scent of someone in the room. She swung around not really afraid, but more startled that there was another person in the building with her. Her foot connected with the shin of the man. She heard him yelp and jump back. She was more concerned when she didn't recognize the stranger. Faith started to stand, hoping there was no need for her to try to defend herself. Before she could, a hand came across her mouth, while the other hand pulled the ear buds away.

"Don't scream. I'm not here to hurt you." He saw the fear in her eyes now. "Promise not to scream, if I remove my hand?" He grinned down at her.

She nodded her head slowly as Faith watched his eyes, and what beautiful eyes they were. Did bad men have eyes the color of the wheat just before the harvest? Surely, criminal's eyelashes weren't as thick and long as this man's. He straightened to his full height as he removed his hand, and Faith knew he towered over her as much as her brother Andy did. The t-shirt fit his broad shoulders like a glove narrowing to a smaller waist. The jeans were well worn, almost threadbare in spots and fit the man like the t-shirt. He had the build of an athlete. She looked back into his eyes, and up to his blond hair noticing it was a bit longer and sun streaked. His chin and cheeks were covered in a scruffy beard she knew he kept maintained at that length. He certainly was not from around here, or Faith would have met him before now.

"Do you always leave your doors unlocked for people to just walk through? I was in the building three to four minutes, before I got tired of waiting for you to notice I was here." He scolded her, his voice a rich, smooth timbre.

"Everyone knows the office is closed at noon on Fridays."

Faith didn't much care for the way the man was accusing her of being careless.

"All the more reason the place should have been locked." He frowned at her.

"Margie just forgot to lock it again. What are you doing here anyway?" Faith asked before realizing the man may be hurt. "I'm sorry, where are my manners? Did you need an appointment, are you hurt?"

"Are you the receptionist?" he asked, not answering her questions.

"No. I'm Dr. Miller's nurse, Faith Thomas. How can I help you?"

The stranger looked at her, clearly trying to decide what else he wanted to say to her.

"I'm looking for Dr. Miller."

"Like I said, the office is closed on Friday afternoons. The doctor is not here. Oh…" It finally dawned on her she was telling this stranger she was all alone in the office. She also knew that he understood what she was saying all along. She saw him take another step toward her still frowning.

"I would have thought a woman old enough to have a nursing degree would have been a little smarter than to tell a man they were all alone. Or did you deliberately tell me all of this for another reason?" Now he was grinning, as if amused by his thoughts, while his eyes raked her body from head to toe.

Faith was angry. She didn't care who this man was, he could not stand there and accuse her of… she didn't even want to think about what he was accusing her. She straightened to her full height of five foot five inches, her dark eyes getting even darker.

"Now, you just stop right there. I have no idea why you are here, but I am not going to stand here and be insulted by a stranger. If you need to see a doctor, I suggest you go next door to the hospital ER. They are quite capable of taking care of any problems you think you have." She poked him in the chest with her finger as she spoke, hoping he would retreat. He just stood grinning at her.

Neither of them heard the door open until the man walking through it spoke. "Rafe, you found the place. I'm glad you have already had a chance to meet Faith. She is the paragon I told you about. Don't know what I would do without her." Doc Miller walked through the door into the reception space where the two of them stood facing each other.

"Actually Uncle Walt, we haven't gotten around to introducing ourselves yet. Faith, I'm Dr. Rafe Miller, Walt's nephew. I'll be taking over the practice when he retires next month." He winked as he held out his hand to her. Faith had no choice, but to shake it, or look foolish. She wasn't prepared for the sensation she felt when she did so, however. Judging by the way his eyes narrowed slightly, Dr. Rafe Miller felt it, too.

Dr. Miller had mentioned a nephew coming to work with him before he retired, but she had expected someone older and more mature. This man looked more like a surfer than a doctor. Surely he wasn't going to leave the practice in this man's hands. Doc Miller was the only general practitioner in the county. People came from all over to see him. Accepting a stranger would be one thing, but someone looking like this would be another story altogether. Of course, there would be more females making appointments just to drool over him, no doubt about that. Faith pulled her thoughts together. Just because he was a beautiful male specimen, there was no reason to let him know she thought that.

"I'm sorry I wasn't here to meet you, son. Let Faith and me show you around the practice. Then we need to get you settled. Have you found a room while you're looking for a place to live?" Doc stepped from the room into the hallway.

"I have a room reserved for at least a month at the Pine Trees Bed and Breakfast you told me about." Rafe heard a slight moan escape from the woman beside him. Looking her direction, he almost missed her eyes rolling.

"Good, good. Faith can show you how to get there. Her folks own the place. Did I tell you that?"

The younger doctor looked back, grinning at the discomfort he knew the nurse was experiencing. This was going to be an interesting month, he felt sure. Taking her upper arm to move her with them, he was ready to see what the practice had to offer.

"Doc, why don't you show your nephew around the place while I finish translating your chicken scratching? I still have a few files to finish before I go home." Faith had no desire to follow these two men around the facility.

"You can do that in just a few minutes. You know where things are much better than I do, especially since you rearranged everything last month. I can barely find my office anymore." He laughed making the last statement to the other man.

"No wonder you are indispensable to the practice if you have changed where everything is located." He mildly accused her.

"Doc, would you mind if I borrow Dr. Miller just a moment? I'll bring him to your office in just a minute." Faith could hardly contain herself.

"Sure, sure. You two take all the time you need. You should get to know one another since you will be working so closely together."

Faith pulled the man into the nearest examining room and quickly closed the door before she turned to face him. "Look, I know we didn't get off on the best foot here, and I'm ready to turn in my resignation just as soon as I can get it typed. But Doc Miller and I have a wonderful relationship and

I don't want him upset. We have to get along until you can find a replacement. Believe it or not, I'm a pretty competent nurse, so you can stop thinking I have sabotaged the place, or that I'm stealing all of the band aids, or whatever you think I have done. You are certainly not what I was expecting either." She started toward the door.

The doctor had sat down with one hip on the examining table while he listened to what the woman had to say. He wasn't ready for her to leave the room, however. He quickly stepped around her and stood with his arms crossed in front of the door.

"Just what were you expecting?"

"What?"

"You said I wasn't what you were expecting. What did you expect me to be like?" He grinned the same infuriating grin he had exhibited since she had first seen him.

"Certainly someone more mature and looking more like a doctor than a beach bum." She stammered.

Rafe actually laughed then. Now, he was laughing at her. She stomped her foot and started to step around him.

Reaching behind him, he started to open the door, but bent down to whisper close in her ear first.

"I won't accept it, you know." He saw the question in her eyes at the statement. "You aren't going to resign. I won't accept you running away." With that, he opened the door and headed down the hallway toward his uncle's office.

Chapter Two

Faith walked out the door waiting for the new doctor to follow her and then stepped back to lock the door behind him. He had turned to lock the door himself.

"Doc already gave you a key?"

"He had sent me a key before I came to town in case the practice was closed when I got here."

She fumed all over again. "So, how do I know you didn't just unlock the door and then jump all over me for not locking the building?"

"You don't. But I didn't need the key. Do you want to talk to the receptionist, or would you rather I do that on Monday?" He stood on the sidewalk watching her.

"I'll do it." She muttered, as she turned away from him.

"What was that?"

"I said I would do it," Faith said not keeping the frustration out of her voice.

"Good idea. I'm sure it will come much better from you than the new guy. Where are you parked? I'll be happy to wait until you get your car."

"I'm parked over…." Faith had forgotten her car wouldn't start this morning. Her dad had brought her to town, and she had planned to call him when she finished at the office. How was she going to tell him without looking incompetent again?

"I take it you don't have your car?" He smirked, leaning his body against the brick of the building.

Faith would rather cut out her tongue than have to

explain to him what had happened. "My battery was dead. Dad brought me to work, and I was supposed to call him when I finished working. I can tell you how to get to the B & B. I really need to do some shopping, anyway."

"Come on. You might as well ride with me. That way you won't get lost."

She didn't miss the insinuation that she would be the one lost, but she decided not to comment on it. She walked behind him slightly as he headed toward a jeep with California tags. At least she felt a little more justified about the beach bum comment.

He opened the door and picked up the trash from the front seat where he had stopped for breakfast. He started to throw it in the back seat, but Faith took it from him instead. She walked over to the trash container just down the sidewalk from where he was parked and threw it away. She could feel his eyes watching her as she returned to the vehicle.

"We like to keep things neat in Lincks." She climbed into the front seat and reached for the seatbelt.

Smiling, Rafe closed the door and walked around to the driver's side, slid into the seat, and fastened his own seatbelt as he started the motor.

"I'm starving. I haven't had anything since six o'clock this morning. Let's stop for lunch before we head to your place." He knew she wouldn't want him referring to the Bed and Breakfast as her home, but he couldn't help teasing her. She was so beautiful, and he enjoyed the way sparks lit up her eyes when she was frustrated or angry. He seemed to know just how to set her off, too.

"We can go to Lucas' Deli or Jerry's Burgers, whichever you want." She wasn't going to give him the satisfaction of commenting on the last remark.

"Let's go to the deli. I have had enough burgers for a few days."

"Fine. Go to the right and circle the square."

Neither of them commented the next two blocks. Rafe pulled into a parking space in front of the building next to a patrol car. Andy and Tom were coming out of the deli as they started toward the door.

"Hi, guys." Faith's face lit up, looking at the two deputies. She hugged Andy throwing her arms around his neck and kissing his cheek, and then hugged Tom in the same manner. Both men lifted her off of her feet as they hugged her back, but they were clearly more interested in the man beside her.

"Aren't you going to introduce us, Sis?" Andy asked.

"Sorry. Dr. Miller, this is my brother, Deputy Andrew Thomas and our friend, Deputy Tom Wallace. Dr. Miller is taking over his uncle's practice at the end of the month."

"Rafe Miller. It's a pleasure to meet both of you." He shook the hand of each man.

"I see you have California tags on your jeep. Is that where you were living before deciding to relocate here?" Andy asked the question both of them were thinking.

"Yeah, I had a practice with another doctor in San Diego. My uncle has been after me for a couple of years to move here and take over his practice. I guess the timing was finally right to do it now."

"Well, welcome to Lincks. Enjoy your lunch. We'll see you later, Faith." He kissed his sister's cheek before walking away. Tom waved not saying anything. She wished the men were just coming in to eat, instead of leaving. It would have been much nicer than sitting at the table by themselves.

"Guess I had better not rile my nurse any further. Looks like you have friends in high places. Although, I'm sure he would be upset to know his sister was alone in a building with it wide open when a stranger walked in unnoticed."

"Will you please drop it? I was perfectly safe, but I will be more careful, now that I know you're in town." She walked into the deli not holding the door for him as she stalked ahead. He quickly caught up with her, still laughing from her remark.

"Faith, it's good to see you, darlin'. How have you been?" Lucas walked with the two to a booth before offering them a menu. She took a seat, but noticed Rafe still standing. She blushed slightly, because she didn't think to introduce the two men. She knew they would see a lot of each other.

"Lucas, this is Dr. Rafe Miller. He's Doc's nephew and will be taking over his practice soon." The two men shook hands before he sat in the seat across from Faith.

"Welcome to Lincks, Rafe. It's nice you're keeping the practice in the family. Walt told me he had finally talked his nephew into joining him. What can I get you two to eat? Mandy made a fantastic new bread recipe today. Want to try some?"

"We'll both take one of the sandwiches and two glasses of tea, please." Rafe spoke up, not waiting for Faith to say anything.

"I wasn't going to order any lunch," she stated between clenched teeth.

"I know you weren't, so I decided to order for you. Are you always this argumentative?" Rafe asked, taking a sip of the tea the waitress brought to the table.

"Believe it or not, most people consider me a nice person. You must bring out the worst in me." She snapped, wondering why he kept goading her.

"Ok. Let's call a truce. Tell me about yourself. Where did you get your degree?" Rafe grinned at her.

Faith exhaled before answering his question. Maybe telling him something about herself would keep him from insulting her any more.

"I went to the University of Illinois at Chicago. I was born and raised in Chicago until a little more than two years ago when my parents decided to move here and build The

Pine Tree Bed and Breakfast. I was working my first job at a hospital in the suburbs. When we moved, I was hired to work at the hospital here in Lincks. Before I could begin working, Doc talked the chief of staff into releasing me, so I would come to work for him. That's about it. I've been with him for two years now." The waitress sat their sandwiches on the table just as she finished talking.

"Do you mind if I say grace?" Rafe asked, surprising Faith.

"Please do." She laid her hands on the table and he reached out for them. Again she felt the sensation as they touched. She bowed her head quickly trying to ignore the feeling.

Rafe thanked God for the food and also for the safe trip and new friends. He squeezed her hands slightly before releasing them.

"Your turn. What should I know about you other than the fact that you are arrogant, overbearing, and bossy?" Faith grinned sweetly at him.

He chuckled slightly as he finished his bite of sandwich. "Like I told your brother, it was just the right time to come. I wanted out of the practice I was in, and Uncle Walt had been asking me to join him for quite some time. I was ready for a change of scenery."

"So you traded warm, sunny San Diego with their beautiful beaches for small town Lincks, Missouri. Running from a woman?" She didn't even know why she asked that. She could care less.

"That's a very personal question. Maybe I should have asked if you left any broken hearts behind, but then I think if there had been someone special, he would have definitely come to get you before now."

"Was that a compliment?"

"I know. Don't let it go to your head." He grinned as she

laughed out loud. He liked the sound of her laughter and looked forward to hearing it more often.

They finished their sandwiches before she realized he had never answered her question.

Chapter Three

Rafe had a hard time going to sleep that night. He kept thinking about the woman he had met that afternoon. Faith had affected him more than any woman had in a long time if ever. His thoughts moved from the dark brown of her long wavy hair to the liquid chocolate of her eyes to the dimples in each cheek. He liked the slight turn up of her nose and the lush fullness of her lips captivated him, even now. He knew his hands could almost span her waistline.

As a doctor, he had always prided himself in being able to read people. His uncle had told him so much about her. He knew she was much more capable than he had given her credit at the clinic. He had really enjoyed getting her flustered, and he looked forward to knowing her better.

Saturday was spent almost entirely with his aunt and uncle. He had left the bed and breakfast before Faith had come down. He figured she was hiding from him, but he didn't comment on it when he saw her parents again. They were both nice people making him feel quite welcome.

It was late before he returned to his room. Nora had mentioned that Faith was out with friends for the evening, so he spent an hour or more visiting with the Thomas' and the other guests before retiring for the night. He had the opportunity to meet her sister as well when Hope came in. Chuck mentioned she was staying temporarily at the home of Greg Parsons, her fiancé as well as their next door neighbor, while he was out of town. He was surprised how closely the two girls resembled each other except for the fact that Hope's face seemed to glow. He assumed that was from the new ring on her finger.

He woke earlier than the others in the household on Sunday morning. Chuck Thomas had invited him to join them for church. Since his aunt and uncle went to a church different than the denomination he usually attended, he decided to accept the invitation.

The coffee was ready and Rafe helped himself to a cup as he headed outside to read his Bible before breakfast. After spending a few minutes in prayer, his thoughts went to the practice he was joining, and the one he left behind. He knew it was time to start fresh, but it wasn't easy leaving the life he'd had in San Diego. The doctor had built a good practice there and had a number of friends. He was a surgeon and being a general practitioner was going to be a different experience. Rafe had prayed about the change for months and felt comfortable that God had led him to Lincks. It would be interesting to see His plans unfold.

Faith heard the back door slide open and she assumed her dad was going to the dock to spend a few minutes in prayer. She often joined him and was especially anxious to talk to him today. She hadn't spent time alone with him in a few days and missed their conversations. She quickly showered, dressed and hurried down to find him. She was already on the deck before she saw the man she had spent the last thirty-six hours trying to avoid.

"Don't run away. Join me," he invited.

"I don't want to interrupt your quiet time." She turned to go back into the house.

"You're not interrupting. God and I had finished talking for now." He patted the seat next to him.

Faith knew it would seem petty to go back into the house, so she took the seat he offered and turned slightly toward him as she tucked her bare feet under her in the loveseat.

"So, are you finding Lincks to be what you were looking for?" She asked, instinctively knowing the job offer was not the only thing bringing Rafe Miller to town.

He peered into her eyes as he contemplated her question. "I'm not really sure what I was looking for, but I have a feeling I'll find it here."

Her pulse accelerated at the intensity of his gaze. She didn't want to be attracted to this man. He would be her boss in a few weeks unless she resigned her position. She hoped she would not be forced to do that. The job was so much more than she had anticipated. Faith loved the people who came to the practice. They were friends as much as patients. The challenge of the career never got old, but Rafe posed a threat to her piece of mind.

He turned slightly toward Faith as well, resting one arm along the back of the loveseat. He picked up a lock of her hair between his fingers. "I like your hair down like this. You looked like a teenager the other day." He spoke more to himself than to her, letting the hair run through his fingers.

"It's not practical wearing it down when I'm at work." She felt herself being drawn more and more toward him.

"I can see that it would be distracting." He didn't add that he knew men would want to run their fingers through it just as he was doing. His eyes moved from her hair to her lips. He wanted to touch them. He moved slightly forward stopping himself as the door slid open. Thankfully, the noise was enough to break where his thoughts were taking him.

Chuck Thomas stepped onto the deck looking across the yard to the water. He noticed a movement to his left and turned his head.

"You two are early birds. Rafe, did you sleep better last night?" The guest had mentioned having trouble sleeping the night before blaming it on the peacefulness of the setting, instead of the owner's daughter.

"Like a log. Thanks for asking." Rafe looked once more at Faith before he stood to join her father. He turned and offered a hand to help the woman to her feet.

"I had better go help Mom with breakfast. I'll see you two in a few minutes." She entered the house before either man made a comment. Her hand still felt warm from Rafe's touch.

Nora and Hope were both in the kitchen. Hope was drinking a cup of coffee as their mother started mixing ingredients for pancakes while the bacon sizzled in the skillet. Breakfast was simple on Sunday mornings since most of the guests were either leaving that morning or heading out to visit someplace. Both ladies were dressed for church.

"Is Greg back yet?" Faith asked her sister.

"He comes home later today. His plane arrives in St. Louis about noon." Hope smiled with a dreamlike expression on her face. Greg Parsons had asked Hope to marry him the same afternoon Andy, Hope's and Faith's brother, had proposed to Casey Newton, Hope's best friend.

Faith knew Hope looked forward to his return later that afternoon. Greg was a professional photographer traveling around the world on different assignments. He had received a call just three days after their engagement, telling him to report to Africa the next day.

While preparing breakfast, the three ladies talked about the wedding plans. Faith was going to be their maid of honor at the double wedding in about three months.

Hope called the men in from outside just as two other couples made their way down the stairs. The meal was served on a large sideboard, where everyone could help themselves to not only pancakes, but selections of eggs, bacon and sausage. Soon the room was filled with talk and laughter.

An hour later, the Thomas family was ready to head to

Sunday school and church. Chuck turned to his youngest daughter. "Faith, why don't you and Rafe ride in together? That way he can find his way around unless you want all of us to ride in the SUV."

Before Faith could respond, Rafe had his hand in the middle of her back moving her toward the door, while Chuck was calling for Hope to hurry up. "That's a good idea. We'll just meet you there," Rafe told the man.

"I have to make a stop before I go to church. Surely you would rather ride with my parents?" Faith didn't need to be any closer to him than necessary.

"Oh, I don't mind taking the scenic route. He moved her past her small sedan to his jeep. "I don't think I can get into that little thing. We'll take my car and you can navigate." He opened the passenger door, waiting for her to climb in.

"Do you always get your way?" She asked sarcastically.

"It's a little too early to know for sure yet." He grinned purposely allowing his eyes to seek her lips. "Where do you need to stop?" He started the car and backed out as her parents and Hope walked out of the house and waved to them.

"I need to run by a friend's house. She lives directly behind the office."

Rafe nodded, not asking any further questions about her destination.

"Do you teach a Sunday school class like your sister and her friend?"

Faith looked at him somewhat surprised. He had learned a lot about her family already. "No, I'm not nearly as good with children as they are. I do substitute for them, when they have to be gone, but thankfully that isn't often."

"What will you do when they are both on their honeymoon at the same time? Your father told me about it this morning." He answered at her astonished look. She was saved from any further comment, as they approached the house of her friend. Faith quickly fumbled in her purse for a key and turned to Rafe.

"I'll just be a moment." She quickly opened the door and let herself out while Rafe turned watching her.

"I don't suppose you want me to come in and meet your friend?" He smiled at her.

"No." She almost shouted as she hurried to the front door, letting herself in the house.

Within minutes, she was back at the jeep ready to leave. Rafe looked at her before starting the car, but never said anything. They arrived at the church and followed the people inside.

"The young adult's class is this way. " Faith looked at Rafe briefly before leading him toward the classroom. The group was large enough now that they were meeting in the fellowship hall. Andy and Casey walked up behind them.

"Good morning Faith, Rafe." Andy spoke to the two ahead of them, forcing Faith to stop, causing Rafe to almost run into the back of her.

"Good morning to you, both. Rafe, this is Casey Newton, Andy's fiancé." Faith introduced them. Casey and Rafe shook hands before Andy extended his as well.

"Are you getting settled in okay, Rafe?" Andy asked.

"I am. I spent some of yesterday touring the town with my uncle. It seems like a friendly place."

Just as Andy started to say something else, the teacher stepped to the door to tell them they were ready to start. The four of them quickly went into the room to find seats. On the way out of the classroom, Andy caught up to Rafe.

"I understand you're looking for a place to purchase. If you are interested in a place with character in an established neighborhood, we have a house you might want to look at. Some of us have a part-time renovating company and are in the process of finishing a place right next to mine." They made arrangements to go by and see the place later that afternoon.

After touring the home and hearing what future plans the men had in mind, Rafe knew it was exactly what he was looking for. He made them an offer they would be fools to pass up. When Andy told him it would be a month or so before it would be ready to move into, Rafe assured him that was no problem, he was enjoying his stay at the bed and breakfast.

Chapter Four

Faith arrived at the clinic fifteen minutes before the doors were to open. Doc Miller had always taken walk-in patients in the mornings and then appointments in the afternoon. Today, they were already lined up down the block. She parked her car in the back of the building and entered through the back door. Rafe stood just inside the door, reading a chart.

"Why haven't you convinced Uncle Walt to stop allowing patients to come for treatment this way?" He frowned as she walked in front of him.

"And good morning to you, too. This has been the way he has practiced for years. The people don't mind. They seem to take waiting in stride. He sees a lot more patients this way. There is no reason to change things. Are you ready for all of this?" She walked toward the receptionist's area to stow her purse without waiting for an answer.

"Are you going to be able to keep up with both of us?" He looked amused as she pulled her hair into the ponytail she usually wore during office hours.

"Let's open the doors and find out. Oh, is Doc here yet?"

"He'll be here soon. Let's start without him." He moved to the back of the office area as Faith went to open the front doors. Patients came in staying in line to sign in and take a seat. Most of the people seemed to prefer coming in the mornings. They sat and visited as they waited their turn. Within minutes, she had the first three patients in exam rooms and had charted their vitals, as well as their symptoms. She walked back to the office area where Rafe stood still reading charts.

"The first three rooms are ready for you. I will have the other two rooms ready in a moment." She didn't wait for an answer, but turned back to walk down the hallway. At the same time, Doc Miller ambled through the back door just behind Margie, the receptionist.

"Good morning, Faith. Getting a head start, I see."

"Dr. Miller was anxious to see the first patients. Do you want to see different patients or are you going into the rooms together?" They hadn't had the opportunity to even discuss how they wanted to handle people meeting the new doctor for the first time.

"I don't see why we can't do different ones. We'll get through twice as many patients that way. I'll find Rafe and make sure that works for him. We have a full room already I see." He waved to the crowd in general and then headed toward the office.

Faith got the next two patients into exam rooms and told Margie she would be right back. She headed out the back door and across the yard to the same house she visited yesterday before church. She had already been to the house before she came into the office. Five minutes later, she sprinted back through the door and checked to see if there were any rooms empty yet.

Knowing the doctors were busy in exam rooms one and two, she waited for one of them to come out, so she could prepare the room for the next person. Seconds later, Rafe and Mr. Bridger walked out of the exam room together.

"Soak that foot twice a day in Epsom salts. That and this prescription should clear that sore up in no time. It was nice meeting you, Sam. Let us know if you need anything else." He patted the elderly man on the back and walked into the next room, but not before he saw Faith standing in the hallway waiting.

At noon, Margie shut the front doors and locked them. She and the nurse had visited just a moment about Friday. She didn't want Faith in any trouble with the new doctor. She told Faith she was heading to Lucas' to pick up their lunch order.

The morning ran smoothly with each doctor seeing patients. Faith was exhausted handling the duties for both men. While Margie was gone, the nurse made sure each room was ready for the afternoon patients and checked on the doctors. They sat talking in the office, discussing the patients they had seen that morning. She just as quickly left the doorway she had entered and headed for the back door of the clinic.

Once again, Faith hurried across the lawn to the house across the alley and entered the building using her key. This time she was gone almost ten minutes before walking back into the practice. She almost collided with Rafe.

"That's three times today you have gone across the alley. May I ask what you are doing over there?" He stood with his arms crossed looking down at her.

"No, you may not ask." She started to walk away, but he grabbed her upper arm stopping her.

"Faith, if you are going to keep leaving the building like this, I think I have a right to know what's going on." He dropped his hand, but still blocked her path.

"What I am doing has nothing to do with you or this practice. Now I need to get to some of Doc's transcribing. Thank you for putting your notes into the computer yourself, by the way." She walked past the man and into the reception office. Sitting down, she started typing some of the notes the older doctor had written that morning. Luckily most of the ailments were simple problems, and she had no trouble deciphering what he had written. She was able to relax when

Rafe finally moved away from the doorway letting her get on with her work. She finished the last chart as she heard the front doors unlock again. Margie was back with their lunch.

The afternoon appointments were many of the same ailments as the morning: colds, sinus infections, or sores needing attention. About half way through the number of patients, the men had caught up somewhat, and Faith was able to catch her breath. She stepped out the door and one more time headed across the street. Five minutes later she was back at the office.

Faith stayed away from the doctors, as much as possible. She kept moving patients into the exam rooms, and making sure they were ready to see one or other of the men before cleaning up the last exam room to be vacated. She was hurrying out of one of the rooms, when she bumped into Rafe. Ducking her head, she tried to move out of his way, but he stopped her, lifting her chin with his fingers.

Swearing under his breath, he wanted to shout at her. "What happened to you? Did one of the patients do that?" He looked at the bruise forming on her cheekbone.

"Of course not, I'm fine. Mrs. Crosby is in room number three. She is seven months pregnant. I'll be right in." Faith walked to put up the last chart before retracing her footsteps. She looked up at the doctor knowing he had not moved.

Rafe knew he was not going to get any answers out of Faith now. He held the door open for her as they walked into the examining room.

"Mrs. Crosby, I'm Rafe Miller, Doc's nephew. I will be taking over his practice in a couple of months. He has asked me to introduce myself. I would like to handle your case if you have no objections." He waited to see the woman's reaction.

"You're much easier on the eyes than Doc is. I might have to come in more often." She grinned at him. She would be delivering her fifth child in a couple of months. The doctor examined her and listened to both the baby's heartbeat, as well as hers. After asking a few questions, he assured her everything was going as expected and told her she could get dressed.

There were three more patients in the exam rooms. Rafe told Faith to have his uncle see them. He needed to run an errand. Then he walked out the back door to his vehicle. Doc Miller handled the rest of the caseload, and the ladies got the rooms in order for the next day. Margie had helped Faith since they were finishing early.

After making sure everything was ready for tomorrow, she headed across the road one more time. This was a trip she made about five times each day, and today was no exception. As she let herself in the back door, she started to call out, but heard voices in the living room. Making her way through the kitchen, she saw two people sitting in the room drinking tea and enjoying a conversation. One of the people was Mrs. Burgess, the owner of the house and the other person was Rafe Miller.

"What are you doing here?" Faith demanded.

"Being new to the area I thought it would be nice if I got to know my neighbors." He smiled innocently. "Mrs. Burgess was just telling me about her husband and how they met."

Faith looked at him trying to decide what to do next. She needed to get back to the clinic, but she wanted to turn Mr. Burgess first. She started toward the bedroom when Rafe spoke again.

"He's just fine. Ms. Agnes and I turned him a moment ago. Why don't you sit down and visit with us a minute?" He had walked across the room to stand in front of her. "Sit down and reassure her you're not hurt," he whispered.

She saw Mrs. Burgess watching them, and she smiled even though she wanted to punch the man standing in front of her. "We'll talk about this later."

"You can count on that," he said taking her arm to lead her toward the sofa.

"Can I get you some tea, Faith?" The lady asked her.

"No, Ms. Agnes, I'm fine. I need to get back to the clinic and transcribe Doc's notes while they're fresh. You know how bad his handwriting is. Will George be home soon?" She smiled at the woman trying to keep her cheek turned away from her as much as possible.

"Yes, I expect he will. He usually leaves the church about four. Today, being Monday, he'll stop by the store for groceries first, but he will be here soon. You two don't have to stay and entertain me. I'll just go read to Arthur for a bit. Rafe, it was so nice meeting you. I appreciate you coming over to help Faith. She is such a slip of a girl, I worry about her hurting herself sometimes."

"Ms. Agnes, I am much stronger than I look. Mr. Arthur is no trouble for me. Our arrangement is just fine." Faith spoke up quickly.

"I have always heard mules were as strong as they are stubborn, but I'll be helping her from now on anyway." Rafe winked at Ms. Agnes and took Faith's elbow. "We'll see you in the morning. He leaned down and kissed the woman's cheek before moving Faith toward the front door.

"I'm walking back to the clinic," she told him under her breath. She didn't want Mrs. Burgess to think they were arguing.

He continued moving her toward his jeep. "She's watching us. Get in the car."

Faith glanced over her shoulder to see if he was telling the truth. Ms. Agnes waved to her, grinning. She waved back and climbed into the jeep.

"Put on your seatbelt." Rafe never looked at her. She started to argue, but saw the look on his face.

"Fine, I'll put on my seatbelt."

When he pulled to the corner he turned left onto the highway, instead of into the alley, where he had been parked.

"I need to get back to the office." She looked at him, frowning. The man beside her never said anything just kept driving further out of town. Finally, he handed his cell phone to her.

"Call your parents and let them know we won't be home for dinner." Still he didn't look at her.

"I will not. You need to turn this car around and take me back to work." How dare he think he could order her around. She wouldn't take that from any man.

Rafe pulled the jeep over to the side of the road and took the phone from her hand. Searching through his directory, he located the inn's phone number and punched the call button.

"Hi, Chuck. It's Rafe. Faith and I are going to grab a bite to eat before we come back. We might be a while." He listened just a moment and replied. "Thanks, I'll tell her." He pocketed his phone.

"He told you to enjoy yourself and not to worry about when you make it back."

Faith stared at the man as he pulled back onto the highway. "I'm not having dinner with you." She stated turning her head to look out the passenger window. Rafe didn't say another word in reply.

They had driven almost to the interstate before Rafe turned down a small dirt road and stopped the vehicle.

"Alright, let's talk. Why are you killing yourself, turning Mr. Burgess every two to three hours?" He waited for her to speak.

"This is really none of your business." She looked straight ahead, not saying any more.

Rafe reached over and turned her face toward him. "I'm making it my business."

"It has nothing to do with the clinic, or my position there."

"Faith, answer my question." She knew Rafe was as angry as she was.

"Oh, for Pete's sake. Mrs. and Mr. Burgess have been coming to the clinic for years. Right after I started working there, Mr. Arthur had a stroke and she couldn't take care of him by herself. George, their son, is the custodian at our church. He lives with them, so he's there nights and most of the time on the weekends. I just go over on Sunday mornings and on weekdays to help turn him. They have lived in their home since they married sixty-two years ago. Ms. Agnes could not stand to put him in a nursing home. I'll help her as long as they are able to live there. Now, can we please go back?"

"And how did you get that bruise on your cheek?"

Faith exhaled loudly before answering. "Sometimes Mr. Arthur gets upset. He doesn't mean to hit me. I just didn't move fast enough today."

"How many times has this happened before?"

"Not that many times."

"How many?"

"I told you not that many times."

"How many times?"

"This is the first time he has hit my face."

"How. Many. Times, Faith?"

"He broke a rib once and knocked me unconscious for a moment one time. That was my fault though because I hit a nightstand." She looked quickly at him before looking away again.

She heard Rafe draw in a deep breath before climbing out of the car. She watched him walk to the front of the vehicle and down the road a little ways. Where was he going? Faith didn't know if this road even led anywhere. She decided to step out of the jeep to see if he was coming back. She saw him stop still not looking back at her. It was two or three minutes before he started walking back toward her. When he did, he looked directly at her the entire time and didn't stop until he was within a step of her.

"You are not to go to that house again to turn the man. You can visit, but if I find out you are turning him, I will get him moved out of the house. Do you understand?"

"You can't do that. This is none of your business." At least she hoped he couldn't do that. She drew herself up as tall as she could.

"I told you before, I am making it my business. I will go to the house and turn him each day at noon. He is fine being turned every four to five hours for now anyway."

"I am not —"

"Faith, don't argue with me. Your parents don't know you are doing this, do they?"

"Nobody knew about it until you had to get involved."

"And Uncle Walt or Margie has never asked where you go?" He couldn't believe she had been doing this almost two years with no one questioning her.

She frowned at him. "I'm not taking that much time from the practice. I stay later to finish transcribing for the day." She assumed he was worried about the time away.

He took her by the shoulders, as if he were going to shake her. "You crazy woman, do you think that is what I am worried about? Faith, that man outweighs you by seventy-five pounds or more. Ms. Agnes is certainly no help to you. We are not leaving until you promise me you won't do this again."

Faith looked at a spot on Rafe's chest refusing to look at his face, until he forced her chin up with his thumb and finger. "You didn't have to drive all the way out here to holler at me. You could have done that at the office."

"I'm waiting for your word." He didn't comment on the last statement.

"Alright, I promise." She almost spit the words at him.

Rafe didn't receive any satisfaction from her acknowledgment. He knew she was furious with him. Surely, she could see that he was just concerned about her. Still holding her chin, he searched her eyes. Maybe he was a little too concerned. This woman was getting under his skin big time. As he stood looking at her, he heard a vehicle slow down to make the turn.

"Get back into the car." He ordered her as a pickup pulled up behind them. Rafe walked to the driver's side of the vehicle and spoke to the man. Faith heard the two of them laugh before she climbed back into the passenger's seat. Within seconds, he was in the jeep pulling on down the road. A house came into view in a large clearing. Rafe pulled over to the side of the drive to allow the man to pass before he waved and turned the jeep around returning down the road they had entered.

Just before they reached the highway, Rafe once again stopped the car. "Do you want to go back to town for dinner or to Rachelle?"

"I don't want to have dinner with you." She scowled at him.

Not saying another word, the man grabbed her by the shoulders pulling her toward him not stopping until his lips were on hers. Faith moaned slightly before he lightened the pressure. He knew he shouldn't have kissed her, but the frustration he felt was stronger than anything he had ever felt toward a woman. *You wouldn't worry about her if you hadn't already started to have feelings for her.* He wanted to ignore the voice in his head. He hadn't moved to Lincks to be involved with a woman.

"I guess that's the only way I'm going to get you to stop arguing with me. Every time you start to, I'm going to kiss you. Now do you want to discuss it some more or go to dinner?" Hopefully, Faith would back down and realize he only cared about her safety.

As Faith opened her mouth to tell him just what she thought of him, he quirked an eyebrow silently, daring her to say something. His eyes moved quickly from her mouth back to her eyes.

"There is a restaurant not too far into Rachelle. We are just a few miles from it."

"I knew you were smarter, than you act sometimes." He tapped her on the nose. Faith slapped his hand away as he chuckled. He turned back onto the highway driving until they reached the town. She told him where to turn and they pulled into the parking lot. Faith quickly opened the door and stood onto the pavement before the doctor had time to get to her side. He only shook his head and moved his hand to her back to make sure she came with him.

While they ate dinner, Rafe asked her about different patients. Several of the patrons in the restaurant spoke to the nurse, and she found herself introducing the doctor often. Dinner took longer, but both of them were more relaxed by the time they finished eating.

They arrived at the office after seven o'clock. Faith turned to Rafe. "Will you please let me borrow your key? My things are locked in the building."

He smiled knowing how hard it was for her to ask so politely. He stepped out of the jeep, walking toward the clinic door. When he unlocked it and turned off the alarm, he reached for the lights. "I'll wait for you to get your purse and follow you home."

"I'm going to stay for a bit and transcribe the files from today."

"You can do that tomorrow. You need to ice that cheek before the bruising gets even worse," he told her.

"I want to get the typing done, while I can keep the

patients straight. I won't stay long." She turned toward the receptionist's office and her computer.

"Did you already forget what I said about arguing with me?" He pulled her toward him. Faith lifted her hands to his chest keeping some distance between them. She smiled at him.

"Please, Rafe. It will be much easier to do the work tonight. I promise to lock the doors behind you and I won't stay long. I only have the afternoon's patient load to do." She moved her hands up his chest slightly. She knew she was flirting with danger, but she wanted to get this work done.

"Don't think I don't know what you are up to. I'll be in the office when you are finished." He moved her hands away from his chest and turned to leave the area. She knew it would do no good to talk further, so she sat down and started her computer. She finished the files half an hour later and walked back to the office to find the doctor.

"I'm heading home. I'll see you in the morning." She spoke to him as he read a journal article.

"I'm ready. I told you I was following you home."

"I know what you said, but that's not necessary. I have driven that road after dark for two years. I will be perfectly safe." She started to turn as Rafe pulled her into his arms quickly capturing her mouth. After a brief kiss, he stepped back.

"I'm rather enjoying this. I think arguing has its rewards." He smirked. As the nurse started to open her mouth, he raised his eyebrows questioning her desire to argue further. Instead, she turned on her heel and headed for the back door with the doctor right behind her.

Driving home she thought about the kisses, more than the promise Rafe had forced her to make. Even though she was sure he meant to punish, she felt the passion behind each one. He made her furious expecting her to do as he said. She had always been able to control the men she knew. This man seemed immune to her charms. It didn't help that he brought out the worst in her. She decided to ignore the way the kisses left her breathless.

She tried to get him out of her head and almost succeeded, when she touched her cheek. It was going to hard trying to explain to her parents how it had happened.

Rafe was at her car door before she could gather her things. She had seen Casey's new car in the drive and knew both Andy and Casey would be there wanting the complete story as well. She glanced up at the man beside her as she stepped out of the vehicle.

"Want me to tell them how it happened?" He knew she was dreading telling her family.

"Thanks, but I can do it." Her voice lacked the confidence her words carried.

They walked into the great room finding it empty. "I'm going to run upstairs and put some makeup on it. That will save a few tempers." She started to turn toward the stairs when Andy walked into the room.

"We thought that was probably—what the—" He used his hand to turn her face toward him, the bruise already darker than it was earlier. Looking first at Faith, his eyes darted to Rafe.

The man threw his hands up in surrender. "She already knows how I feel."

Andy took her arm and moved her through the room to the outside deck where the others were seated. Rafe followed, determined she wouldn't gloss over the story.

Before she could even greet the others, her brother turned to her. "I want the entire story, and you had better tell me the truth." He looked even madder than the man standing beside her.

"Let's have a seat first." Rafe moved her away from

171

Andy and sat down with her on a loveseat. "You need to tell them, Faith."

Andy scowled at the way the doctor had become so comfortable with his sister, but he let the feeling pass when he saw the way Rafe looked at her. The man really did care about her. He didn't even try to hide his feelings. He also saw the way Faith looked at him as he placed his hand over hers on the cushion.

"It's no big deal, really. I have been helping a neighbor with her husband, and he accidently hit me this afternoon as I turned him. I probably should ice it down." She started to get up, until Rafe moved his hand from hers to her shoulder.

"Faith." He left the rest of the words unsaid, but she knew she had to tell the rest of the story.

"Okay. It wasn't the first time I've been hurt, but he doesn't mean to strike out like that. Mr. Burgess had a stroke almost two years ago. He just hasn't been the same since."

"What else happened?" Andy and her father asked at the same time.

When Faith ducked her head and didn't say anything, Rafe spoke up. "She had a broken rib once, and he knocked her unconscious another time."

"I told you, that was my fault. I hit the corner of the nightstand." Her head snapped up to see the man beside her, her family forgotten for a moment, as she looked at him a conflict of emotions going across his face.

"And you knew about this, Rafe?" Andy grilled him.

"Not until this afternoon. She is very protective of her friends. It took some persuading to get this much information, and I'm still not sure I know the whole story." He looked from her brother to her father before shrugging.

While the three men looked at the woman, Casey and Nora looked at each other and grinned. They had seen the expressions the two latecomers had on their faces. Rafe had only been in town for four days, but both of the women knew Faith had met her match. She had always been the strong independent one, never letting anybody tell her what to do, or how to do it. Nora knew that had already begun to change. She stood and walked into the kitchen to get ice for her daughter's cheek.

"So, obviously, she will not be allowed to do this anymore. What can we do to help?" Andy directed the question at Rafe.

"I'll go over during the lunch break and turn him myself. I'm told their son lives there and helps nights and weekends. Once during the day isn't ideal, but I'll keep an eye on him."

"I have done this for two years and been hurt less than a handful of times. I know what I'm doing. I would never forgive myself or you, if Mr. Arthur developed bed sores." Faith turned in the seat to plead her case.

"Faith, do you really want to argue with me about this here?" Rafe intentionally kept his voice low.

"You wouldn't dare. Besides, what do you think you can do to stop me, if I want to go over there?" The words were out before she thought about it.

Rafe swooped down and kissed her before she had a chance to move. It was brief, but had the effect he wanted. As he pulled away, she blushed red.

"Don't think I won't stop you." He said just loud enough for Faith to hear.

Andy started to rise from his seat. He wasn't about to let a stranger take such liberties with his sister.

Before he could move, Chuck put a hand on his son's arm. He and Nora had already discussed the couple. They knew there was an attraction between the two. "Rafe, I'm not sure I appreciate your methods, but someone has to help Faith see how dangerous this is. I don't know how we missed knowing about the situation before now."

Rafe grinned at Chuck. "Arguing with her has become

much more pleasurable for me, anyway. Your daughter is used to getting her way, I have a feeling."

Faith took the ice her mother handed to her and stood up walking out into the yard. Rafe saw her wipe across her face and knew she was crying. He hadn't wanted to upset her. As he approached, Faith held up her hand.

"Please go away." She didn't want to talk to anyone right now, and especially not the doctor. She was having a terrible time controlling her emotions. Rafe put a hand on each shoulder and turned her into his arms.

"Honey, I didn't mean to make you cry. I just can't take a chance on you getting hurt now that I know what you're doing." His words made her cry even harder, and he wrapped his arms around her, pulling her close where her head laid across his heart. He figured she could hear the effect she was having on him.

"Rafe, I can't let Ms. Agnes think that Mr. Arthur could hurt me or ever has hurt me. She would be devastated. I have to keep helping, or she will insist they move him when she doesn't want to. It may come to that soon, anyway, but I need to be there until then." She cried even harder trying to tell him between sobs.

"Okay, baby. If it means that much to you, we will both go every couple of hours. You can come into the room with me, and I'll do the turning. How my uncle let you get by with this is beyond me." His soothing words began to help her relax, and she slipped her arms around his waist before speaking again.

"Doc didn't know I was doing this. When Mr. Burgess had the stroke he asked me to find someone to assist them. Ms. Agnes told me Mr. Arthur wouldn't allow anyone to help him. He was a very prideful man. She agreed he might let me since I had been their nurse, so I did it. Lately he has become a bit more aggressive. I worry about Ms. Agnes bathing and cleaning him. He doesn't know people like he used to." She rested her head against his chest and was comforted by the beat of his heart. Rafe laid his chin on her head, enjoying her in his arms until they heard someone approaching.

Faith stepped away from Rafe and looked at Andy. She knew he would be the one coming to make sure she was okay. He had always been her protector.

"Faith, what can I do to help? You could teach me how to turn the man and I would be happy to go by once or twice a day to do that." Andy saw her red eyes knowing she was upset. Chuck had told him what they suspected about Rafe's feelings toward his sister before he walked toward the couple.

She turned toward him and hugged his waist. "I love you, Andy. Rafe just told me he would go more often and let me help. Mr. Burgess is uncomfortable around strangers. If we need help later on, I'll be happy to let you know." She squeezed him a bit harder before stepping back. She hadn't hugged her brother like that since the first day he returned from the service.

"You're taking care of the situation then?" Andy turned to question Rafe. Both men knew he meant more than just the patient they had been discussing.

"I've got it completely under control if that works for you." Rafe extended his hand toward Andy, thankful he shook it.

"I think I'm good with that." Andy had already looked into the doctor's background and knew he was a man to be trusted. He felt like he had just handed over his sister's heart to the fellow.

The three of them headed back toward the house where Casey was standing. Chuck and Nora had gone inside. She hugged Faith when they reached the deck and turned toward her fiancée. They were ready to leave.

"So the wedding is the middle of October, huh?" Rafe stopped the two with the question.

"It is, less than three months." Casey answered the query, wondering why he was curious now.

"Hopefully, that will be enough time." He made the statement more to himself than anyone.

"Time for what?" Faith asked.

"I'll let you know one of these days. Right now, I think I will turn in for the night. Good night, Andy, Casey. Faith, I'll see you in the morning." He waved to the three as he headed into the house.

"I've never met a man that wants to control everything more than he does." Faith said to the two beside her.

Casey laughed. "You have never met a man you couldn't control, you mean." Andy joined her laughing, while Faith scowled looking in the direction he just went.

Chapter Five

July turned into August, and with it came hotter temperatures. The clinic saw several patients with heat-related symptoms. Rafe was dealing more and more with the clients, while Walt took more time away. A big retirement party had been planned by Faith and her mother in just three days. All of the patients from the clinic had been sent an invitation. Of course, the party was to be held at the Pine Trees Bed and Breakfast.

Rafe had been true to his word and went to the Burgess residence with Faith at least four times each day. He noticed how the man's condition had deteriorated the last month, and he had tried to brace both Ms. Agnes and Faith, but didn't think either of them would be ready to accept the likelihood of another stroke.

Two nights before the big celebration, the doctor awoke to his phone ringing beside the bed. It was Ms. Agnes. Mr. Arthur was acting quite strange and having trouble breathing. He assured her they would be right there.

He threw on his clothes and rushed down to the room he hoped Faith slept in, knocking on the door softly. Rapping a bit harder, he heard footsteps approaching the door. She looked adorable in the oversized t-shirt and her hair all tossed from sleep, but he had to concentrate on his reason for disturbing her.

"It's Mr. Burgess. Ms. Agnes needs us." He saw her eyes become fully alert.

"Give me two minutes." She was ready in one and a half.

Rafe drove as quickly as he dared. He had already called the ambulance. He knew Cindy Guthrie was on duty at the hospital and called her as he drove explaining the situation.

"We'll go by the house and if the ambulance isn't there, we'll head to the hospital," he told the woman praying beside him.

The ambulance was still at the house when they arrived. Both of them rushed in and went straight to the bedroom. Mike Guthrie, the fire chief, was the paramedic tonight.

"He's agitated and won't let us do anything to help him." While Mike talked to Rafe, Faith walked around to the other side of the bed.

"Hi, Mr. Arthur, it's Faith. How are you feeling tonight? I think we need to check you out just a little bit. Dr. Rafe is here. Would you let him listen to your heart?" She had been rubbing his hand while she talked, reassuring him all the time she checked his pulse. He was not nearly as upset as he was when they came in.

"Rafe, his pulse is weak. His pupils are dilated and his skin is clammy. Do you have a sedative in your bag?" She hadn't changed her tone of voice and continued to stroke the patient, knowing it was not the words, but the calm attitude that was helping him.

The doctor handed her a stethoscope and told her to listen to his heart. She told the man what she needed to do and warmed the end of the instrument before placing it on his chest. Faith told him what she heard and Rafe pulled a vial and needle out of the bag he carried preparing the shot for her.

"Mr. Burgess, we're going to give you a little something to help you rest. If you let me give you a shot, I'll get you a lollipop like I give the children." She giggled and was relieved to see him smile. At least, he understood what was going on.

"We need to take you to the hospital for a checkup. Ms. Agnes and George will be coming, too. Will that be okay with you? Either Dr. Rafe or I will ride in the ambulance with you. Oh, I felt that. Good choice, I'm much nicer than he is." She leaned down and kissed his forehead. "Mike and Drew, the paramedics, are going to put you on the gurney now and get you outside. I'll be right beside you all the way."

Rafe wasn't happy that Faith was the one riding in the ambulance, but the patient seemed to be much calmer with her in the room. He helped Ms. Agnes and George get ready. George put his mother in the car and pulled in behind the ambulance. The doctor took off ahead of the ambulance and was parked by the time they were backing into a bay.

He stood at the vehicle door and lifted Faith out, setting her in front of him. "Are you okay? You were wonderful with him."

She only smiled her thanks and turned toward her patient as they removed the gurney. She took his hand once more and told him she was right there. She explained they would have to see a doctor before he could see Ms. Agnes or George, but they were just inside the waiting room ready to see him when the doctors were finished. The sedative had calmed him considerably, and he just nodded watching Faith put an IV into his arm and told him she was going to get his son and sweetheart. He smiled back at her. All three of the medical team left Ms. Agnes and George to visit with the patient.

The doctor walked up and put his arm around his nurse. "You calmed him down when Ms. Agnes couldn't. He depends on you a lot more than I thought. He is more alert than he has been in quite some time, too. I think we can leave him with Cindy now. You look exhausted."

Faith punched him lightly on the arm. "Compliment me and then tell me I look bad. Some bedside manner you have."

"You always look beautiful to me, Faith. Let's get you home. We only have a few hours until it's time to open the clinic. I think you need to stay home today. Margie and I can handle it."

"Of course, I won't stay home. I have a job to do, and I'll be just fine. You've been up as long as I have."

"I just stood back and watched you work. You were amazing." Rafe brushed the hair out of her face and cupped her cheeks before lowering him mouth to claim hers. Faith wrapped her arms around his waist as he pulled her closer deepening the kiss.

"Excuse me. Doctor, I need your signature on this paper to move your patient." The charge nurse, a good friend of Faith's, stood behind them smiling.

The couple separated both blushing slightly. Rafe signed the paper, took Faith's hand and walked out of the hospital. Neither of them commented on the kiss.

Chapter Six

Faith was already in the office, when Rafe walked in the back door. Patients filled most of the chairs in the waiting room, and she was ushering a gentleman into the third exam room.

"I thought I told you not to come in today."

"You already have patients in three rooms. You need to get busy." She spoke as if he had said nothing. She walked into exam room number one with him. Little Molly Chambers was in the room with her mother. Molly had cut her foot on some glass. The nurse wasn't sure who was having the most problem with the injury, the child or the parent. Mrs. Chambers was white, and the girl just kept crying.

Faith had removed the bloodied sock Molly was wearing. She had hoped the bit of padding had kept the wound from being as deep, but she could tell it would need stitches and had already prepared a suture kit for the doctor.

"Molly, are you and your parents coming to the house on Saturday for Doc Miller's big party? There will be a big cake and lots of candles. Maybe Doc Miller will let you blow out some of the candles, when I tell him what a big girl you have been." She continued to talk to the youngster and her mother while Rafe examined the foot. He sprayed the cut with a spray and shot it with a needle after the deadening took effect. Molly jumped, but didn't cry any louder. The nurse had her enthralled with a story about the big dog that lived next door and how smart he was. Within minutes, the doctor was wrapping the wound and told her mother she could take her home.

"What a great job you did, Miss Molly." Faith pulled two suckers from her pocket offering them to the child. Mrs. Chambers picked up her daughter and thanked both the doctor and nurse for their help. Rafe told her to bring her back in a week, and they would remove the stitches. As they left the room, he turned back toward Faith.

"You told me you weren't good with children. Nobody could have handled that little girl better. You made my job easy. Now, I wish you would go home and get some rest."

"You were up just a late as I was. We'll both be fine. We'll sleep tonight." She stood on her tiptoes and kissed his cheek. "That's for not arguing with me." She grinned and walked out the door to get the next patient.

Later that afternoon Ms. Agnes called to tell them Mr. Arthur was able to come home. Rafe had talked to Mike about using the ambulance to transport him home since they lived so close. The men made sure he was comfortably in bed before leaving again.

By the time the last patient was seen, both doctor and nurse were exhausted. Faith and Margie readied the exam rooms for the next day, and called it a day. Rafe had decided to leave the emails he had over the course of the day until tomorrow as well. The only thing left to do was return phone calls. When Faith brought them to him, she had sorted them giving him only the most important ones. She would call the others back herself. He noticed the stack still left in her hand.

"Are those more phone calls?"

"They are the ones I can take care of myself. You have enough calls to make." She turned to leave the office.

"Faith, I'm glad my uncle insisted you come to work for him. You are the paragon he bragged about. Thank you."

She just grinned at him blushing a beautiful shade of

pink before leaving the room. Thirty minutes later, they were both ready to leave when she received a call from her mom. Rafe had walked out of his office to join her in the hallway as she answered the phone.

"Hi, Mom," Faith commented before listening to the conversation from the other end.

"Okay, give her my love. Don't worry about it. You know I can take care of it." Again, she listened for just a moment.

"Love you both. Drive safely."

"Something wrong?" Rafe startled her when he moved up beside her.

"No. Well, yes. My grandmother in Chicago fell and broke her hip. Mom and Dad are driving back there tonight to stay with her. They won't be back for a few days."

"Then we need to postpone the party." He knew that was worrying Faith.

"We can't do that. Mom has most everything ready and it's too late to contact the guests. You and I will just have to be the hosts. I can finish the last of the food preparation. Andy will help you get the yard and everything else prepared. I know he and Casey will help all they can. We'll be fine. It is more tonight I'm concerned about. They still have two more couples staying at the house. I need to get home and finish the meal for them." She fumbled in her purse, looking for her keys. The doctor jingled them as they hung from her hand.

"Take a deep breath and relax. The couples will understand. I'm sure Nora had the majority of the meal prepared by now. We'll finish it together and worry about the party afterward." He wrapped his arm around her shoulders and started moving her toward the back door.

"Mr. Arthur. They will be expecting us." The nurse just remembered.

"I'll handle that. You go on home and finish dinner. I will be just a few minutes behind you." He kissed her forehead

183

and opened the back door.

Rafe also took time to run by the new place Andy was renovating to see how progress was coming. He hadn't said anything to Faith about purchasing the house yet. He could only hope she would like the home as much as he did. Maybe he should bring her by soon to see what it looked like.

By the time Faith turned into the driveway, she was back to normal. She knew she could finish any meal her mom had started. Nora had insisted that all three of the children learn how to cook. Hope didn't like to cook very much, but she could in a pinch. Andy enjoyed it but didn't practice often. Usually it was Faith in the kitchen, working with her mother, and Casey always helped when she was at the house as well.

Faith was in the kitchen pulling things from the refrigerator when Rafe walked in. She turned and smiled at him.

"I've got this under control. Why don't you go up and take a shower before dinner? It will relax you." She had pulled out everything she needed. Thankfully, Mom had planned a simple meal of steak, baked potatoes and salad. The salad was already done and the steaks were marinating. She would start wrapping potatoes as soon as she got Rafe out of the kitchen.

"Why don't you let me help you get the potatoes ready, and we can both take a shower while they're baking?" He rested one hip against the island, waiting for her answer.

"Are you arguing with me?" She walked up to him laying her hands on his chest.

"I was thinking of it as a compromise, but if you want to think of it as arguing, I'm all for that." He quickly moved her hands to his neck and wrapped his arms around her waist before lifting her to his lips. He held her body against him as he changed the chaste kiss into something more hungry. They never heard Andy and Casey walk through the door.

"I think we may be interrupting something here." Andy laughed as the couple separated slightly; Rafe still holding Faith in his arms off of the floor. He grinned against her lips as he kissed her briefly once more before placing her back on the ground. He liked the rosy blush on her face as she turned toward her brother.

"You two are just in time to help finish dinner. Casey, if you will start washing potatoes, Andy, I need you to get the grill ready, please. Rafe, you go take your shower." She turned away after giving out the orders to each one. She started counting out the potatoes for Casey.

"Wow. Who put her in charge?" Andy laughed as he headed out the door to do as he was told. Both of the others laughed before they went in different directions.

With dinner out of the way, the guests had decided to go see a movie. The four quickly got the kitchen cleaned up and headed to the family room to visit. Casey wanted to know how she could help with the retirement party.

Andy and Casey sat close together on the sofa. Rafe had sat down on the loveseat. When Faith came in, she headed toward the recliner her dad usually claimed until Rafe grabbed her hand pulling her down next to him.

"How is Mr. Burgess doing this afternoon?" Faith asked the man beside her. She hadn't had a spare moment to question him until now.

"He asked about you and wondered where you were. I told him what had happened. He gave me no problems when I went to turn him. He even tried to shake my hand. He seems much better the last few days. I just hope it lasts." Rafe told her.

Casey asked about the plans for Saturday and the four of them started talking about the party. Faith grew quiet and within seconds Rafe felt her lean into his body. She was sound asleep. She had already told him she would have to get up earlier to prepare breakfast before she came to work. Casey had told her she would be over early to clean up after the breakfast was finished. They would get Hope to help Casey prepare lunch and start dinner. Faith had decided lasagna would be the simplest thing to fix. She would have that ready while the others made garlic bread and salad. Nora always had plenty of desserts for emergencies. Casey had taken two pies out of the freezer as they prepared dinner tonight.

The two couples were due to check out on Saturday morning right after breakfast. The two new couples coming in the same morning had plans to be gone until late Saturday evening.

The three talked for a few more minutes. Then Andy told Rafe he had better wake Faith up, so she could get to bed. He wasn't comfortable leaving his sister asleep in the doctor's arms no matter how much he liked the man. He knew Rafe had strong feelings for the woman.

Rafe figured he should wake Faith as well, but he was really enjoying the feel of her next to him. He ran his finger down her cheek not wanting to startle her awake. He called her name. She only nuzzled closer to him like a kitten.

"Casey, will you help me get her up to bed. I don't see any reason to wake her if she can sleep." Rafe scooted off of the loveseat supporting her body until he could turn and pick her up. Again, Faith just cuddled into his arms. It took all of the control he had to keep from kissing her awake. He had fallen head over heels for this woman, and he wanted to make her his.

Casey moved up the stairs in front of him and turned the bed down. Rafe laid her gently onto the bed, but not before he kissed her forehead. Casey patted his arm as he walked past her to head back downstairs.

"Do you want Casey and me to spend the night, Rafe?" Andy asked.

Rafe grinned slightly at Andy. "I'm not going to compromise your sister, Andy. But I will tell you right now, I am going to marry the woman."

"Have you told her that?" He wasn't surprised with the looks he had seen the two share.

"Not yet, but soon. How do you think Hope and Casey would feel about a triple wedding instead of a double wedding?"

"I think we would love that." Casey exclaimed as she walked down the stairs. "Don't wait too long though. Nora will need time to add to the arrangements."

"So you think Faith will say yes?" Rafe was sure about his feelings. It was hers, he questioned yet.

"I can't say for certain, but I've seen the sparks flying between you, too. She either hates you or loves you and that can be a very fine line."

"Well, let's just hope its love she's feeling. Knowing her, she will argue about it anyway," he stated.

"You have a pretty effective way of dealing with those arguments though," Andy stated, as the three of them chuckled.

"We had better get out of here and let you get some sleep." Andy joined his fiancée by the door. Rafe walked to the outside door with them and made sure it was locked behind them before checking the sliding doors. He flipped off the lights and walked upstairs to his room.

Chapter Seven

The weather for the retirement party could not have been more beautiful. The skies were clear with just a slight breeze blowing. The celebration wasn't scheduled until six that evening, plenty of time to get the last minute foods prepared and everything ready.

Faith had been up earlier than usual to prepare breakfast, both yesterday and today. She had just set the last of the breakfast items on the sideboard for the guests when Rafe walked into the kitchen.

"I had planned to be up in time to help you this morning. I didn't expect you to be so fast." He poured himself a cup of coffee and went to stand beside her. "You have to be exhausted. I know you were up late last night as well."

"I couldn't sleep, thinking about the plans for tonight. I want this to be a special time for Doc."

"Honey, it will be a great evening. I don't want you to worry anymore about it. You will have all the help you need if I have to bring in a catering staff from St. Louis. I know a couple of good ones in San Diego. Want me to fly them out?" He teased her, but then the idea didn't sound that bad, either. If he had thought about it earlier, he would have made it happen. As it was, it would probably be too late to get a private jet to bring them.

"If I said yes, you would probably make it work, wouldn't you?" She took the cup from his hand setting in on the counter. "Just kiss me long enough to make me forget all about the party for fifteen seconds." She wrapped her arms around his neck and stood on tiptoe to reach his mouth.

Even though the request surprised him, Rafe was quick enough to react. He pulled Faith's body close to him, as he touched his lips to hers softly until she moaned slightly in protest. Then he increased the pressure, kissing her with passion and desire. By the time she moved back slightly, both of them were gasping for air. He turned his attention to the graceful neck before him; kissing and nibbling as he made his way down to her collarbone and back up.

"I think we had better stop before I forget everything." She kissed his cheek before moving her hands away from his neck.

Rafe took her face between his two hands. "You, woman, are becoming too addicting. We had better do something about this."

"Oh, and what do you suggest we do?" She teased.

"I suggest we get married." He still held her face watching the emotions in her eyes.

"Married? Are you proposing to me, Rafe Miller?

"Yes, I am. Would you do me the honor of becoming my wife, Faith?"

"Rafe, we have only known each other a few weeks." She didn't know what to say.

"I knew I was going to marry you the day I walked into the office. I fell head over heels in love with the most argumentative, stubborn woman I have ever met. But if you need more time, I'll give you all the time you need. If you want to argue about it, I will be happy to handle that, as well." He grinned at her.

"Are you sure about this?"

"As sure as anything I have ever done in my life."

"Oh, Rafe, I love you, too. I would be honored to become your wife."

He drew her into his arms again, kissing her with a passion neither of them had expressed before. Just then Andy and Casey walked into the room followed by Hope and Greg.

"We came to find you two, but it seems we keep interrupting." Andy shook his head grinning.

"We were just celebrating. She said yes." Rafe smiled at the couples.

"You're getting married? You're getting married!" Hope ran into her sister's arms hugging her. The men congratulated Rafe, while Casey took her turn hugging Faith.

"So this is going to be a triple wedding, now?" Andy asked the newly engaged couple.

"Actually we hadn't gotten that far yet." The doctor laughed. "What do you say, sweetheart? Do you want to share a wedding date with your brother and sister?"

"Y'all wouldn't mind?"

They all assured her they wouldn't mind at all.

"Think how much easier it will be for us guys to remember our anniversary, if they are all on the same date. Mom and Dad will only have one date to remember like they have one birthday." Andy laughed.

"We were all three born on the fourth of July." Faith explained to Rafe.

"That does make it convenient, doesn't it?" the man said.

"Okay, then. I guess we all wait until the middle of October for a huge wedding." She grinned at the group.

"We came to see what we can help with this morning for the party." Casey brought the thoughts back to present.

The women sat at the kitchen island and talked about the plans for the food while the men decided to go in and have breakfast. Faith was already cooking more food for the guests.

By noon, everything that could be prepared ahead of

time was done. Faith was decorating the big cake when the doorbell rang. She wiped her hands on the apron she was wearing and went to answer it. The person on the other side of the door stood impatiently.

"I'm looking for Rafe Miller. I was told he is staying here." The woman looked at Faith with a scowl on her face. She was tall, willow thin and dressed to the nines, making her look completely out of place in the environment.

"Rafe is staying here. Please come in, and I will see if I can locate him for you." Faith had already decided this woman was trouble. She knew she had to be from San Diego, and she wondered just how well they knew each other.

"Please have a seat, while I let him know you're here." Faith turned from the woman, knowing she would not sit and wait. She headed to the deck to see if he was out there with the men.

Spotting him at the boat dock, she walked part way across the yard before he saw her coming. He said something to the other men and started walking toward her.

"There is a woman here to see you." Faith stated watching his eyes. She saw them narrow slightly before she turned to walk with him back to the house his hand in the middle of her back.

The woman stood in the doorway to the deck watching them. "Hello, darling. I thought I would surprise you and see if you were ready to come home." The woman wound her arms around his neck pulling Rafe into a kiss. He backed away, but not before she had marked his mouth with her red lipstick. "Darling, you don't act happy to see me. Did I embarrass you in front of the help?" She linked her arm with his pulling him into the living room leaving Faith alone standing in the kitchen.

"What are you doing here, Cynthia?" Rafe asked in an angry tone.

191

They had moved too far for Faith to hear the answer. She wanted to follow them, but knew Rafe would tell her what was going on as soon as he could. She tried to concentrate on finishing the cake, but messed up the decorations twice having to repair the damage. Minutes later he walked into the kitchen.

"Faith, do you have a room Cynthia can have for the night? She will be leaving in the morning," he asked. Then he added, "I'll explain later."

On top of trying to finish things for the party, now she had to go upstairs and clean another room. She smiled and assured him she would have a room ready in thirty minutes. She moved the cake into the walk-in refrigerator and went upstairs to prepare the place. Anger made her work faster, getting the suite ready in fifteen minutes. The only space available was directly across the hall from Rafe's.

She walked down the stairs and into the great room, where the two sat. "Your room is ready. Would you like for me to show it to you now, or do you want to wait until later?" She tried her best to be friendly.

"You may get my bags out of the car, and I will see the room later." She turned her attention away from the woman standing in front of them.

"Cynthia, Faith is not one of your servants. She does not get bags. Her parents own this Bed and Breakfast and she is helping them while they handle an emergency." He stood and walked to her side. "Faith, this is Cynthia Foster. We shared a doctor's office in San Diego." Before he could say any more, the woman interrupted laughing.

"Darling, we shared so much more than that."

"Cynthia, this is Faith Thomas my nurse, and as of this morning, my fiancée." Rafe picked up her hand and kissed her palm.

"Well, well you certainly worked fast enough this time.

Faith, you and I will have to have a little talk about your new fiancé." The woman almost purred.

"I think I know just about everything I need to know about Rafe, don't I, sweetheart?" She wiped the woman's lipstick off of his mouth before she stood on tiptoe and rubbed her cheek against his. "You better have a good explanation." She whispered in his ear before kissing him briefly. Before she pulled away, he wrapped his arm around her waist, kissing her much longer than she kissed him. Faith was clinging to him by the time he let her go.

"I had better go finish things in the kitchen. The guests should be arriving in less than an hour." She ran her hand down his cheek before walking away.

Faith was furious. How could she have fallen in love with a man and known so little about him. She didn't know anything about his past, even if his parents were still alive or not. For all she knew, he could be married to that piranha in the other room. How could she have been so stupid? She started pulling out the trays for the food, wanting to bang them on the cabinets, but she didn't want to give Cynthia the satisfaction of thinking she was upset.

Casey and Andy walked through the great room on the way to the kitchen. They had gone to pick up the breads Mandy and Maria baked in their bakery especially for the party. Rafe had introduced everyone and Casey knew her friend would be angry. She just didn't know how angry until she saw Faith.

"I assume you didn't know anything about Cynthia?" Casey asked Faith. When she only shook her head, Casey said, "I'm sure Rafe will explain everything as soon as he can."

"I'm sure he'll try." Faith commented. She wasn't certain she even wanted to hear an explanation she was so upset with him. She arranged the breads to go with the meats and

193

cheeses. She already had relish plates prepared and big bowls of different salads ready to go onto the tables set up on the deck. Baked beans were heating on the stove. Andy had carried the ice to the tubs filled with all kinds of sodas. She put the last slice of bread on the tray as the doorbell rang. Knowing Rafe was in the great room, she let him answer the door. He was supposed to be hosting anyway.

The first guests to arrive were Doc Miller and his wife, Frieda. Hope met them in the great room. It seemed they already knew Cynthia, as they stood talking. She turned back to the kitchen to help Faith start moving things outside. When Doc and his wife walked through, Faith smiled at them. Both of them hugged her and thanked her for the party.

"Rafe just told us about your parents being gone. This was too much for you to do on top of work. We should have postponed it." Frieda was the one to comment.

"Nonsense, Mom had most of the work done already. You know I wasn't about to let my favorite doctor down." She wrapped an arm around both of them as she walked them to the back of the house.

"Favorite doctor indeed, I just heard you agreed to marry that scallywag nephew of mine in mid-October. I couldn't be more thrilled. That will make you my favorite nurse and favorite niece, you know. Just ignore that vulture in there with him. In fact, you need to get him out here with you." Doc Miller told her. She kissed his cheek for making her feel so much better. Undoubtedly, the couple didn't think much of her either.

Other guests began to arrive, some coming through the front door, but most of them walking around the house to the backyard. Cynthia walked through the kitchen not speaking to Faith as she made her way to the deck. The spike heels she wore would not be too practical, but she decided not to say anything. Rafe walked through a couple of minutes later watching Faith as he approached her.

"Sweetheart, I'm so sorry. I never dreamt she would show up here. I don't even know how she knew about the party, or if it was coincidence. I would like to explain about her, but this is not the time or the place. We'll talk about it later." He tried to pull her into his arms.

"You can count on talking about it later. Right now, you need to go visit with your guests." She avoided his hands as she picked up another tray. She heard his sigh before walking outside. As she started to take the tray out, she spotted the Bible verse hanging next to the door.

Trust in the Lord with all your heart and lean not on your own understanding; in all your ways acknowledge Him, and he will make your paths straight. Proverbs three, verses five and six.

Her parents had taught her those verses when she was just beginning to talk, and she had held them close to her heart ever since. She knew God had brought Rafe into her life, and He would not let her down now. She walked out the door with a smile on her face greeting everyone with enthusiasm.

By the time all of the food was outside, Rafe was exhausted just watching Faith. She had worked like a whole catering party and still was smiling. He had offered a silent prayer that she would trust him to make things right. He had fully intended to tell the woman he loved about Cynthia. Everything had happened so quickly, he just hadn't had the chance to do so yet. He hoped he would have the opportunity to talk to her before Cynthia could do more damage.

Faith found Reverend Jenkins and asked him to say grace over the meal. He walked to the deck with her and called for silence in a loud voice. Andy let out a shrill whistle that got everyone's attention. The pastor thanked everyone for attending and asked them to bow their heads for thanks.

Heavenly Father, we thank you for this time of fellowship together. We thank you for the doctor who has meant so much to all of us over the years and for his beautiful wife who has sacrificed so much for our community. We thank you, too for the food we are about to receive and for the hands that prepared it. In Jesus' name. Amen.

Faith asked Doc Miller and his wife to start the line and people gathered behind them, each taking a plate, filling it with food. She noticed Cynthia was close to the head of the line picking through the food as she went. Rafe stood over to the side of the crowd talking to Andy and Greg. She walked over to them wrapping her arm around the man she loved. He looked at her and then kissed her forehead placing his arm around her shoulders. He knew God had answered his prayers, and they would be able to work things out. He fell in love with Faith a little more if that was possible.

Rafe helped Faith bring out the cake she had baked earlier. Little Molly Chambers watched from the crowd. When Faith quickly explained the promise she had made the youngster, Doc called her to the deck. She still had the stitches in her foot, so her father carried her up the steps.

"Molly is going to help this old man blow out all of the candles, one for every year I have practiced. I'm surprised you don't have your fire truck here, Mike."

"I've got them on standby, Doc." Mike called out from the crowd causing laughter across the yard. Faith and Rafe were busily lighting the candles. Molly and her dad stood with Doc and Frieda as they started blowing. Faith and Rafe helped as well. Within seconds, all forty-eight candles were extinguished. A roar went up through the crowd. Doc hugged his wife first and then his nurse. Both women kissed his cheek at the same time, as if rehearsed creating a second cheer. Faith backed into Rafe's arms as he wiped a tear from her cheek. He hugged her to him before she stepped forward once again to start cutting the cake. It took close to thirty minutes to make sure everyone had a piece.

Exhausted but happy with the way the party had gone, Faith looked across the yard. Casey and Hope had helped her put away the leftovers while the crowd lingered. Nobody seemed in a hurry to go home. It was close to ten before the last of the guests had left.

Faith carried a large plastic sack she was using to clean up the plates and cups people had set down instead of using large containers for their trash. Andy and Greg had cleaned up the majority of the mess earlier, but she wanted to make sure there was nothing for the animals to get into or to blow into the neighbor's yards or the lake. When she was satisfied she had everything, she started back into the house. Rafe was just coming out to find her.

"I finally got Uncle Walt and Aunt Frieda to leave. That man can talk. I think he remembers the name of every patient he has ever seen." Rafe moved close to her before pulling her against his body. "Faith, I can't thank you enough for everything you did tonight. It is something everyone will remember for a long time. You were amazing." He laid his forehead against hers.

"I enjoyed doing it, Rafe. I love your uncle, too."

"Are you ready to go to bed?" he asked.

"I don't have much more to do. I finally got Andy and Casey to go home. Hope went upstairs a few minutes ago. You go ahead. I'll make sure everything is locked up and be ready in just a bit. I'll see you in the morning." She kissed his cheek and smiled at him. He wanted much more than the chaste kiss she gave him, but he decided not to push it. He could tell she was exhausted, but she wasn't going to let him finish up. He headed up to his room.

Chapter Eight

Faith made sure everything was secure, and that the last of the food was safely stored in the refrigerator before she walked up the stairs herself. Her parents always made a habit of walking quietly through the guest quarters to make sure all was well there before turning toward their own wing of the house. She made that walk herself. She noticed the light under Cynthia's door and saw the shadow standing on the other side.

Before giving herself time to even think about it, she knocked quietly on the room across from hers and entered as the door knob turned.

"I'm sorry it took me so long to get up here, sweetheart. I hope I didn't keep you waiting long." She put her finger to her lips motioning to the door. Then she moved further into the room. She spoke to him in a whisper.

"I hope you weren't waiting for Cynthia, because she was waiting for you. I saw this in an old movie once, and I didn't even stop to think before I knocked. I will leave if you want me to." She was embarrassed that she was in here with Rafe alone. Her parents would have a fit. And she wasn't sure her new fiancée wanted her in the room.

"I remember seeing that movie, too. I don't remember how they passed the time, waiting for the vulture to decide she didn't get the man. Do you have any ideas?" He stood next to her wanting to take her in his arms.

"Nothing you are going to get to practice." She giggled.

"You can spend the time telling me about that woman and just what your relationship is." She heard the door creak across the hallway.

"Oh, sweetheart, you know how much I love it when you do that. Hmm." Faith giggled again as they heard the door slam.

"You would think she would have seen that movie herself, wouldn't you?" Faith smiled. "Now I think you owe me an explanation."

"I do. Cynthia and I were partners in a practice in San Diego like I told you earlier. Our parents were good friends and thought the two of us should be married. Cynthia was all for the idea. I promise you, sweetheart, I never loved her and never encouraged her. As you can probably tell, when she decides she wants something, she doesn't like taking no for an answer. She very much likes getting her way. She came to Lincks to talk me into returning to San Diego with her. She figured I was tired of playing small town doctor by now."

"What about your parents? Are they disappointed you didn't marry her?"

"My dad died in a car crash five years ago. He was Uncle Walt's only sibling. Mom never really got over the death and passed away almost a year ago. When she died, I had nothing more in San Diego to keep me there. It took a few months to sell my share of the practice and apply for my medical certificate in Missouri. As soon as it was official, I called Uncle Walt and told him I was on my way. I think Cynthia was as disappointed about not getting her hands on my money as my name. She has never loved anything but herself."

"So, you aren't a poor surfer, doc?" She grinned.

He laughed. "I used to love surfing when I was going to college. Later, there was no time for it. But no, I'm not poor, either. Dad owned his own company that was doing quite well. Mom asked me to sell it for her and invest the profits. You, my dear, are engaged to a wealthy man if you care." He ran his hand down her cheek.

"You know I don't care. All I care about is that you love me and that we're happy. What are you going to do to get rid of the piranha?" She chuckled.

"Somehow, I think you have effectively taken care of that little problem. Thing is your reputation is ruined now. I will have to do the decent thing and marry you. I'm not sure I can wait until October." He reached for her.

"We both know nothing is going to happen. We just have to wait a little while to make the story believable. Could we please sit down though? My feet are killing me." She slipped her shoes off and started rubbing her feet.

"Lie down and let me do that." He turned her in the bed and picked up a foot massaging her toes first and working his way down her foot to her ankle and then to her calf. He heard her moan slightly as she relaxed. Before he finished the second foot, she was sound asleep. He didn't have the heart to wake her. He couldn't carry her to her room because she and Hope shared a Jack and Jill bathroom. He was afraid she would hear him carry her in. He decided to lie down beside her and was asleep almost as quickly as she was. He woke to find Faith cuddled snuggly in his arms. He watched her just a moment before kissing her cheek. Her eyes fluttered awake grinning as she looked at the man beside her.

"Good morning." She said dreamily. Then it dawned on her where she was. Her eyes flew to the window. "Oh, Rafe, it's morning. How did this happen? I mean I know how it happened. Nothing happened. No, nothing happened. We are both fully dressed. I have to leave. What time is it? Oh, no. It's seven-thirty. Hope will be up already. What am I going to tell her?" Finally Rafe laid his finger across her lips.

"Sweetheart, it's okay. I will explain to Hope how you saved me from a fate worse than death. She will understand. Now, I think you had better leave before she comes looking for us. I'm going to take a shower and start breakfast. I'll see you in a few minutes."

They both walked to the door. "I love you, Faith. I'll see you in a few minutes, sweetheart." He kissed her quickly. She giggled as she started to leave. Rafe pulled her back to him. "That was not for her benefit. I meant it. I love you." he whispered it in her ear, kissing it before releasing her.

She made it to her room. Hope was still asleep, so she quickly slipped her clothes off and took her shower. She was drying her hair when she heard the knock on the door. Faith opened it smiling at her sister. She let Hope have the bathroom while she went to get dressed.

As she entered the kitchen, she found Rafe whistling while he fried bacon and mixed pancake batter. She walked up behind him slipping her arms around his waist.

"Do you always let women hug you like this?" she teased him.

"Only when the woman is my beautiful fiancée and I saw her reflection in the toaster." He sat the bowl down and turned to take her in his arms. Just as he started to kiss her, Cynthia walked into the room.

"Well, aren't you just the domestic one. I need a cup of coffee." She pulled out a stool from the island and sat down looking at the couple.

Rafe kissed the woman in his arms briefly before turning back toward the cabinets. "I'll be happy to pour you a cup of coffee to go, Cynthia. I know you won't want something as heavy as pancakes and bacon for breakfast. As soon as we finish eating, we'll be going to church. You are welcome to join us, but I doubt that you are interested in that either." He sat a to-go cup in front of her.

She glared at them, before stomping into the hallway to pick up her bags. She walked out the door leaving it standing wide open. Hope closed it as she came down the stairs.

"It seems our guest is leaving in a bit of a hurry." She commented before they all broke into laughter. "Faith, could I speak to Rafe privately just a minute?"

"No, Hope. You can speak to both of us. I will be happy to explain about last night. It was my idea and Rafe had nothing to do with it."

"He had nothing to do with the fact that you never came to bed last night?" Hope scowled at her sister. "Were you not with him?"

"Well, yes, but it is not what you think. Remember that old movie where the heroine saves the man from the woman after him by going to his bedroom late at night? Well, that is what I did. Only thing is I fell asleep, rather we both fell asleep and didn't wake up until this morning. I thought you were asleep when I came in." Faith explained.

"So you two slept together to save Rafe from Cynthia?" Hope had her fist on her hip by now. She was none too happy.

"We didn't sleep together. Well, technically, I guess we did, but we were both fully dressed and nothing happened except when he kissed my cheek to wake me up. Hope, you know me. Besides I am a woman grown, and this is really none of your business." Faith was beginning to get mad herself. She shouldn't have to explain to her sister.

"Hope, Faith is right. This is between the two of us and God. He knows it was perfectly innocent. But I will be more than happy to marry your sister tomorrow or even today if we can arrange it. I love her and nothing is going to soil her reputation." Rafe looked at the woman across from them.

"I'm sorry, both of you. You're right, it's not my business and for what it's worth, I believe you. You really did pull that off with the old battle-axe? I love that scene and I can't even remember what movie it's from. It served her right. I don't know how a person can be so hateful and call themselves a doctor."

"She's a very good doctor, but certainly not known for her bedside manner. She told me yesterday her new partner was already trying to sell his share of the practice."

Faith turned the bacon now quite crispy while her sister poured each of them a cup of coffee. Rafe started cooking the pancakes. Just as they finished dishing up the food, the doorbell rang and Greg walked in.

"The door was unlocked and I smelled bacon. I hope there is enough for another person. I figured I would be safe since your guest left in such a huff." He grinned at the others. They set a place for him and Rafe gave thanks blessing the meal and his friends.

Chapter Nine

After church, Rafe asked Faith to pack them a lunch and change into her swimsuit. He found a blanket in the back of his jeep and shook it out to make sure it wasn't too dirty. He thought about inviting Hope and Greg to join them, but decided he and his new fiancée had plenty that they needed to talk about.

He changed his church clothes for a pair of swim trunks and a t-shirt, and went in search of Faith. She had changed her clothes as well, and was finishing packing their lunch in a basket. She had a cooler ready to fill. Rafe added the drinks he and Faith preferred before picking up both containers.

They headed out of the house after telling Hope they would be back in time to help with dinner. "Where are we going?" Faith asked as Rafe held the door to his jeep for her.

"It's a surprise. You will just have to wait and see." He headed the vehicle away from town when he pulled onto the highway. He didn't go too far when he turned down another road that circled the lake. Driving about two miles he turned down a road that looked like no more than a path cut between trees. "Hang on. I hear this is pretty rough." He grinned big like a kid with a new toy.

She braced herself as the driver took off over the ruts. They bounced and slid over the uneven terrain finally coming to stop at an open area with the lake in front of them. Rafe grabbed the basket and cooler while Faith took the blanket laying with the things. She loved the idea of a picnic. They walked to the edge of the clearing. There was a sandy beach perfect for swimming. She quickly pulled off her shorts and top to reveal her suit underneath. The red swimsuit was one piece, but fit her like a glove. The color complimented her skin to perfection, and it was all Rafe could do to stop from staring at her. She was more beautiful than any woman he had seen on the beaches in California, and she loved him. He thought himself to be the luckiest person in the world at that moment. He removed his shirt running to join her in the water.

As a nurse, Faith had seen plenty of men's bodies, but Rafe's took her breath away. He had a flat abdomen and beautiful muscles with broad shoulders. She didn't know how he stayed in such great shape being at the office all day. *He must exercise when he goes to his room.* All she wanted to do was look at him. She wanted to run her hand across his chest but her emotions had her hesitating. She had never been drawn to a man like she was this one.

Rafe made the decision for her. He grabbed her around the waist and held her above the water. She laid her hands on his shoulders to keep from falling. Then he slowly lowered her into the water in front of him. She locked her hands behind his neck, as she slid down his body until their lips touched. Rafe pulled her as close to himself as possible as he deepened the kiss. He had wanted her touch all morning. He barely gave her time to take a breath before he kissed her again. Finally he had to pull her away. He was losing control. Maybe this hadn't been such a good idea after all. As they stood staring into each other's eyes, a ski boat cut its engine and started floating toward them. It was Hope and Greg.

"Is this a private party or can anyone join you?" Greg was the one to call to them. Hope stood in the boat watching the two of them. She saw the passion on their faces and was thankful they had come when they did. Greg steered the boat onto the shore before he jumped out and helped Hope over the side into his arms. He would have kissed her, but he didn't think she would welcome it with the cold stare she was giving Rafe. He tied the boat to a tree to keep it from drifting and reached over the side for the basket of food Hope had packed for them. He also found a blanket for them to sit on.

Faith asked Rafe if he was ready to eat. "Yeah, I think we had better. Are you two going to eat now or swim first?"

"I think I need to swim a little first." Hope turned away from the two and swam out into the lake. She wanted to talk to Rafe, but knew Faith would never stand for it. All she could do is hope her sister knew what she was doing.

Would you have been any better if you and Greg had been here by yourselves? The thought came from nowhere and it surprised her. She wanted Greg and knew he felt the same way Rafe and Faith did. She couldn't judge them. She just hoped they knew what they were doing and stayed out of temptation's way like she and Greg needed to do.

She swam back to shore, where Greg was floating in the water. "Better?" He asked knowing what she had been thinking. She grinned, nodding her head.

They walked onto the shore. "Y'all were here first; if you want to be alone we understand." Hope spoke to both of them.

Rafe took the blanket from her hands and spread it next to theirs. "I think there is plenty of room for all of us." He grinned, knowing Hope had calmed down. He really couldn't blame her. He was close to losing control, and he knew he could have taken Faith with him. He would have to make sure they were not in such a compromising position again.

After an awkward moment, the four of them had an enjoyable lunch. They swam and played Frisbee until Rafe's phone rang. It was the answering service. Mr. Burgess was in the hospital. Faith started gathering the food as soon as he mouthed the problem still listening to the caller. She pulled her clothes over her damp swimsuit and started carrying the things to the jeep.

"How bad?" She asked as he hung up.

"He's unconscious. His breathing is labored. They're doing a heart test now to see if it was another stroke." He knew the situation was grave.

"Rafe, can you drive a boat?" When he told Greg he used to own an inboard, Greg walked over to the tree to begin untying it. "You two take this. Hope and I will bring the jeep back. Just leave the boat at the dock, and I'll get it later."

"Thanks, Greg. I'll leave the keys on the kitchen island." They ran to the boat and he helped Faith in before he climbed aboard himself. Within minutes, they were at the Inn's dock. They raced up the hill and into the house to quickly change into dry clothes. Two minutes later, Rafe was squeezed into Faith's little sedan racing to the hospital.

The nurse on duty had just brought the patient back to ER when they arrived. Cindy Guthrie was the doctor on duty and was familiar with his case. "It's not good guys. It looks like he's in a coma. He's not responding to stimuli." Faith went to his side hoping he might respond to her voice.

"Mr. Arthur, it's Faith. I need you squeeze my fingers so I know you're hearing me. Mr. Burgess, can you squeeze my hand? I saw Ms. Agnes sitting out there waiting for you to wake up and look at her." She watched his face for a sign of recognition even the slightest movement of his hand, but she felt nothing, saw nothing. A tear slipped from her eyes as she rubbed his arm with her other hand.

Rafe wrapped his arm around her waist, wishing he could do more to comfort her and help his patient. Mr. Burgess was in God's hands now. There was nothing more they could do, but wait.

"Faith, I want you to go be with Ms. Agnes and George. Let them know he's not hurting." She nodded not taking her eyes off of her patient. Finally, Rafe moved her away from the room. She looked up at him with tears glistening in her eyes. He hugged her close before letting her walk to the waiting room. He turned back to his patient to check his vital signs and see if there was anything to be done to help the man.

"It's alright, Faith. He has lived a long time and we have had a wonderful marriage. George and I told him goodbye before the ambulance came for him. We knew he was slipping from us. God will take care of him." Ms. Agnes hugged the woman as Faith stood there with tears streaming down her face. She was the one that was supposed to be strong for her patients, but she couldn't do that now.

"I've never known a man that loved his family more. Every time either of you walked into the room, his eyes would light up." Faith grabbed a tissue from the stand and wiped her face. She had to be stronger than this. "Please, let's sit down. Can I get either of you anything?" She needed to keep busy. George sat by his mother gently patting her hand. Faith smiled at him, and he grinned back. She knew their son had some mild mental problems, but he was such a good man and people couldn't help but love him. He had taken good care of his parents.

Faith looked up to see Rafe walking toward them, his face solemn. "I'm so sorry, Ms. Agnes. We did all we could." He wrapped the woman in his arms as she stood to hug him. He just let her cry. George took Faith's hand, and she moved to sit beside him while Rafe held his mother. She prayed for the family as she sat there. She knew God was already bringing comfort to them all.

Rafe asked Ms. Agnes if she and her son would like to spend some time with Mr. Burgess.

"No, Rafe. We told Author goodbye at home. His body

is all that's in that room now. We'll see him in heaven soon enough." Ms. Agnes laid her hand on Rafe's arm and reached up to put a quick kiss on his cheek. "Thank you for taking care of him."

George moved to his mother's side. "Are you ready to go home, Mom?" George patted her arm. She smiled sadly at him and nodded her head.

"Did you drive to the hospital, George?" Faith asked. She knew he drove to and from work stopping by the grocery store, but that was just about all he ever did.

"Mom said I could. I can get us home safe." He smiled at the nurse.

"I know you can. Ms. Agnes, will you call me if you need anything before tomorrow? I'll be over in the morning to help you make arrangements." She knew the woman would want George to go to work. Mondays were busy at the church.

"Thank you, dear." She hugged Faith for several seconds. "Arthur appreciated all you did for him, as much as I did. I love you, Faith." She and George walked out of the emergency room doors.

"Are you alright, sweetheart?" Rafe wrapped his arms around her from behind as she stood watching them leave.

"I want the kind of marriage they had, Rafe. I want to grow old with you, loving you as many years as God will give us." He pulled her closer to him, as he told her he wanted that as well.

Chapter Ten

Angie Murdock from the hospital was usually the one Faith called when she couldn't make it to work. Monday was no exception. She had contacted the woman before they left the hospital. Faith planned to spend the morning helping Ms. Agnes deal with her husband's death and the details of the funeral.

Faith made sure the clinic was ready and opened the door herself. After helping Angie get the first few patients settled, she told Rafe she was going to Ms. Agnes'.

"You call me if you need anything. We can close the clinic for a couple of hours." He kissed her briefly before she left.

It took about an hour for Ms. Agnes to decide on the arrangements she wanted. They didn't have as many friends as they used to because many of them had already passed away. She decided to have graveside services only. With Reverend Jenkins and Faith by her side, she chose the things necessary to complete the details. Then the three of them sat down to visit about Mr. Arthur and his life. Ms. Agnes told them that her sister and brother-in-law should be arriving soon.

"She's my baby sister. It's just the two of us, now. We used to have six more brothers and sisters all together. She'll stay for a few days, I expect." When the doorbell rang, Faith went to answer it and introduced herself. Not long afterward both Reverend Jenkins and Faith told the women they were going to leave and let them visit.

"You call me if you need anything, okay?" The young woman instructed her friend.

"I will, dear. Now go give that handsome young doctor a kiss from me. We will be just fine." She hugged Faith before she left.

By the time she arrived at the clinic, the last patient for the morning had already been seen. She walked in the back door to find Rafe and Margie digging through the files looking for something.

"I don't know how it could be missing. We had the file Friday." Margie sounded almost frantic.

"Well it's not here now, is it? Someone needs to find it." Rafe was almost yelling.

"What are you looking for?" Faith stood at the door watching the pair.

"Thank goodness, you're here." Margie exclaimed. "We can't find the Archer file."

"Did you look under T? Remember she got married last month. Her name is Annie Turner, now." Faith pulled the file and handed it to Rafe who was staring at Margie. He turned without saying anything to either of them and went to his office.

"I forgot she got married, Faith. Undoubtedly she did too, because she signed in as Annie Archer." Margie was visibly upset.

"It's okay, a simple mistake. Where's Angie?"

"Dr. Miller sent her home an hour ago. She had been throwing up for thirty minutes." Margie told her.

"Why didn't one of you call me? I could have come back. I feel awful." Faith went in search of Rafe.

"Rafe, why didn't you call me when Angie got sick?" She walked into his office closing the door behind her.

"You were busy. Next time you have to be gone, we'll just

close the office." He walked around his desk and reached for her.

"You silly man, you can't close the office every time I have to be gone."

"I don't see why not. What would you do if I were sick?"

"We would have to close then. But, I'm not indispensable like you are. Angie did just fine, didn't she?" Faith grinned at him.

"She was not you. Next time we close the office. Now, how was Ms. Agnes this morning? Did you get all of the arrangements made?" He started to nuzzle her neck.

"She is really doing well considering, and yes, all of the arrangements have been made. The funeral will be graveside at ten o'clock on Wednesday. Her sister came while I was there. You have to stop that." She was trying hard to evade him, but it didn't seem to be working.

"I have decided kissing you is better than practicing medicine." He grinned as he tried once more to get to her neck.

"Doctor, we have a practice to run here. Are you ready for your next patient?" Faith pushed him away, and stood as tall as she could; trying to look quite prim.

"Spoil sport. Did you eat any lunch yet?"

"We have a pretty light schedule this afternoon. I will grab something to snack on later. Let's see the first patient." She walked out of the room after taking his hand to move him with her.

"Margie, will you please print a notice that the office will be closed Wednesday morning? Post it on the doors, and by the sign-in tablet, please." Faith knew Rafe would want to go to the funeral with her. She unlocked the front door and held it for the pregnant woman.

"Mrs. Crosby, is it already time for your next appointment? You're having trouble, aren't you?" Faith hurried to walk her through the door straight into an exam room. The woman looked pale and was breathing heavy. Faith got her settled in the room and stepped into the hall to call the doctor.

Rafe quickly examined the woman asking questions as he checked her. He turned to Faith, telling her to call an ambulance. "Mrs. Crosby, your body is trying to go into labor. It's too early. Let's get you to the hospital. Hopefully, we can stop the contractions and give this little one some more time to develop."

Faith had already told Margie what to do and was back into the room to assist the mother-to-be with whatever she needed. Within a minute, Mike and Drew walked into the office, stopping to knock on the exam door.

The doctor and nurse helped the woman into the hallway and onto the gurney. Mike strapped her down and they started out the door followed quickly by Rafe. Faith walked beside him to see what he wanted to do about the afternoon patients. Doc and his wife had gone out of town to try out their new motorhome.

"Let's reschedule those who can wait, and you help everyone you can. I'll be back as quickly as I know she's out of danger."

While Margie called patients later in the day to reschedule their appointments, Faith talked to each of the ones due in within the next hour. She was able to help three of them, and rearranged the schedule for Rafe to see them tomorrow.

Rafe walked through the door just as Margie hung up from the last phone call.

"How are Mrs. Crosby and the baby?" Margie asked the question before Faith could turn around to ask it herself.

"We stopped the contractions this time, but she will be on complete bed rest the remainder of her pregnancy. I talked to Cindy about the procedures in place for preemies. She said they have to be flown to St. Louis. That is totally unacceptable. Some changes will have to be made."

Faith tried to calm him down. "We've been fortunate so far. I only know of one baby born premature and she was close enough to term the doctors were able to treat her here with some pretty innovative methods. She is a healthy two-year-old little girl now."

"I have some phone calls to make. I can't accept this situation." The doctor headed toward his office while the two women looked at each other.

It was almost six o'clock before Faith saw Rafe again. She had already sent Margie home and called Hope to prepare dinner for the three families staying at the lodge. Since she had ridden into town with Rafe, she finished as much in the office as she could while she waited for him.

When he walked out of the office, he acted surprised to see her still working. "Why haven't you gone home, Faith?" He walked into the reception area where she was occupied with the accounts.

"We rode together today, remember? Besides I wanted to make sure you were okay. You seemed frustrated when you came back. Debra Crosby will be alright, won't she?"

"I feel sure she will, thanks to God and a lot of prayers. What scares me is the fact that the hospital is not equipped to handle a preemie with complications. Waiting for a life flight is not an acceptable option. I will do everything within my power to have a physician in place with the equipment he or she will need within six months. I have been on the phone talking to two doctors this afternoon. Hopefully, one of them will be willing to open a practice here."

Three days later, Rafe sat at the dining room table and announced a new pediatric wing would be added to the hospital and a new physician would be in town within two months. His office would be opened in the physician's building adjacent to the doctor's offices there now.

"Blake Turner had been looking for a place to locate. He will be bringing some of the equipment necessary with him and the rest will be supplied to the hospital through donations. Very little equipment will need to be purchased at this point." Rafe was beside himself with happiness. "No more babies will be without medical care. Since he will be seeing children, too, they will have a place to go more fitting than our clinic. What do you think, have I forgotten anything?" The family grinned at his enthusiasm. To accomplish everything he planned in that length of time seemed impossible, but Faith knew enough to realize when Rafe decided to do something, he would make it work.

"Adam Reynolds was just finishing the strip mall in town, so he'll start on the hospital wing tomorrow. The office building is already in place and just needs to be renovated. Andy, I was hoping your group could handle that project. There is not really a lot that needs to be changed. What do you say, would you consider this a project worth tackling?"

Andy was a little awestruck. They were just about finished with the renovations on Rafe's house next to his, so they would be looking at another job soon, anyway. "Let me talk to the others and see what they think. Having a pediatrician in town is certainly a great idea. I'll talk to them today and get back with you."

As the couples talked about the plans for the new additions to the medical community, the door opened and Nora and Chuck walked through. All three girls rushed to hug them, while Andy got up to shake hands with his dad. Everyone was glad to see them. Nana was doing much better. She had a caregiver coming in twice a day to help with physical therapy and to make sure she was eating properly. The couple was more than ready to get home to their own family.

After eating some of the leftovers from the evening meal, they all sat down to catch up on the events they had missed. Nora's first question had been how the retirement party had gone. They talked over an hour about the party itself, Rafe's unexpected guest and how Faith convinced her she was not really needed. They told them about the newest engagement. The ring Rafe had given her had been passed down from his great-grandmother. She fell in love with it instantly as did Nora and the others. Nora and Chuck had expected the declaration, but maybe not quite as soon as it happened. They were thrilled with the announcement and welcomed Rafe into the family with open arms as they had the others.

"Does this mean there will be a triple wedding in October?" Nora asked the question as the three women nodded. "I had better get busy then. Girls, we have to go dress shopping and quickly. I think we should talk to Reverend Jenkins about using the church for the ceremony and then having the reception out here. What do you think?"

Andy spoke up for the first time. "Mom, we have talked about this quite a bit. We think the reception should be at the church as well. You will have your hands full trying to get three brides ready. We're taking care of the reception. Rafe has already been in contact with friends in San Diego. They are insisting they will handle all of the preparation and the catering. We want you to concentrate on the wedding parties themselves. You can supervise the flowers and the set-ups and things if you want, but that's all you need to do. Will you be okay with that?"

Nora gazed at the family around her. "I will be fine with that. I just want my children to be happily married and to give us grandchildren in the not too distant future." She grinned as each of them blushed slightly making comments under their breath.

"How many people are we expecting to invite?" Faith asked the question. "Many of the people will be on at least two if not all three of our lists. Maybe we should be working on that. After all, we have less than two months before the wedding. When do invitations need to be mailed?" Nora grabbed a tablet for each of the ladies to start writing people to be invited.

Chapter Eleven

The women decided to make a trip to St. Louis on Saturday. They had six weeks to find dresses they would each like to wear. They had already decided they would not have attendants stand with them. They wanted all three couples at the altar at the same time repeating their vows together.

They got up early Saturday morning leaving the men in charge of the bed and breakfast. Casey had done a lot of research online and told them about the dress shops she had found in the St. Louis area. They decided to take her SUV since she knew best where they wanted to go. The first shop had only one dress Hope liked, but nothing for the other two.

At the second shop, the girls started by looking in their particular size. Casey wore one size larger than Hope's size and Faith headed to the petites. The clerks stood back waiting with Nora to see what the girls would choose. Within minutes, each of them brought the dress they wanted to try on. When they looked at each other, they first gasped and then started laughing. Each of them had chosen exactly the same dress.

The clerks provided them with the necessary undergarments needed for the dresses while Nora took a seat waiting for them to come to the pedestal in front of the three way mirrors.

Casey had her dress on first. The dresses had lace cap

sleeves with a sweetheart neckline. It was fitted through the bodice and down to the hips where it flared slightly flowing onto the floor all around the dress. The fabric below the lace bust line was covered in a pearl design. The back laced together like a corset. The dress was both flattering and sensual. Casey's dress fit her as if it had been designed to mold her perfect curves.

Hope's dress also fit her like a glove. Faith's dress was a bit too long for her petite height, and the body of the garment fit her a little looser than it should. The three women looked at each other. "Do we want to look for similar styles to compliment these dresses or do we want to all dress alike? Hope raised the question. Nora stepped up toward the platform with tears in her eyes.

"These dresses fit you to perfection as if each one was designed for your body. Unless the idea of dressing alike bothers you, each of you look magnificent. I personally think it will beautiful for the three of you to dress the same. I am sure you will prefer a different color and style of flower for your bouquets. That will be what will make your wedding unique. The men can wear vests to match the colors of your bouquets. But you girls need to be the ones to decide if you want another dress or not."

"I love this dress." The girls spoke at the same time. They grinned at each other.

"We are fine with wearing the same dress for the wedding, then?" Casey asked the question looking at the other two. They both nodded, and it was settled. The three clerks checked each dress for any alterations that might be needed. Faith's dress would need hemmed a couple of inches to match the other two. It also needed taken up in the waist an inch or so. Casey and Hope both were satisfied with the fit of theirs. They talked about veils, but all three had decided they would rather not wear one.

While they were at the shop they looked for the perfect dress for Nora. She preferred a suit to a dress and after several attempts, they located an ensemble that excited all of them. Casey took a picture of Nora in the outfit to send to her mother so she would have some idea of what she wanted to wear. She wished she could have been with them today as she shopped. She felt as close to Nora as her own mother, but she knew Marge Newton would have enjoyed being a part of the group as well. No matter, they would have time to talk before the wedding. Her parents planned to arrive a few days early.

On the way back to Lincks, the women talked about the flowers and the type of cakes they preferred. Each of them definitely wanted different arrangements for the bouquets.

"I have always wanted bright pink roses as the main flower in my bouquet." Casey could almost picture the flowers in her mind.

Hope spoke up next. "Purple hydrangeas have always been my favorite flower. That is what I would love to use."

"You know my favorite flowers are gerber daisies. I think I would like to use pinks and lavenders to complement each of your bouquets. We could also add carnations in those two colors to tie the three arrangements together." Faith didn't know if it would matter if they coordinated or not, but she was always one who liked symmetry in everything. The others thought that sounded like a great idea.

Nora asked them if they had thought about how they would stand at the altar. After tossing ideas back and forth, it was decided Casey and Andrew would stand at the right facing the altar, Hope and Greg to the left and Faith and Rafe in the middle. The men were quite similar in height, but Faith was shorter than Casey and Hope. Again, they decided to keep the appearance balanced as much as possible.

They were back in Lincks before the discussion of the

cakes was brought up. Nora was determined she would take care of those herself. She appreciated Rafe handling the catering, but she wanted to do this much for each of her girls and her son. She would sketch out a couple of ideas she had in her head, and let the ladies decide which one they liked best.

Chapter Twelve

With wedding preparations well underway, the Labor Day festivities were upon them all too soon. Hope and Casey were preparing their classrooms for the new three and four year-olds they would soon have in class. They had their rooms decorated and set up for school to begin in two days. Tomorrow was Labor Day and they poured all of their energy into helping where they were needed.

After church, all three of the ladies headed back to the house to help Nora with baking. She had volunteered to make the cakes and brownies for the annual event held each year on the town square. Vendors came from around the area to set up carnival rides for the midway. Craft booths dotted the square and most importantly, the town provided a meal for anyone wanting to partake in the festivities.

Nora had already baked a dozen cakes, half chocolate and half vanilla. Today they would be baking brownies. She wanted another dozen recipes of those, ready for the crowd. Mandy and Maria had also promised lemon bars and cookies to round out the desserts.

Andy was on duty until three that afternoon. He hated missing church on Sundays, but thankfully his shift didn't fall on that day, too often. Garrett tried to be sure it only happened once every four to six weeks at the most. He liked his men to spend time with God as much as with their families.

When he and the other deputies had cordoned off the square for tomorrow, Andy got in his patrol car and started driving the streets around town before he planned to head out of town to patrol further. His jurisdiction was the town and western areas today. Each deputy was assigned a section of the county to cover.

Bethany, police dispatcher, called him over the radio to report two men fighting on the corner of the street. He was only two blocks away. He called dispatch to let her know what he saw and stepped out of the vehicle.

"Sheriff's Department. Both of you on your knees and lock your hands behind your head." He had his hand on his gun, but had not pulled it yet, expecting the two men to obey his order. As he walked up closer to the scuffle, he realized something was off. The men were rolling back and forth rather than throwing punches at each other. Before he had an opportunity to pull his revolver, he felt the shot hit in his side. A second bullet hit his thigh as he drew his weapon. Although he had dropped to the ground, he was able to fire two rounds hitting each of the men. "Shots fired. Officer down." He called over his radio before he lost unconsciousness.

Cindy Guthrie was in with the family. The waiting room was full of family members and other police officers. "He's lost a lot of blood. The one bullet cracked two ribs. But neither of them punctured his lung. He was lucky. Rafe has taken him into surgery now. He should be able to remove the bullets easy enough. All of you have a seat, and we'll let you know as soon as we know something."

Rafe didn't do surgeries any longer, but since he had been a surgeon in San Diego, he wasn't going to wait until a doctor could get there from St. Louis. He wasn't even licensed for surgery in Missouri, but he would worry about that later. Andy was family and they took care of their own.

Faith refused to wait outside of the operating room. She had scrubbed and was assisting him with the surgery. Both of them tried to not think about who lay on the table, but concentrated on doing what was needed to keep the patient alive. Andy had been luckier than the two men he shot.

As much as Garrett and Owen wanted to be at the hospital awaiting word about the deputy's condition, they decided to handle the crime scene themselves. They checked with neighbors to see if anyone heard or saw anything. A couple said they saw the two men in what looked like a fight, and heard the officer tell them to stop, repeating what Andy had said to the men. They saw where the deputy had dropped to the ground and took photos of the positions. Garrett looked at Owen. "How did he manage to stop them with two bullets in him already?" The two victims were still in the same position they died in, one laying across the other one. Each of them had a gun in their hand, indicating they had both fired a shot. Both men had been shot in the head, killing them instantly.

The men continued to process the crime scene. Garrett located a car with out of state tags about two hundred feet from the corner where the men were killed. They dusted the car for fingerprints and had Lester tow it to his impound lot. After they had finished, Garrett told the medical examiner he could remove the bodies. It had taken more than two hours to process the area, and they still had not heard anything about Andy. Both men headed toward the hospital.

The sheriff and deputy reached the waiting room just as Rafe walked toward the family. "He's going to be just fine. I had some trouble locating the bullet in his thigh. It ricocheted off of the bone. He has the two broken ribs, but I'm sure Cindy told you no major organs were hit. He'll just be mighty sore for two or three weeks. Faith is with him now. As soon as he regains consciousness, you'll be able to see him."

"I know all of you want to be there with him, but I can't let anyone in there until I have had a chance to interview him. Faith can stay with him until he is awake. Rafe, he's part of an official investigation. I'm sorry, folks." Garrett felt bad especially for his parents and Casey, but he didn't want anyone telling him what had happened until they could talk.

—⁂—

Andy blinked a couple of times, trying to figure out where he was. He tried to talk, but his throat was so scratchy no words would form. He closed his eyes trying to remember what had happened.

"Do you want some water, Andy?" It was Faith's voice he heard. He nodded slightly, trying to make his eyes stay open. She held a straw to his lips and he sipped. All too soon, she pulled it away from him. "You can't have too much at a time. We don't want you vomiting."

Andy looked around the room. He was in a hospital room, but why? His mind seemed to be in a fog. He closed his eyes, hoping to drift back to sleep.

"You need to wake up, Andy. A lot of people are concerned about you. I need you to wake up and talk to me." The voice paused for just a moment before speaking again. "Andy? Can you hear me? It's time to wake up now. Are you ready for another sip of water?" He wanted to tell Faith to leave him alone. It had been a long time, since she had pestered him this much. She kept speaking to him and rubbing his hand or cheek or shoulder. He finally came to enough to focus on her.

"I guess you're going to just keep bugging me until I wake up, huh?" He grinned slightly at his sister.

"I guess I am. How's your pain?" He thought about her question. He hadn't really noticed any pain, until he tried to move.

"No. Lie still. We don't want you moving around too soon. Andy, do you remember what happened to you?"

He tried to focus on her question and things started coming back to him. He remembered why he was here. "I

225

need to talk to Garrett."

"I'm here, Andy. Do you feel up to talking?" Garrett stepped across the room to the bed.

"We need to get my statement taken care of, sheriff." Andy wiped his hand across his eyes as if to wipe his mind clear. "Faith, I need for you to go let the family know I am doing just fine and send Owen in, please."

"Andy, don't...."

"It's okay, Sis. I need to talk to Garrett. Then I want to see Casey and the others. Tell them I love them and will see them in a few minutes." He watched as she stepped out of the door. "Do you want to wait for Owen?"

"He'll be here in just a minute. Why don't you tell me what you had been doing since you came on duty this morning?"

"You must be really bored." Andy grinned just before he grimaced as he tried to get more comfortable. "Tom and I got all of the barriers set up to block off Main Street. I heard him call into Bethany that we were finished and would be starting our patrol. He headed out the highway, as I climbed into my patrol car." Owen walked into the room as he was talking.

"Go ahead Andy. What did you do after you got in the vehicle?" Garrett asked.

"I headed toward Jefferson Street just driving the neighborhoods to make sure everything was quiet. Bethany called me over the radio to report two men fighting on the corner of Jefferson and Eighth Street. When I got there, I confirmed the fight with her and stepped out of the car identifying myself as a deputy sheriff. I told them to get on their knees and lock their hands behind their heads. I had my hand on my revolver, but hadn't pulled it yet. Then I noticed neither of them was trying to punch the other one, they were just rolling back and forth against each other. Next thing I knew, I felt a bullet slam into my side. I pulled my gun as the second bullet hit my thigh. I fired two rounds. By that time, I was on my knees. I called it in and passed out before I could do anything more. What happened to the two men? Are they going to be okay?"

"Andy, did you see anyone else around them? You didn't see them pull their guns?"

"That was what was so strange. It took me just a second to realize I couldn't see their hands at all. I saw one throw a punch at the other one as I drove up, but they tucked their arms between their bodies. They rolled slightly apart, as I saw the weapons aimed at me. It was so fast I didn't have time to do anything before the first shot. The second one was a second or two later than the first one. No more. I don't know if it was one man or both that shot me, it happened so quickly. What are you not telling me Garrett? Am I in trouble here? I thought it was just a fight between two neighbors until they fired on me."

"You didn't do anything wrong, Andy. You shot in self-defense. You know the district attorney will have to investigate and the state may want to question you as well. But that is nothing unusual."

"There's something you are not telling me, Garett."

"Andy, both of the men you shot are dead. You shot both of them right between the eyes."

As the news absorbed into his brain, Andy paled and closed his eyes. He knew he had killed men overseas; had seen them die through his telescope, but he had never taken the life of an American citizen. He felt like he could throw up, but didn't want to disgrace himself in front of his superior and fellow deputy. He practiced the breathing techniques he had learned in the service until the feeling finally passed.

"Do you know anything about them yet? Please tell me they weren't locals." Andy didn't know how he would feel killing someone from the town. It was bad enough knowing two men were dead because of him.

"Their IDs showed they were from St. Louis, but the car we found down the street had California tags on it. It's really early in the investigation, buddy. From what I can tell now, I know the kill was a righteous shoot. Both men still had their guns in their hands. Witnesses said they heard you call out to the men. They used the same wording you used. Right now your job will be to get better and get out of here. Let the rest of us examine the evidence and see what we can come up with. You ready to see that beautiful fiancée of yours?" Garrett patted his officer on the shoulder. "I'll be in tomorrow morning to see how you're doing. You do what they tell you and get some rest." The two men walked out of the room. Faith and Rafe stood outside the room.

"He's all yours, Doc." Garrett shook his hand as he spoke to the doctor. Then he gave Faith a quick hug. "Take good care of my deputy there. I'll send the rest of the family in."

Garrett walked to the waiting room where the relatives waited. "Folks, you can go see him now. He is not going to want to talk about what happened. Don't push him for details. He'll let you know when he's ready to tell you more. Just know he's going to be fine."

"Thanks, Garrett." Chuck shook his hand as the ladies headed toward his room.

"He'll be okay, Chuck. It will just take some time to recover mentally. He's one of the best officers I have ever had the privilege of working with and a really good man." The sheriff patted him on the back as he and Owen started out of the hospital.

"Something is not adding up here. Those weren't just two men fighting. I have a feeling they knew Andy's routine and staged this whole thing. It's almost too bad he is such a good shot. I sure wish I could have talked to those two men," Garrett told Owen as they waited for the elevator. "I know one thing. After today, kevlar vests will be mandatory. It wouldn't have saved his thigh but that second bullet wouldn't have done that much damage."

Owen nodded. "I worry that Andy is going to be hurting as much mentally as physically. Shooting someone even in the line of duty has to be hard to deal with."

"I agree. It's something you never get over fully."

Chapter Thirteen

Casey stirred when the nurse came in early the next morning to check Andy's vital signs and to draw some blood.

"You had to give me blood because I lost so much and now you are drawing it out again. You would think someone could make up their minds." Andy grumbled.

"If we didn't do crazy things like this, we would be bored out of our minds." Angie, Faith's good friend, patted his shoulder and smiled before she walked out of the room.

"How are you feeling this morning, sweetheart?" Casey had moved to his bedside as the nurse left the room.

"I would feel a whole lot better, if I could wrap my arms around you and kiss you." He grinned at her.

"I think we can accommodate the kissing part at least." She leaned over the bed and placed her lips on his. Just as he started to return the kiss, the door opened and Rafe and Faith walked in.

"Oh dear, it looks like we might be interrupting something." Faith giggled turning to the man beside her. "What is it they say about paybacks?" All four of them laughed as Rafe walked over to check on his patient. Casey and Faith walked down to get a cup of coffee while the doctor examined his wounds.

"How is the pain today, Andy?"

"It doesn't hurt much if I lie still. When I try to get more comfortable, I feel like I have been shot." He grinned.

"I want you to stay on the pain meds for the next two or

three days, at least. This evening we'll get you up and into a chair for a few minutes. By tomorrow, I want you up walking hopefully. Everything else doing okay? Did you sleep alright? No nightmares?"

"Who has time for nightmares with a nurse in here every two hours? Seriously, Rafe, I'm fine. I'm sure you know what happened. I just want to know why. I wonder if it might be related to some undercover work I did a few months ago. If it is, Casey and the family could be in trouble as well."

"Faith told me about the drug ring you broke up. She said you weren't able to arrest all of the major players though. Surely they wouldn't come after you no higher up the chain than you got?"

"Two of the guys talked when the DEA stepped in. They might be still investigating for all I know. There were more arrests involved than we first thought. Garrett will get to the bottom of it all. I just worry about those I love being hurt."

"I could hire some protection until we know more if it would make you feel better."

"Let me talk to Garrett about it first. I appreciate the offer."

"What offer is that?" Faith and Casey walked back into the room.

"I told him we would take you home for a while to get some rest and get cleaned up." Rafe told Casey.

"I don't want to go home yet. I'm just fine staying here for now." Casey winked at Andy.

"Sorry, doctor's orders. His parents will be up here soon. We'll bring you back this afternoon after you have slept some. I know you didn't sleep any better than he did. He is going to take a good long nap, too. We'll give you five minutes to say goodbye for now. Faith, give your brother a kiss. We'll wait for you in the hallway, Casey."

"Thanks, Rafe." Andy said.

"Get some rest." Faith kissed his forehead.

"I will, sis."

The two of them stepped out into the hallway while Casey moved back to the bed.

Andy took her hand and pulled her closer. "Now where were we?" He pulled her face down to meet his.

The nurse came into the room just as Andy was waking from a coveted nap. Each time he tried to sleep, someone needed something else from him. They wanted more blood or needed to check his dressings or brought him a meal. He was ready to lock everyone out of the room including his family.

"Dr. Miller wants you up in the chair for a little while this afternoon. Ready to try that?"

"I'm ready to do anything to get me out of this bed." He started to swing the covers back only to realize he was hooked to several wires and had nothing more than a gown to cover himself."

"I'm going to unplug a few wires, and then an orderly will be in to help you into the chair." Just as she started to disconnect some of the different tubes attached to him in various places, Garrett and Owen walked through the door.

"Going somewhere?" Owen asked the question while Garrett just smiled.

"They're finally going to let me get out of this bed. I'm going crazy laying here."

"Andy, it has been less than twenty-four hours. How about some patience?" Garrett made that statement.

"Hey guys, how about helping me over to the chair?" Andy asked as soon as the nurse left the room. Just then an orderly walked through the door. He turned the patient in the bed and had him in the chair before anyone was able to say anything more.

"I'll be back to help you into bed in a couple of hours unless you need me sooner."

When it was just the three of them in the room again, Garrett walked over and locked the door. Usually people knocked before entering, but he didn't want them to be overheard.

"We made some positive ID's on our two guys. This was not a random fight, Andy. These two had rap sheets longer than our arms, mostly for drug trafficking. It looks like a very sloppy hit job. They must have been watching you for a while to know where you would be patrolling. They called the fight in themselves. Anyway, the DEA is going to take over the investigation. We want to get whoever put the hit out on you. I guess we disturbed more business than we thought with that undercover investigation." Garrett shared what little facts they knew.

"Rafe asked about hiring a security team to watch the family. Do you think it will come to that?"

"Can he afford that?" Owen was surprised.

"Yeah, he comes from money, though you would never know it. He's paying for the new wing to the hospital, and the renovations we just finished to the physician's offices. He doesn't want that to be public knowledge though."

"I would like to tell him there's no threat to your family, but I can't, in all honesty. Hopefully, there will be a break in the case early. DEA agents will be coming in tomorrow to talk to you more about what happened and see if there is anything we missed. Personally, I think we covered all of our bases and then some, but it gives them a place to start anyway," Garrett answered the question.

"The wedding is just a few weeks away. I want this settled before that day comes."

"Garrett and I want that, too, Andy. We will do everything we can to push the investigation along. In the meantime, you

get yourself out of here, so we can keep a better eye on you."
Owen spoke for the first time.

"I'll talk to Rafe and see what we can do about getting me released. I want to be at home, where I can keep an eye on things. Problem is school started today, and Faith and Rafe have to go to work every day, too. You men find this guy and I'll work on getting my family safe. Thanks for keeping me in the loop. I appreciate it, guys. How long will it take to get me reinstated?"

"You have to be released for duty first. I will need for you to talk to a counselor. I have a good friend who can handle that for you. Then you will have to pass the physical."

"I need my gun, Garrett. We only have rifles and shotguns at the house, hunting guns."

"I'll get you what you need. Right now, you just concentrate on getting out of here."

The men each shook Andy's hand with a pat on his shoulder before they left. Andy sat in the chair thinking about how best to protect those he loved.

Chapter Fourteen

Three days after the shooting, the patient was on his way home. His dad picked him up so they could talk. Andy shared the concerns the department had that the incident was a possible hit attempt. He also told Chuck that Rafe had protection covering all of them beginning that morning. Actually the doctor had insisted upon it.

Rafe had hired one of the best security firms in the nation. Their employees had either military backgrounds or had been trained by the government themselves. The three sent to Lincks were well aware of the situation before they arrived in town.

The men were staying as guests at the Inn. Mark Walker was there as a doctor friend of Rafe's looking into starting his own family practice. Sean Gibbons drove the teachers back and forth while he was "auditing" the school records. James Renfro slept during the day while Andy was at the house and kept watch when the entire family was at home during the night. He passed himself off as a writer that always wrote better at night than during the day. Greg was safe on an extended assignment with a whole crew of people. They had their own security.

"I'm sorry I got our family in this mess, Dad."

"You were just doing your job, son. They will catch this maniac, and it will all be over soon. In the meantime, we have plenty of time to catch up on things. We just don't need to share everything with your mom though." The girls had to know about the protection detail to allow the men to travel with them, but everyone agreed Nora had no reason to believe they were any more than Inn guests. With each of them in their own room, the bed and breakfast was full and there was no need to worry about extra guests.

"The men finished Rafe's house yesterday. They're ready to turn the keys over to him. He's not moving in until after the wedding. He wants to wait until Faith can share it with him. He was going to take her shopping for furniture this weekend. Walker will have some excuse I'm sure to tag along to St. Louis. Gibbons and Renfro will just plan a quiet weekend around the place."

By the time the men made it home, Andy felt like he had been run over by a truck. He told his dad about the gun, showed him where to find it, and went into the den to rest on the sofa. He was fast asleep when Hope and Casey arrived at the Inn.

Casey kneeled down beside the couch and gently kissed her fiancé's lips. As he stirred, she pressed her lips tighter to his until he responded. She felt him grin as she continued to kiss him.

"It's too bad every patient can't be awakened that nicely." He moved to kiss her once more.

"I was surprised to see you home this soon. I didn't think Rafe was going to let you out until tomorrow."

"He got tired of me whining, I think. I told him I would be on my very best behavior if he would let me out early."

Rafe and Faith walked through the door in time to see Casey in Andy's arms.

"I gave orders for the patient to rest and not get all excited by the visitors. Am I going to have to put you back in the hospital?" Rafe grinned at Andy.

"I thought this was the medicine you prescribed for me. I feel better already. You're a great doctor." They all laughed as Casey stood to join the others.

"Casey, let's go check on dinner while these two talk." Faith walked with her asking how the first day of school went.

"Rafe, I'm going to have to be up and around more. I can't lay here waiting for something to happen."

"I understand how you feel. Let's talk to Garrett, and see if we can't devise a plan to get this thing moving along."

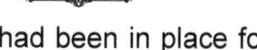

The security team had been in place for a week. Mark Fuller had just locked the doors to the clinic and was headed back to check on Rafe, when he heard the jingle of the doors opening again.

He stepped back into the small office area as he heard Faith say, "I'm sorry, you men need to go next door. ER can handle the problem much better than we can here."

The two men at the door pushed, one grabbing Faith as the other one grabbed the door. "No, lady. You are all we need. Now be quiet and come with us. Make a sound and we shoot that doctor you seem to care about so much." The larger of the two men wrapped his arm around Faith's waist and hoisted her onto his hip while the second man looked up and down the street. They headed to the van parked in front of the building.

Mark cursed as he grabbed his cell phone. The men had been too close to Faith for him to take a chance on shooting. He could have hit one of them but the other one would have surely shot Faith at the same time. He hit the button calling Garrett Austin's private cell number. "They just took Faith. They're driving north on the square heading toward the highway. It's an Oklahoma tag ZZZ-12 something. Couldn't get the last number. Van is an old Dodge, mostly faded black. One tail-light is busted and driver's door is dented. Rafe and I will be following as soon as I can get him in the car." He disconnected the call and raced to Rafe's office. He wasn't at all excited to tell his employer what had happened.

Garrett put out the call to all deputies while he was running to his own cruiser. His next call was to Andy. He could let the other two men know to keep an extra close eye on their people. Then he called his friend at the DEA. They needed to start putting pressure on the men they had in jail. Someone had to know who put out the orders to kidnap one of the family. *I can't imagine what they think they will accomplish with this crazy stunt. It just adds to their sentence.* He started praying for Faith as he headed toward the highway.

Faith wasn't at all happy she had let these two goons kidnap her. She should have known better than to open the door. All she saw was the arm bleeding and wanted to get them help as quickly as possible. "You two are crazy if you think this is going to help anything. Just stop the car and let me out right here. I can't call anyone before you could be long gone. Surely, you're not that stupid, are you?"

"Lady, you sit back there and keep your trap shut. We have our orders." The big guy had turned to yell at her.

She couldn't help it, Faith started to giggle. Then the giggles turned into laughter until tears ran down her cheeks and her sides hurt.

"You crazy woman, what do you think is so funny?" The big guy asked.

"Lady, you sit back there and keep your trap shut. We have our orders." Faith imitated the man as best she could using a deep voice. "Honestly, you sound just like a scene out of an old black and white comedy." She tried to stop the giggles but was having a hard time.

"Ya know, she's right, Merv. Ya sound just like that." The second man was driving and made the comment before he started laughing.

Before she could move, a big fist hit Faith in the side

of her jaw. She blinked once before darkness overtook her. "Yeah, ya see that in the movies, too," Merv said, a satisfied grinning spreading across his face.

"What did you do that for? Nobody said anything about hurting her. We're just taking her to the boss. He'll deal with it. How you gonna explain that big bruise she's gonna have on her jaw?" The driver shook his head before glancing at the man beside him once more.

Rafe had started toward his office door when he heard Mark's voice on the phone. He knew something was wrong when he saw the man at his door.

"They got her, Rafe. We need to get going." Mark didn't wait to see if the doctor followed him or not. He ran to the back door of the clinic and was in his car as the man reached the passenger door. "Tell me Faith is wearing that pin you gave her."

"She had it on this morning. How did this happen?" Rafe didn't know if he wanted to scream or pray.

As they headed out of town, Mark told him what had transpired. "I can't imagine why she opened the door, Rafe."

"Unfortunately, I can. Faith is too trusting. She sees someone needing help and that's all she thinks about. Her safety is nothing she ever considers. Have you picked up her signal yet?" Rafe had not told the ladies they each wore a GPS signal in the pins he bought for each of them. He had told them how much it would mean to him if they would each wear it every day. Andy knew about them and encouraged each one to wear it as well."

"Yeah, we have a good signal. They're headed toward St. Louis." Mark tossed his phone into Rafe's lap. "Let Garrett know, will you please?"

Rafe made the call putting the phone on speaker. "Garrett, we have a tracking device on Faith. She doesn't know what it is but we have a pretty strong signal. They're headed toward St. Louis," Mark told the sheriff.

"I just got off the phone with the DEA. They are taking over the chase. As long as the men don't stop, they want to follow the vehicle. They are already tailing them. Rafe, I'm so sorry. It's important they arrest the people orchestrating these crimes. I know how I would feel if Faith was my woman."

Mark heard the frustration in Garrett's voice. "You can't take a chance following in your cruiser, Garrett. We can travel behind them with the tracker. We're about ten miles away from the van now. We'll stay back enough to not alert them. You might want to let the agent in charge know we're here though. Who are you working with?" Mark asked.

"Anthony Tarvis is the agent in charge. All my information has been through him."

"Tony and I went through training together with the FBI. He transferred to DEA a couple of years before I left the agency. He's a good man. He'll take as much care as possible with the situation."

"I'll let him know. I'll also pass on your phone number if that's okay?" Garrett said.

"Thanks, Garrett. We're within two miles of the van now. I'm going to back off on the pedal just a bit. I don't have time to get stopped now." Mark laughed. "We'll keep in touch." He nodded to Rafe, who disconnected the call.

"They're doing the right thing, Rafe. This has to stop or the whole family will never feel safe. They hadn't hurt Faith when they left and they have been traveling ever since. I'm sure their instructions were to take her to someone. Tony will have enough eyes on them, nothing is going to happen to her." Mark hoped he was right. This was his fault. He should have stressed the importance of staying safe. None of them expected it to come to this.

———— ❧ ————

Faith blinked her eyes trying to get them to focus. She slowly started to remember where she was and why her jaw hurt so much. *It's your own fault, you crazy woman. You can't go around making these guys mad.* She laid there with her eyes closed listening to the men, hoping they would give her some idea of where they were going.

"This one's pretty enough to fetch a nice price. If we can get to the other two, maybe the boss won't be so mad about the money he lost in the drug raids. I sure wouldn't want to be in Alfonzo's shoes when he gets to prison. Figure he knows his days are numbered?" Merv asked. "Pauly, I'm getting hungry. How soon we stopping for gas?"

"How's the gal doing back there? She coming around yet?" the driver asked.

"Nah, she must be a real softy. She hasn't moved yet." Merv glanced in the back seat before turning back to watch traffic. "Let's pull into a burger joint before we hit St. Louis. I'm hungry, and I also gotta go. My bladder will pop if we try driving through the city this time of day." Merv started fidgeting in his seat.

"We'll stop the next exit with a station. I swear I'm buying you Depends, Merv. You got the tiniest bladder of anyone I ever knew." The man laughed at his joke.

"Shut up, Pauly. You know it's from getting too many punches in the kidneys. Doc told me it would happen." Merv whined.

"Yeah, yeah. Reach back there and shake that gal. I want her going the same time we do so we don't hear any crying about needing to stop."

Merv reached back and grabbed Faith's arm, shaking her best he could across the seat. "Wake up, woman. I didn't hit you that hard."

Faith felt the bruising on her upper arm. *This guy doesn't worry about making a mark.* She had heard what the men said about getting a good price for her. *They're taking me someplace to be sold. I assume we're headed to face the leader of the mob. Somehow, I've got to get away.* "You're hurting me, you big idiot." She pulled her arm away as best she could feeling Merv's fingers release her.

"I'm telling you right now, I'm real tired of that smart mouth of yours. We might have to make a little detour and I'll teach you a little respect." Merv reached for her again.

"Not now, Merv. I'm going to pull into that station ahead. You go take care of business while I get the gas. Then me and the gal will go in." Pauly caught Faith's eyes in the rearview mirror. "You behave yourself or I might let Merv have you." He laughed at the shiver Faith tried to contain.

Chapter Fifteen

Mark's phone rang as he and Rafe continued to follow the van. He nodded to Rafe to answer the call.

"Rafe, I'm Special Agent Anthony Tarvis. I know you're worried about Faith, but Doc, we have eyes and ears on her right now. We've been watching these two for a few days. We have a very good bug planted in their van. I have to tell you, your beautiful fiancée is giving those two what for. She's not letting them get by with anything."

"Faith doesn't know about the device she's wearing either. It's only GPS but we are staying within a couple of miles of her. Looks like they're pulling off the highway," Mark said.

"Yeah, the big guy, Merv, is complaining about needing to use the bathroom and he's hungry. We're pulling in right behind them for gas. I already have a woman headed to the restroom. She'll let Faith know she's safe. Rafe, will you trust us to make sure your woman is going to be okay?" Tarvis didn't want him trying anything that would get him arrested for interfering with the investigation.

"Doesn't seem like I have much choice. This has got to come to an end. I don't want any of our family to have to look over our shoulder constantly worrying something else is going to happen." Rafe was more afraid than any time in his life. The woman he loved was being held in a van not two miles ahead of him and he could do nothing about it.

Mark turned the car toward the exit the van had taken

moments before. While the vehicle and the DEA pulled into the first station, he passed them and drove to the smaller station across the road. "Rafe, see if we can get anything to eat while I fill up with gas. We'll want to be on the road as soon as they pull out."

He was thankful the doctor was following his requests. He wasn't sure he would be as accommodating if it was someone he loved in that vehicle. As the tank continued to fill, his thoughts turned to Shelly. He had stopped dating her when his feelings got too strong, too caring. *Maybe I'll give her a call when I get back. See if she'll give me another chance. I'm tired of constantly traveling, never having someone to go home to. Maybe....*

Rafe, looked at the van across the road. The driver opened the back door and pulled Faith out of the vehicle. Then he said something to her before wrapping his arm around her waist. He took a step forward as Faith tried pulling away. The man wrapped her tighter against him and laughed before heading into the building.

"I know it's hard, Rafe. But let it be. They have her covered. That creep can't move without guns pulled on him in every direction if it comes to that. Get in the car. I'm running inside real quick and we'll be ready before they are back outside." Mark hoped he didn't have to stop the man from going after Faith.

Faith was warned to take care of business and get back out the door within two minutes or Pauly was coming in after her. She moved into the door and noticed a woman standing inside the first stall. She had a badge on her waistband.

"Shh. I'm Special Agent Marianne Harper. We're following you. We know everything that is being said in the van. You're safe, Faith. We just need to get you to the man who gave the orders. Are you tough enough to stay with them?"

"I thought I saw Rafe and Mark across the street. Are

they following us?" Faith wasn't sure what she was feeling right now.

"Seems the pin Rafe gave you has a tracker in it. They've been right behind you since the beginning. I promise you this will all end just fine if you can keep your head. Don't push Merv too much. He's not as stable as Pauly. Now you take care of things before he comes in looking for you. Just do as they say. Things will be fine. We're hearing everything said in the van. If it gets dangerous, we'll pull them over within seconds." Harper patted Faith's arm trying to reassure her.

"Then you know they plan to sell me?" Faith felt her lip quiver.

"Yeah, we heard. That won't even come close to happening, Faith."

"Okay, I have to trust you. It's my own fault I'm in this mess. I'll see if I can get them to talk some more. Maybe they'll give you more to work with." Faith looked at the woman. "I need to help somehow."

"Just don't make them mad. You've been extremely brave so far. I think I'm more concerned about that bruise on your jaw than anything. That man of yours is not going to be happy about that." She patted Faith's arm and moved back into the stall so Faith could use the second one.

⚜

It was two o'clock in the morning when Mark saw the dot they have followed for the last nine hours stop moving. The caravan had driven to Chicago. At the same time, his phone beeped with a message.

Rafe punched the icon and read. "We have the leader in custody. He was at the warehouse waiting for the van. Faith got the men to talk enough about what was going down, we didn't have to wait. Plus one of his own gave him up. It's over. Tell Rafe to come get his woman." He turned to Mark and asked, "What are we waiting for?"

245

Special Agents Tarvis and Harper sat back in their chairs after giving each other a fist bump. The man they had been following for the last two years was in custody along with most of his mob. It felt good. They not only had this gang off of the streets but had found two dozen women being held captive until they could be sold.

Mark looked at Rafe with his arms wrapped around Faith as they waited for the chopper to take them home. Mark would be flying back with them. His car was a rental and catching a ride with one of the other two men from the agency Rafe hired would be no problem. "Faith, I'm so sorry this happened to you. If —"

"Stop right there, Mark. This is not your fault. I was the one who didn't think. I opened the door. But God was in control the whole time. We would still be looking over our shoulders if this hadn't happened. No one was hurt and they took a lot of horrible people off of the streets. Not to mention the woman who were saved. All in all, I think it worked out pretty well." Faith said before she laid her head against Rafe's chest hugging him closer.

Both men looked at her shaking their heads.

Garrett got to the house early that morning. He seemed excited as he asked Chuck to gather everyone into the room including the bodyguards.

"Faith and Rafe are both safe and on their way home with Mark. The DEA has arrested the man who ordered the kidnapping. Seems one of the low life arrested earlier is in prison already. He is a cousin to Marco D'Angelo, one of Chicago's high-ranking Mafia bosses. The FBI and DEA have both been watching him for months. He visited his cousin, Antonio, in jail a couple of weeks ago.

"The two goons you shot, Andy, have been on D'Angelo's

payroll for years. When Antonio was confronted with ordering the hit, the little weasel started talking. His family loyalties were not as strong as Marco's, it seems. He told what Marco had said about getting the guy that shut down the ring and taking him out permanently. They arrested Marco early this morning." Garrett waited for the murmurs to quiet down before he finished his news.

"They also apprehended most of the gang and saved twenty-four women already in a crate ready to be shipped overseas. Not only was the gang into drugs, they were also heavy into human trafficking. It's over, folks. I don't think you will need to be watching over your shoulders any longer."

The family cheered as they all began talking at once. Andy gingerly stood and walked over to his boss and friend. "Thanks, Garrett. That is great news. I'm ready to start taking steps to getting back on duty. What do you want done first? Talk to the shrink?"

"Yeah, you can do that while you recuperate. I don't think Rafe is going to release you for duty for a couple more weeks anyway. Then there is still the physical. We've missed you running with us."

"Turns out Rafe is a runner, also. He and I met in town several mornings to run for a couple of miles each day. He has a black belt in karate, so he stays pretty fit. Faith is all ga-ga over his muscles. With the wedding five weeks away now, it will be good to think about more practical things like the kind of cake we want." Andy rolled his eyes as he made the remark. "Seriously, though, I hope this all behind us now."

"We feel sure it is, Andy. You get some rest, so you will be strong enough for the physical when it's time to go through it. Your Army training came in handy. Keep up that tough spirit and you'll be back on duty in no time." The sheriff told the family goodbye and let himself out the door.

Sean Gibbons looked at the James Renfro. "Think we

ought to get our stuff together and be ready to leave when Mark gets back?" They had just finished a meal with the group.

"Spend one more night guys, this evening is on the house." Chuck suggested. They immediately agreed. They had enjoyed the family, the great food and the location. Gibbons even booked a weekend next month to bring his wife for a couple of days.

Chapter Sixteen

The wedding was two weeks away. Andy was back on duty healing well from the gunshot wounds. And Nora was getting excited. She had been in contact with the caterers about the menu three times, each time making a change here or there. She had shown her drawings of the cakes to the girls. They had discussed the plans several times and finally the preparations were underway.

Casey had wanted a white cake with fudge filling between the layers. Hope loved her mother's red velvet cake and asked for that. Faith had asked for a spice cake with an apple filling. Nora had her work cut out for her. They had decided all three cakes would be decorated with the white icing and flowers matching all three bouquets. Over two hundred RSVPs had been returned, so they expected the majority of the three hundred guests would be attending.

"Nora, what can I do to help you prepare for the wedding? I don't want you to run yourself ragged and be too tired to enjoy the festivities." Casey was in the kitchen with her future mother-in-law. "How about I clean the rooms from the guests that just left?"

"I have already handled that, darling. You have enough on your hands preparing things yourself. Do any of you girls have your clothing packed for the honeymoon?"

"The men won't tell us where we're going. It seems Rafe has taken this in hand with full cooperation from each of the men. All we know is we are to bring two swimsuits and lots of comfortable clothing for warm weather. We assume we are going to a beach, but we have not been told where or even if we are all going together."

"That's the way it should be. Be thankful they didn't pack for you or you might not have had that much to take." Nora grinned as Casey's face blushed a sweet shade of pink.

"You're probably right. Are you going to start baking the cakes soon? I would love to help you with them."

"Each layer of your cake is already in the freezer, I am going to work on the spice cakes for Faith today. I want to wait until closer to the wedding to do the red velvet. It doesn't freeze as well as the other cakes do. Have you seen Rafe and Faith around this morning? I have not seen them at all."

"Blake Turner arrived early this morning with a truck full of equipment. The men and Faith are over there helping him set up the spaces."

Dr. Turner couldn't say enough about the new hospital wing and his practice. Rafe had everything built to the specifications Blake had sent. Now the county of Lincks would not worry about treatment for preemies or their young children.

Rafe was thrilled to have his buddy practicing in town. They had known each other since going through med school together along with Blake's wife, Megan. The men had been good friends since medical school. He served as best man at Blake and Megan's wedding. Rafe was godfather to their four-year-old daughter, Carrie.

The death of Megan had shook Rafe almost as much as it did Blake. She had been killed on a missionary trip to Africa more than a year ago.

Faith took to Carrie immediately. The girl was shy, but within minutes was telling Faith all about her dolls and animals packed and waiting for her. Their personal furniture was due to be delivered in two days.

Faith took her fiancée aside. "Rafe, where are they going to live? We have to find a place for them. Carrie needs her things with her, not in some storage building."

"Remember the house Andy and the crew was working on before they renovated the offices? I had planned to surprise you with that home for us. They have already started on the one on the other side of Andy's house. Do you think you could wait until they finish it to move in instead of the first one? Blake could purchase the house, if he's interested. Or Casey's apartment will be available soon."

"Casey's apartment is only a one bedroom. Let's take them to see the place when the truck is unloaded. We had better talk to Andy, though and make sure the other house is available still. I want a place to live with my new husband as quickly as possible. I love that old neighborhood, and it's close to work."

Faith caught Andy right away and told him about the situation. They already had most of the demolition they planned to do finished and would start the renovations in the next couple of days.

"We should be able to have the house ready to move into by the time we're back from the honeymoons or soon after." Andy told her. "I guess Rafe wasn't able to keep the house a secret any longer."

"Carrie needs a home to move into, not just a room or two. It is more important for her than for us right now. I'll have a home soon. This way I get some say is what is done there, don't I?" Faith grinned.

"You can as long as you are not over there constantly telling the guys what to do. They might just nail you into a closet for Rafe to let out later." Faith punched Andy in the shoulder for his comment before they both laughed.

After the truck was emptied and the equipment set

into place, Andy, Rafe and Faith took Blake and Carrie to the house just finished. Faith had not seen it yet either, so she was excited to see what it looked like, and what the possibilities were for their home. All three had the same floor plan in the beginning.

Blake walked through the house carefully looking at the details. Carrie found her room immediately and decided to stay in there. Faith liked the layout of the rooms and the attention to details the man had put in the house. But she was also thankful she had the opportunity to make a few changes. She quickly grabbed a scrap paper from the floor and began to sketch what she wanted the layout of the kitchen to be. The master bathroom was one other detail she wanted changed, even if it meant they lost just a little of the huge walk-in closet.

The doctor was thrilled with the house and ready to purchase it right away. Since Andy's company had asked that Rafe wait to sign the papers to buy the house, it would be easy enough to sell the house to Dr. Turner instead.

Faith insisted she see the house on the other side of Andy's even if the demolition was not completely cleaned up yet. She walked from room to room, talking to Andy about what she wanted changed, and what she liked about each room. Rafe stood behind her with his arms crossed as he grinned.

"I guess it is a good thing I didn't try to surprise her, or you would have been renovating the renovation before we could have moved in."

"I loved the other house, darling, but the kitchen was not quite as handy as it could be for cooking. I wanted more space in the master bathroom, so we could get ready together in the mornings. Do you mind if I make some changes?"

Rafe pulled Faith into his arms. "We can tear the house down and start over if it makes you happy, sweetheart." He leaned down and kissed her thoroughly.

Andy walked to the door, "I'll make sure I get your plans drawn up, and that they will meet your approval before we go any further. Let's go see if Blake and his daughter are ready to leave."

Chapter Seventeen

By the time the bridal party was ready to head to the church, the sunny day was beginning to have a crisp, clean feel to it. The wedding was being held on a Wednesday evening so the couples would have as much time as possible during fall break. Blake Turner volunteered to keep the clinic open while Rafe was gone.

The men had spent the night at Greg's house enjoying their last night as bachelors, and because they had been kicked out of the Inn. Knowing a limo was due to pick up the ladies any minute, the men had already headed to the church.

As the doorbell rang, the ladies all looked at each other. "This is it." Marge, Casey's mother said to the group standing there. "Let's go have the most beautiful wedding this town has ever seen." They walked out to the limo all piling in. With the dresses and other necessities already at the church, they had plenty of room for everyone. Before the driver shut the door, he handed a stack of envelopes to Nora.

"I was asked to give you these," he said.

Each envelope had a name on it, each in a different handwriting. Nora passed them out. There was one for Marge and one for herself as well.

"If Rafe Miller makes me cry on my wedding day, I'm going to make him so sorry." Faith smiled already tearing up at the thought of a message from him. Each of the other women wiped the corner of their eyes before even opening their envelopes. Though none shared what the others said, everyone knew the messages were profoundly sweet sentiments from the men they loved. It was a beautiful way to begin the event.

Mack Newton, Casey's dad, and Chuck met the ladies at the limo helping each of them out with a kiss and a hug. They escorted them into one of the classrooms, where they would be changing since the bridal dressing area was not large enough to accommodate three brides at one time. The bride's mothers were already dressed. The fathers of the brides had rented tuxes with black vests from the shop in town. Each of the grooms would wear a white vest because the ladies couldn't decide what color they wanted their respective groom to wear.

All three of the girls had chosen to wear their hair down since the men had often told them they liked it that way. Their makeup had to be retouched after reading their letters, but that didn't take long.

Finally it was time for the ceremony to begin. The mothers walked arm in arm down the aisle. They hugged and separated to sit on each side of the aisle. Then the wedding march began to play. Casey and her dad walked down the aisle first. She smiled at Andy as he stared at her with a huge grin on his face. He winked just as she and her father approached the platform. They both turned as well to watch Faith and Hope walk on either side of their father. The men grinned at their brides as the women smiled at their grooms. When the three had reached the stage, the fathers placed the hands of their daughters into the hand of the waiting man in front of them. The ladies took one step up to join the men on the platform.

"Who gives these women to be wed to these men?" Pastor Jenkins asked.

Both Chuck and Mack said, "their mother and I." They

took their seats beside their wives and the wedding continued.

As the Reverend read the vows, each of the three recited their parts at the same time. All too quickly, the ceremony was over.

"You may kiss your bride." Each man turned to his bride and reverently kissed her.

"Ladies and Gentlemen, at this time I would like to present to you Mr. and Mrs. Greg Parsons, Dr. and Mrs. Rafe Miller, and Mr. and Mrs. Andrew Thomas." Each of the couples walked down the aisle ready to greet their guests.

The pastor invited the guests to the fellowship hall for refreshments, while the wedding couples had their pictures taken. To move things along, three photographers were used. They had been busy with the candid shots before the wedding, so the bridal shots went fairly fast. Shots were taken of the three couples together, separately and with family members. Then the wedding party moved into the fellowship hall to greet their guests.

Andy and Casey found Ms. Ruth as quickly as possible. They knew she and her son would want to head back to St. Louis early. They each gave her a big hug and kiss on the cheek. Andrew shook hands with Jerome again and thanked him for bringing his mother.

"I think she would have walked if need be to attend your wedding. She thinks the world of both of you." Jerome chuckled.

"No more than we think of her. She is one special lady and a privilege to know for sure," Andy returned the compliment.

Faith and Rafe were soon joined by Ms. Agnes and George. She looked well and said she was doing just fine. George had been a big help. She was planning on selling the house, and the two of them were going to live with her sister. Faith was happy for them, but knew she would miss their friendship. Walt and Frieda Miller returned from their extended vacation to make sure they were in time for the wedding.

More than half of the police force families were there to greet Andy and Casey. The women hugged Casey commenting on how beautiful she looked. The men patted Andy on the back, or gave him a "bro" hug.

By the time the couples had greeted their guests, it was time to cut the cake. More pictures were taken as each couple fed their spouse a bite as was tradition. Then came the bridal bouquet toss. All of the single women in the audience lined up ready to fight for one of the arrangements. At the count of three, all three bouquets sailed through the air. Angie caught Faith's and Bethany, the dispatcher, caught Casey's. Hope's landed right into the hands of a brand new teacher to their school, Missy Fulton. The girls giggled like children.

Nora had insisted each of the girls have a garter as well. Since there were no best men to assist, the women stood in front of their groom while he got down on one knee. She raised her dress and placed the foot with the garter on their thigh while the groom pulled it from her leg to the delight of the men in the audience. All of the single men then lined up ready for their chance to catch the coveted item. The men turned their backs and shot them into the air behind them. Blake Turner was quick to grab the one Rafe let fly. Bud Reynolds caught one and the last one landed right into the hands of Reverend Jenkins much to the surprise of him and the entire assembly of people.

By the end of the evening, the three couples were exhausted. They had reservations at a hotel in St. Louis and then would be flying out early tomorrow morning. The men had never told them where they were flying. They loaded into the limo Rafe had rented and headed toward St. Louis.

———❦———

The plane was due to take off at six-fifteen that morning.

Thankfully, they had their boarding passes, because the trio of couples didn't make it to the airport with much time to spare. They made it through security and to the gate as the last group of numbers were called. Rafe had surprised even his brother-in-law's by upgrading all of the tickets to first class. Each couple had a row of seats to themselves, but they were all together within easy talking distance of each other.

The ladies discovered their destination when the pilot announced the weather in San Diego would be a beautiful eighty-five degrees. The men were duly thanked for their choice. They explained that Rafe still had his home on the beach there. It had four bedrooms, three of which were master bedrooms with on-suite bathrooms. It would be like a private hotel room with beach privileges. The only thing it didn't come with was a cook, but they all promised to help with that. Greg knew some fantastic locations with beautiful scenery and Rafe was ready to teach them how to surf.

By the time they arrived at the house, everyone was bursting with excitement. The first thing they did was head to the beach. The neighborhood was gated and had its own private beach area. This time of the week the three couples had the area completely to themselves. They swam and sunbathed until noon. Rafe spent the time teaching Faith how to surf. She picked it up quickly and they spent each morning surfing together. Then they dressed to explore the sights before coming back to the house for dinner. The evenings usually consisted of moonlight strolls. Each day was fun-packed and the nights were just for loving. All too soon it was Sunday afternoon and time to board the plane for home.

Rafe and Faith didn't have a completed home yet, so they were given the honeymoon suite at the Pine Trees Bed and Breakfast. Rafe carried his bride across the threshold of the room before he kissed her passionately.

"I love you. Thank you for sharing your city with me. I loved surfing with you, Doc."

Epilogue

Casey had just finished preparing her classroom. Another school year would be starting in about six weeks. It felt like the last year had just finished. As she picked the last of the boxes from the floor to set in the closet, Hope waddled into the room.

"I just completed all of the preparation my room is going to get this year. I need to get my feet up. This baby is pushing something terrible. Rafe said he wouldn't let me go too much longer, but I'm ready for this boy to be born."

"I'm ready to head home as well. Is Greg going to be here soon? I would love to bum a ride. Andy is on duty until three. I hate to call him if I don't need to. He's trying to finish his shift before we go to the hospital. Rafe said he would induce me at seven this evening since I'm two weeks past due. He should have the clinic cleared out by then."

"We'll be happy to drop you off. I really should check on Faith. She stopped working two weeks ago, husband's orders. He didn't want her on her feet any more than necessary." Hope's cell phone rang just as she finished her sentence. "Greg is out front waiting on us. Are you ready?"

"More than ready. Let me grab my purse and oh, oh... Hope, my water just broke." Casey looked at her friend as a puddle formed at her feet.

"I'll call the front desk to get someone to clean it up. You call Andy and get him here now."

Hope talked to the secretary who told her they would

have a custodian in there quickly. Just as she started to put her phone away, Faith called.

"We are on the way to the hospital. I'm in labor and my water broke. Can you come?"

"We were just waiting for Andy to get here. Casey's water broke, too. Grab a big room when you get there. I'm not waiting any longer either."

Hope made one more phone call before Greg walked in with Andy. "Dad, grab Casey's parents and head to the hospital. We're having babies tonight."

Andy helped Casey to the patrol car and sped away to the hospital. Greg and Hope walked at a little slower pace. "Greg, Rafe is going to have to induce my labor. If the other two are having their babies today, I want Michael Gregory to share their birthday, too."

"That's fine with me, sugar. I'm ready to meet this little man of ours." He got her in the car and they headed toward the hospital. They pulled into the parking lot just as Faith and Rafe drove in. Instead of waiting for a wheelchair, Rafe scooped her into his arms and carried her to the chair. Andy already had Casey checked in. Seconds later, Blake walked out of one of the hospital doors.

"What's this I hear about babies being born today? Hope, what's your problem? What are you waiting for?" The big man teased the women.

Just then, Hope doubled over with a pain as water trickled down both legs. She looked up at Blake with a scowl on her face. "You could have at least waited until I got my clothes off." She turned to Greg. "How did he do that?"

"I don't think he had a thing to do with it. Our son didn't want to be left behind it seems."

All three ladies were moved into a large room usually used to hold six beds in an emergency. Everyone decided it would be easier if they were all together. It quickly became a race to see which baby would decide to be born first. Hope and Greg knew they were having a boy. Faith and Rafe were also having a son, Mitchell Wayne after Rafe's father. Casey and Andy decided to wait until the baby was born to know if it was a boy or girl.

Blake checked on the babies and Rafe checked the moms periodically. He had been the doctor to take care of all three of them since there were no gynecologists in the area. He was thankful the pediatrician was here to take care of the babies when they were born. He would have his hands full taking care of the three mothers.

It was after midnight before the first baby decided to make an appearance. Since Andy was the oldest child it was only right that his daughter should be born first. Katrina Ruth Thomas was born at twelve-sixteen on July twenty-first. She was named after Andy's biological mother and their sweet friend, Ruth Simmons.

Rafe had barely finished with Casey, when Hope was ready to push. Fifteen minutes later, Michael Gregory Parsons was screaming at the top of his lungs. Both mother and baby were doing just fine.

Faith smiled as her husband walked over to her. "How are you doing there, sweetheart? You have been so quiet. Pains aren't too bad yet? You've been in labor quite a while."

"I think you had better check on our son. I think he's ready to be born also." She gripped his hand.

"I haven't heard a peep out of you."

"You've had your hands full until now. Let's do this, Doc."

Rafe walked to the end of the bed and blinked. "Faith, push with the next contraction." Seconds later the doctor held his son in his hands. He cleaned the baby's mouth and listened to his good, healthy screams. After clamping off the umbilical cord, he wrapped the baby and laid him on Faith's chest while he finished what he needed to do.

Blake walked over to take the baby. After checking him good, he brought him to Rafe, patting him on the back. "Good job, my friend."

Dear friends,

Welcome Home and Surfer Doc were so closely tied together, we had to make them into one book for you to truly enjoy their stories.

I hope you liked getting to know the Thomas family as much as I enjoyed introducing them to you. Andy had served his country well for ten years, but he was ready to meet the woman God had waiting for him. Casey was ready for a family in her life. They fell in love at first sight.

Faith was a different story. She was happy enjoying her work and loving the town patients. A man was the furthest thing from her thoughts until Rafe Miller.

Life is like that. We never know when something will suddenly change our circumstances for the better or the worse. But we never have to face those changes by ourselves. Jesus wants to walk with you through every event in your life, good or bad.

I hope He walks with you daily. If not, He's there waiting for you. All you have to do is invite Him into your heart. Remember Edie? Her life was a disaster but Jesus was there. None of us are so perfect that we deserve eternity in Heaven but God loves us just as we are, mistakes, sins and all.

If you don't know Him personally, find a church, a friend, anyone who can introduce you. If you don't know who to reach out too, email me. I would love to help.

Thank you for reading these books.

God bless you.

Carol Clay

carolclaywrites@gmail.com

Carol Clay, author on Facebook

Enjoy this excerpt of

After God Called

Book Seven of the Lincks Series

Chapter One

"Rafe?"

Rafe Miller instantly recognized the voice, but that couldn't be. Megan Turner had been dead for three and a half years now.

"Megan?"

"Oh, Rafe, I'm so thankful to reach you. I can't find Blake." She breathed deeply trying to stop the tears that threatened to fall.

"Megan, is it really you? We all thought you were dead."

"I...that must have been what he wanted the world to believe. It was all a well-executed plan, Rafe. I was held a prisoner for the last three years, eight months and thirteen days." Megan knew. She had kept track of the time.

"Where are you?" He pulled the phone away from his ear to look at the phone number before quickly moving it back again.

"I'm in D.C. The government is finally through with us. They say we can go home, but I can't reach Blake. Rafe, I don't know if I even have a home to go to. I tried Blake's number, and it belonged to another person. Even my parents must have a different number. Yours is the only other number I could remember. Can you help me find Blake, Rafe? I need to see him and Carrie. I need to hold my family." She couldn't hold the tears back any longer as she sobbed into the phone.

"Megan, sweetheart, you've been gone for more than three years and a half years. You can't just call Blake out of

266

the blue and tell him you're alive. I'm coming to get you."

"Rafe, he's remarried, hasn't he? Is that why you don't want me to see him? Nothing has happened to him or Carrie, has it?" She felt the panic filling her chest.

"No, no. They're both just fine. Megan, let me tell him you're alive. One of us will be there to get you as soon as arrangements can be made. Can I reach you at this number?" Rafe wasn't sure how he would break the news to his friend.

"I'm calling from the Embassy. The men brought us here when we arrived back in the United States. I don't know if you can call back at this number." She didn't know what to tell him. "Can I call you later tonight? It's four o'clock here, so it must be noon there, right?"

"Megan, a lot has happened since you left. Blake doesn't live in San Diego any longer. We both live in a small town in Missouri called Lincks. That's one reason you couldn't reach him." Rafe wasn't sure he should be the one to tell her all of this. Her husband needed to explain everything. "Call me back in a couple of hours. I'll talk to Blake before then, and I'll know which one of us will be coming to to bring you home."

"I'm not alone, Rafe."

"There were others taken when you were?"

"Yes, but—"

"Megan, you bring whomever you need to bring with you. We will find a place for them and get this all sorted out. I can't believe you're alive. That's the important thing. You've been gone more than three years."

"I will call back in two hours. Thank you."

Rafe punched the button to release the call as he dropped down in the chair behind him. He had been pacing his office since his phone rang.

Faith walked through the door as he sat there. "Honey, are you okay? We have patients waiting. Rafe?"

He looked at his wife standing beside the chair. He

267

pulled her onto his lap and rested his forehead against hers. "I just talked to a ghost."

"Sweetheart, what are you talking about? You're scaring me."

"I just got off of the phone with Blake's wife, Megan. It was her, Faith. I recognized her voice as soon as she said my name." He pulled her a little closer.

"Did she give you any explanation? Where has she been for the last, what has it been, three almost four years?"

"She only said she had been held a prisoner, something about a well-executed plan. She wants to see Blake and Carrie."

"I'm sure she does after all these years. How's Blake going to take the news, Rafe?"

"That's something I can't predict. Blake encouraged Megan to go on the trip even after he broke his foot and couldn't travel with her. They both felt strongly they were called to the missionary field when whooping cough got so bad in Africa. Children and adults were dying. As pediatricians, they didn't want to see the disease spreading to the United States. They wanted to help stop it there." Rafe looked across the room in a vacant stare before he spoke again.

"Blake only heard from her once after she left. She wanted to let him know she had arrived safely. They were due to Skype the night the village was burned to the ground, supposedly by some rebel forces in the area. Her passport was found in the charred remains along with those of another doctor and two nurses. All four of them had traveled together to the village that begged for help. Blake has always blamed himself for not being there with her."

"Are you going to tell him?" Faith hadn't heard the story before, knowing it hurt both men to talk about it. Rafe had told her he loved Megan like a sister. He and Blake were closer than a lot of brothers.

"I have to be the one. I can't just let her walk up to him and say "Hi, I'm home." I don't know how he's going to take it."

"I never mentioned it to you because nothing came of it. But one day, I tried to get him to take Angie Murdock out to dinner. He told me he wasn't dating anybody. He was waiting for Megan. He didn't believe she was dead."

"The Government investigated the incident. They brought him what was left of her passport. The bodies were burned so badly there was no way to identify anyone. He's never mentioned that to me, thinking she was alive all this time." Rafe looked into his wife's eyes.

"Rafe, I think God told him to wait, to have patience. Blake truly believes she never died."

"That explains why he would never purchase a burial plot for Megan, even when her parents insisted. He put the money from her life insurance in a savings account. He wouldn't touch it. He never would talk about her death to me."

"Maybe he thought you would talk him out of the belief she was still out there somewhere. If this is how he feels, what joy your news will bring him. You have to go see him, now. I'll take care of the patients. We can reschedule them."

He put a hand on either side of Faith's cheeks and smiled at her. "Do you know how much I love you?" he asked as he pulled her face toward his, kissing her with passion. He broke the kiss only to pull air into his lungs.

"You'll just have to convince me of that love tonight," she giggled as she stood. "Now go make our friend a happy man." Faith kissed him quickly on the forehead before she left the room.

CPSIA information can be obtained
at www.ICGtesting.com
Printed in the USA
FFHW011610060319
50807075-56265FF

9 781945 620584